DECK THE MALLS WITH MURDER

William J. and Martha Q. Schafer

"You mean Beaugard is dead? Then it's murder, all right!"
—Groucho Marx, in Animal Crackers

"God bless us, every one!"
—Tiny Tim, in general

1/3/14 2:33 PM

ISBN 978-0-9911918-1-9

Cover design: Mary Ellen Niedenfuer

www.uridesigns.com

Forward

Deck The Malls With Murder is the second book in the Richard Poole mystery series, the first one being *The Process of Murder*. If you have comments or corrections, please contact the publisher at amarich@notecloud.com.

Deck The Malls With Murder

Santa's Little Helpers

THE FIRST ELF Richard Poole saw was floating face-down in the greenish water of the central atrium fountain in the vast rococo rotunda of LeeLand Mall. The second lay doubled in a red-white-and-green heap beside a yellow plastic litter can. His belled fool's cap was crushed in his hand, and Poole felt strangely moved at the sight of the tiny man's nearly bald head and fringe of white hair.

Both elves were stone-cold dead. Both elves had been strangled. The taped-music system in the long, empty hall played softly—"It Came Upon a Midnight Clear."

The carol did not serenade phalanxes of anxious shoppers. Someone had tripped the music system, the escalators and the advertising-sign lights when they had turned on the overhead lighting in the mall. Opening time for LeeLand Mall was hours away, and the huge plaza was occupied by investigating teams from the Leeland city police, the PawPaw County sheriff's office and the Illinois State Police. They had set up powerful spotlights, and men in white lab coats crept on hands and knees across the acres of travertine floor.

Poole had been admonished to stay out of the way, so he stood a dozen yards from the fountain before a B. Dalton's bookstore, trying to light his recalcitrant pipe. When he heard his name called, he abandoned the effort and thrust the battered briar into his jacket pocket, where (if past experience was trustworthy) a lurking coal would smolder and eventually burn out the lining of the old coat.

"Mr. Poole—this is my boss, Howard Buxtrider."

Poole was being introduced by Deputy Sheriff Wilma Breithope, a trim blonde who had met him at the mall. The man she pulled toward him was thick and muscular, in his mid-thirties, with a Tom Selleck mustache and curly brown hair.

Buxtrider thrust out a big grain-farmer's paw and said, "Hiya. Wilma says you're working for the mall now. We'll keep you folks posted as we unravel this case."

Poole shook the hand carefully, to avoid a crushing contest. Buxtrider maintained steady eye contact through the ritual. *This guy has read his Zane Grey carefully,* Poole decided.

"I'm not exactly *with* the mall. I just flew in from Pittsburgh. I represent the company with a controlling interest here, Sheriff Buxtrider. TransAtlas Corporation. Here's a card, and I'll be happy to have my status confirmed…"

"Whatever," the sheriff said with a careless wave. "Call me Buck. Everybody does. I told Wilma she should liaise with you on this job, so you check with her on whatever you need."

He shot his deputy a megadose of brilliant smile then donned a khaki Smokey Bear D.I. hat and zipped his bulky down jacket.

"I'm heading back to the office, Wilma. I'll have the day-shift guy out as soon as I can. Glad to meet you, Toole."

He strode down the corridor, away from the cone of light blazing at the murder site. Wilma Breithope stared after him, hands on her hips. Poole decided she looked like Johnny in the old Philip Morris ads, *sans* pillbox hat. Not that he would tell her that, because 1) she was far too young to recall Johnny and 2) she looked tough enough to cosh him with her baton, clip him to her come-along and drag him to the PawPaw County line for dumping.

She smiled at Poole. She was compact and sturdily made under the shapeless formalism of the deputy's rig. Shaking her head, she said, "Buck is working hard to become a local character before he hits forty. Figures it keeps sheriffs in office in this part of the world. And he has a peculiar notion I'm eager to star as his comic sidekick."

"You don't remind me a bit of Gabby Hayes."

She gave Poole an odd look and said, "I'm the professional token woman on Buck's staff. Just another uniform, he says. Old Buck is careful to treat everybody equally—which comes easy when you believe the universe revolves around you."

She walked Poole toward the bustle of technicians and uniforms around the fountain. The coroner and an aide bundled the small corpses into black body bags, which looked weirdly deflated with those under-sized contents. Two city policemen helped a forensics technician dismantle spotlights, and a photographer stood to one side shooting with a Haselblad, aiming at chalked outlines on the floor. The taped music murmured "We Three Kings."

A tall, slightly stooped man detached himself from conversation with the police captain and approached Poole. This was Gregory Samsa, who had waked Poole from his jet-lag-induced stupor at the SleepyEye House Motel an hour earlier and exhorted him to rush to the mall.

Samsa wore a rumpled blue suit and a rumpled expression on his narrow face. His tie was twisted like a rope. He brushed ineffectually at his clothing. His hands trembled.

"Thank God you're here, Poole. It's a miracle. We've got to keep this from destroying the season. The mall entered the peak sales period as of yesterday, and this kind of…incident could devastate us." He plucked a show handkerchief from his breast pocket and mopped at his forehead. He patted his lips and shivered.

"Why would someone kill the, er, elves?" Poole asked.

"It's a plot to ruin the mall. Discredit us. Spread fear and panic."

Samsa smiled uncertainly at Wilma Breithope. Poole nudged her elbow.

"The sheriff's office says they'll cooperate in every way. Deputy Breithope, this is Mr. Samsa, the mall manager."

Wilma nodded, "I've known him for ages. I was in the Miss PawPaw finals in 1979, if you don't recall, Mr. Samsa. When you were still with the Chamber of Commerce."

"Yes, yes—I certainly recall, Miss Breithope. A splendid competition. We had an unusually...rich field of entries that year."

Samsa looked further unstrung. He glanced at the police myrmidons as they cleared their equipment. He shot his cuff and peered at a large thin watch.

"We open in two and a half hours," he said, "and I've stalled our maintenance staff an hour already. Mr. Poole, I've told the workers you're here as a safety inspector."

"Right. I'll just drift this morning, but I need to see you to get oriented."

Wilma Breithope said, "I'll be with Mr. Samsa to get his statement for our office first."

"Okay. Chase me down when you finish," Poole said to her. "I'll buy you coffee—or breakfast—and get the sheriff's office perspective."

* * *

LeeLand Mall is an enormous complex, fabricated like a colossal steamboat (appropriate for its location), a vast building trimmed in gothic gewgaws, with tower and porticos and crenellations, as fanciful as a monster wedding cake deposited whimsically on the alluvial Mississippi River flats, where the oceanic Illinois prairie ends. The river flows back of the mall site, nearly a half-mile wide, purling and innocuous, its smooth surface maculated by oil slicks, iridescent patches from chemical spills and random litter.

Two miles north, the city of Leeland (without the second capital L) squats on a slight rise, enrolling 110,000 souls in the 1980 census. What is now Leeland was in the 1840s a minor steamboat landing—

a wood yard cleared among gigantic sycamores. Young Sam Clemens, learning as a pilot-apprentice, may have navigated past shoals and deadheads in the broad river here. Today, Leeland's waterfront is a tangle of closed-down rail yards, mucky swamp and the ubiquitous non-biodegradable litter of a small manufacturing-mercantile city.

The brown god flows on heedless, but no one drifts past on a raft, and no fire-breathing sternwheelers stop to load cords of hardwood to feed the boilers. Contrails etch the skies from east to west. The river is no longer either a barrier or a passageway.

Richard Poole left the building and circumnavigated the site. In the weak wintry light, the huge structure rose like an apparition, the ghost of a deserted castle from a creaky tale. Acres of asphalt surrounded the building like a frozen black moat, now dotted with a few cars—earliest employee arrivals.

Poole surveyed the domain: the parking lots, segmented by entrance roads, were labeled with cartoon signs to aid shoppers emerging from mall narcosis. Each lot bore a generic name, after a bird species—Heron Lot, Nighthawk Lot, Oriole Lot, Robin Lot, Mallard Lot. Behind the bulk of the mall stood a low brick edifice labeled *MAINTENANCE*, housing electrical systems and other vital organs of Leviathan. Poole returned to the mall from the river side, passing under an oriflamme emblazoned *COUNTDOWN TO CHRISTMAS*.

Inside the big doors, Poole stopped at an electronic map with a lighted schematic of the building. It showed four levels, each leading from an octagonal central rotunda and divided into cell-like patterns of the stores ("franchises," Poole reminded himself, to get the jargon straight).

Without trying to memorize the beehive configuration of the organism, Poole scanned the list of venues in the mall: basic familiar ones, giant magnet-merchandisers like Sears and JCPenney, smaller avatars like B. Dalton's, Radio Shack, J Riggins,

Baskin-Robbins, Computerland, Florsheim. Then smaller cells assigned to local or novitiate enterprises, with bizarre names, language bent to yearning: Pursey's, Mr. Pretzel, Sounds Exciting, The Diaper Bag, Kay's Krazee Kandies, Gerbils Unlimited, Popcorn Anonymous, Handyman Harve. Poole suppressed a shudder of anomie. Soon the monstrous arcade would fill with shoppers, miles of fluorescent tubing would flicker, night security grates would rattle up and the sound of electronic cash registers ("merchandising points") would chirp a treble ostinato over the constant mutter of the music system.

He walked down the corridor, past The Happy Humidor, Lingerie Heaven, Seth's Gulper (Biggest & Best Bratwurst 'n' Bubbles), U-Pick-Em Shoes and End Games. He reentered the rotunda from a new angle, under a looming pastel-painted sculpture that insulted the memory of Alexander Calder, behind a bank of lush tropical foliage like a stage set left from a Tarzan movie. The fountain spurted in a bowl of palms and ferns. The bubble of its rills and falls rose above the taped Christmas anthem.

He stepped onto the escalator behind the fountain and rode up three levels, looking out across the height of the mall, feeling like Satan making his first reconnaissance flight through the hollow earth, an orc's-eye view of pandemonium. Soon the space below would fill with marching battalions of the doomed—holiday shoppers out on a spree, overspent from here to eternity.

At the top, Poole found stairs marked Credit-Financing-Management. He followed them to an aerie atop the atrium, small windowless offices heavily carpeted, humming with ozone-charged air. From behind a large CRT, a blonde girl with flopsy-mopsy hair and prominent chewing gum peered at Poole.

"To see Mr. Samsa—Richard Poole."

"He's on a line," she twitched a smile, "but I'll buzz you in as soon as possible."

Poole circuited the anteroom, observing the decor: posters from assorted stores, framed certificates and awards from over-initialed organizations. Large glossy photos of the mall from earth-level and from the heavens. An easeled studio portrait of a man looking like a non-benevolent Colonel Sanders. The eternal piped music now cycling through the maddening strains of "The Twelve Days of Christmas." A giant flip-over calendar at the end of the room showed the music premature: December 1.

Strolling back, Poole observed the receptionist, who crouched at her CRT, which revealed a series of small maps with spots of flickery light. As he approached, she said, "Check-in time. This shows me who's in and on-line."

Shutting down the program, she turned and said, "You're the guy from TransAtlas. Is it true what they say about a robbery last night?"

Reading her embossed desk nameplate—*ALICINE MUNGO* —Poole said, "Who told you that, Alicine?"

"Not seen, silly—it's Alice-*sin*. But call me Lissy. I don't know— somebody down at the door. Maybe Fred Toller. He's the security chief."

Poole said, "No, there was no robbery. But you be careful about spreading rumors. I'll bet Mr. Samsa's a stickler on that, huh?"

Alicine-Lissy smiled broadly, showing Poole bejeweled braces, an orthodontist's blessing. She fluffed the left sprig of bottle-blonde hair and said, "Greg knows I would never ever betray a confidence. He said I was mature enough to be a really, really good executive secretary."

Poole pulled a chair over and sat next to her. With the keyboard of the CRT between them, he felt like a parlor pianist about to engage in a recital of four-handed music—or four-handed foreplay. Forehanded. He reminded himself dizzily that Little Missy Lissy was only a very recent graduate of the local jailbait academy.

"Tell me, Lissy—were you in the, er, Miss PawPaw contest?"

"Oh, that's old hat. *Old* women enter that! But I was hostess for LeeLand Daze last summer."

"And that's when Greg—Mr. Samsa—hired you?"

"Oh, no—I already worked here. I'd been a year with Chocolate Frenzee. That was a stone bore. I hated it, and was getting, you know, acne. Zits. I didn't *eat* any of the stuff, but I had to handle it and breathe in the fumes. It still makes me gag to walk by and smell it."

"So, Mr. Samsa picked you up—out—when you'd been hostess?" Alicine drew back. "Hey—what's all the questions? I had my application in, and Mr. Samsa interviewed me and all that stuff."

"Okay, okay. I'm here to, er, review and evaluate the management structure. A little efficiency interfacing study and infrastructure cross-correlation, see?"

"Oh. Yeh." Alicine turned away and tickled her keyboard.

An orange grid lit up, with a small pulsing box in one corner. "See that? SantaLand's untended. Old Heck Ogden must be off on a toot again." She cleared the screen and entered numbers and letters.

A door behind them opened and Poole turned to see a small, squarish man with slicked-back Valentino black hair peek out. The door was labeled Associate Manager. He stared at Poole and cleared his throat.

He advanced, saying, "I'm Cosgrove—Don Cosgrove."

Poole shook his soft hand. He gave a capsule brief of his mission for TransAtlas, through AmeriMall, a wholly-owned subsidiary, which in turn held majority interest in LeeLand Mall. Cosgrove followed the jack-built tale with a nervous grin.

"Gregory—Mr. Samsa—asked me to talk with you till he's out from under his conference call. I've got Deputy, er, Breithope with me, and some..." He glanced at Alicine and nodded toward his office. Poole grinned as Alicine made a face at Cosgrove's back. Poole followed into a small room full of flesh.

Poole met in turn Dr. Marty Grimes, State Police Medical Examiner, and Len Howells, homicide dick on the Leeland force. Grimes wore a battered off-the-rack blue suit that might as well have been stenciled "work clothes." Howells wore a natty charcoal-gray suit two grades too good for an honest cop. Grimes was fat-and-forty, with dutch-blond hair cut *en brosse,* Howells nearer fifty, ferret-thin and without animated expression. The men ignored Cosgrove. Poole spotted Wilma Breithope on a stubby couch and slipped in next to her. Grimes and Howells slumped in fake Breuer chairs running to rust and rips.

Howells stared at Poole and said, "You're a company snoop? Jesus—what next? The CIA? The Sureté? Holmes and Watson? This is already so goddam complicated we'll be tripping on our... falling on our asses."

"The State Police came in when you called," Grimes said in a bored voice. "I was in East St. Louis, scheduled for Springfield, or you'd never have gotten me down to this ass-end of the world before dawn."

Wilma nudged Poole and whispered, "Grimes is a real hot-shot forensics guy. Lots of TV time and headlines on his cases."

Cosgrove, trying to mediate, was saying, "...sure we need all the help we can get from law enforcement agencies. I can't over-stress the importance of clearing this up neatly and quickly."

"Yeh—you don't think I *like* being on one of these cross-jurisdictional nightmares, do you?" Howells said. "If you want a ruling from the county judge, fine. But since no one can agree if the mall is in or out of the city corporate limits, I'm in. Buck sent Wilma down to keep his hand in. Grimes is a leaner. Now we deal Poole in to keep the money-men happy. Donnie—you're the real fifth wheel here."

Cosgrove scrubbed a hand over his greased hair and sighed, "I've got to keep Samsa posted, don't I?"

"Oh," Howells smiled thinly, "I thought you were here to keep an eye on Daddy's money."

Cosgrove glared. "The bank, of course, has a deep interest in the mall's future."

Howells laughed and shook a Pall Mall from a pack. "Yeh—the way I have a deep interest in staying alive."

Grimes shifted in his chair and said, "I'm due in Springfield by noon, gents. You want my quick-and-dirty statement or not?"

"Please," Cosgrove sighed.

Grimes flipped through a small leather-bound notebook, then looked at a point on the wall behind Cosgrove and recited: "The two victims were abnormally small, white males, early middle age, in general good health. Deaths by strangulation, with ligatures. Some struggle. Evidence of battering—bruising and contusions. Both asphyxiated, probably from behind. Both killed elsewhere and placed on-site. Both dead between six and eight hours when I examined, which was at six a.m."

Howells said, "How long before a complete P.M.?"

Grimes shrugged. "I'll be in my lab tomorrow morning."

"What kind of ligatures?" Wilma asked.

"Can't say exactly. Heavy plastic—nylon rope from any hardware store, I'd guess. We'll try to pin it down."

"But...but," Cosgrove sputtered, "where could they have been killed? Why put them here?"

Grimes stared at Cosgrove as if he were a slide in an ME's exhibit. "Your boss keeps saying somebody's trying to sabotage the mall. As to where they died—that's what this army of cops is for."

Poole asked, "Anything unusual about their clothing or effects?"

With a mirthless snicker, Grimes said, "You don't think *elf-suits* are unusual enough? Okay, I get you. Pockets empty, and the only *effect* I found was a merchandise inventory tag in Doc Number Two's hand. Here—" He flipped a sheaf of photocopy sheets onto Cosgrove's desk. "I knew you'd all want a genuine, heavy-duty clue. Be my guest."

Grimes rose and pulled on a baggy overcoat. "I must hit the road. Someday our governor will see the wisdom of booking me full time on a chopper, but now I get to drive myself across these interesting cornfields. Via con dios."

He left, Cosgrove fluttering behind, and Howells blew a smoke ring at his back and muttered "Prick!" He winked at Wilma.

Poole asked, "What's the story on Cosgrove and the bank?"

Wilma said, "Just that his father is president—the Leeland Merchant's Bank has been in the family since Abe Lincoln rode circuit around here. Everybody assumes Charles Cosgrove sent his son to watch-dog the biggest investment in PawPaw County. The bank, you see, owns all these lovely acres that are leased to the mall."

Howells stood, lifted a crisp Burberry from the coat rack and shrugged into it. Cosgrove returned, wringing his hands.

Howells buttoned his coat, stubbed his cigarette in Cosgrove's ashtray and whacked Cosgrove on the back, booming, "Hey—don't sweat it, chief! We gotcha covered seven ways to Sunday. With all these cops on the job, you're as safe as Fort Knox, right? Between the smokies, me, Buck's office and this big-money cop, we can track down some raving lunatic who gets off on snuffing midgets. And Christmas is coming. Whoopee. Season's greetings!"

When Howells stomped out, Cosgrove slumped into his chair, mumbling, "Unpleasant SOB. I wouldn't trust him to take out the garbage. Will the sheriff's office stay in, Miss Breithope?"

"Call me Deputy. And yes, Buck says we're in for keeps."

Cosgrove attempted a smile that turned feral. He started to speak, when Gregory Samsa entered, leading a squat man in a loudly checked yellow sport coat and baggy blue trousers. He moved with a fat man's violent grace, almost pushing Samsa's stick-man form ahead of him, like a truck push-starting a small car.

Samsa stood by Cosgrove's desk, and the fat man dropped into a mock-Breuer chair, nearly splaying its steel legs.

"Mr. Poole," Samsa said, "this is our security chief, Fred Toller. I've asked him to keep lines open with the Leeland P.D. and the medical examiner's office."

Toller shook Poole's hand enthusiastically and nodded to Wilma. He shifted a toothpick in the corner of his mouth, cleared his throat and said, "I got a call from your Harvey Lewis, Poole. About twenty minutes ago. I filled him in on this damn crazy situation. You know what he said? 'Who the hell would kill a

Christmas elf?—Ebenezer Scrooge?' He wants you to call and keep him posted."

Samsa said, "Please, you can compare notes later. Now I want to be informed of procedures you'll use to…alleviate this situation."

Toller shifted laboriously and craned at Samsa. "Jesus, Greg—you thinking of artificial respiration? Or a Lazarus act? I don't think anything can be done to *alleviate* strangling, do you?"

"You know what I mean." Samsa sighed and glared at Cosgrove. "You," he said, "must speak with the newspaper and TV people. There was an *Eagle* reporter on the phone. I stalled him, but there'll be a mob of vultures by noon. St. Louis, Chicago—" He shuddered.

"A *flock*," Poole said absently.

"What?"

"Vultures come in flocks," Poole said. "But old Harvey had a good question: who *would* kill Santa's elves?"

Toller handed Poole a sheaf of papers. "I copied files on key personnel—the store Santa, maintenance crew, night security man.

And the damn elves."

"Who were they?" Wilma asked.

"A couple of rent-a-elves from St. Louis," Toller said. "Sent up last week by a theatrical agency. Both had experience with Christmas work and came with good recommendations."

"So—they weren't local? No connections with Leeland?" Poole asked.

"As far as I can trace," Toller said, "they didn't know a soul here before last week. When Heck Ogden turns up, we'll ask him if they mentioned people here. He's the only one who had much contact with them."

Samsa paced next to Cosgrove's desk like a clockwork figure in a shooting gallery. He glared at Cosgrove and said, "If we can't contain this disaster, Christmas will be a write-off. I don't need to spell out what that means in terms of the mall's financial viability."

Poole nudged Wilma. "You folks carry on with your crash course in catastrophe economics. I'm going to absorb this data and view this wonderland in operation."

Toller heaved to his feet, flashing a greasy smile around his toothpick. "You come out to my office in the maintenance annex when you need help. I'm waiting to hear from the State Police and the local cops."

As Poole and Wilma left, Cosgrove and Samsa burst into acrimonious cross-talk. In the anteroom, Alicine Mungo beamed a platinum smile at Poole, eliciting a snort from Wilma.

"You've gone and captured the heart of our queen of the mall-rats," she said. "Did you make a heavy burger-and-fries date with her?"

"I exuded native charm. What's a mall-rat?"

"You'll see. Kids who make a career of hanging out. They spend more time here than at home. Or in school. Ask Fred Toller to give you a guided tour of the Pizza Tower or Ali Baba's."

"Ali Baba's?"

"The game parlor on level one. Or hang around the fountain. You'll see them fragging the geeks. That's what they call making total assholes of themselves. Toller's crew runs a sweep and pitches them out every afternoon."

"You run into them in the line of duty?"

"Buck comes by and hassles them about once a week. The truant officer shows up with the skipper-mobile. But you can't keep 'em out. They *are* like rats."

They rode the long escalator down the side of the rotunda. The huge concourses rattled with shuffling feet, voices, beeping merchandise points, against the saccharine jingle of taped carols. They stood by the big fountain, where heavenly light fell in glories from clerestory windows high above, and the space was a bizarre church sheltering a restless congregation.

"I almost married a woman who knew all about Netherland church paintings," Poole said absently.

Wilma stared in mild astonishment and said, "My ex runs the Big Eagle Bowlarama," as if seeking a capping *non sequitur.*

"Your ex? Then you're...free?"

Wilma smiled. "You look like a man deciding if he could go out with a lady who works in an all-wool monkey suit." She slapped the holster for her .38 revolver.

"You could appear in mufti."

"And you don't have a date with Miss Crazee Daze of 1984?"

Poole shuddered. "I'm looking for a good woman to save me from a life of shame. Deliver me from nymphets."

"I go off shift at three-thirty."

"Why don't you call me? Through Toller's office. Or at the dear old SleepyEye House. Leave me any new ideas on this mess and tell me some essential details like your address and phone. I'll knockoff for supper, if you pick out the niftiest eatery in town. Always assuming there is one."

Wilma grinned. As she walked away, Poole admired the rear view. A little romantic imagination could transmogrify the uniform into elegant jodhpurs and riding boots. *Riding to hounds. Polo. Ind-jah.* Glancing back, she called, "I hope you'll recognize me when I'm transformed. Don't faint."

Poole wandered around to look at SantaLand, a red-and-green plywood gingerbread house atop a flight of stairs with a cordoned path that ended in a tall, gilded throne. A placard read

SANTA'S IN HIS WORKSHOP

BACK AT _____

The splash of water in the fountain evoked deep woods in which monsters lurked, where death waited for small creatures too far from home. Poole stifled a yawn and trudged through the madding crowd in search of lunch.

* * *

The employment forms identified the elves as Morris (Moe) Weiner, age 52, and Jacob Greene, age 49, both of St. Louis. They had been contracted through Cosmo Attractions, a booking agency of that city, on a four-week contract. An entry identified their job description as "to greet and entertain children" while acting as "Santa's Helpers" and "to assist parents at a properly organized holiday display." The contract indicated that LeeLand Mall would furnish appropriate costumes, equipment and accessories.

Cosmo Attractions vouched for the experience and character of Weiner and Greene, listing references on file. Past employment cited for each man included work in TV and films. Weiner was described as a singer and dancer, and Greene's talents included "comic juggling" and ventriloquism. Both were acrobats with circus and carnival experience. Weiner was described as WM 4'6", 81 lbs., Greene as WM 4'3", 74 lbs.

As small as children, Poole thought.

Poole had seen a sufficiency of dead men, women and children in his work. But never a dead...*dwarf? midget? little person?* He wondered what the two had been, technically. What were the distinctions of nomenclature and semantics? Did they matter?

Easy to strangle two tiny men with a stout cord. Anyone could do it—man, woman or reasonably strong adolescent. Why? There were easier ways to discredit the mall, to sabotage Gregory Samsa's brummagem empire.

Poole pushed away his half-eaten DomeBurger. He sat in a back booth at Paradise Dome, a fast food concession on level two. The ventilating system futilely emitted bursts of ozone to combat the dense haze of grease in the air. Behind the counter, late adolescents clad in green uniforms and abbreviated green stovepipe hats shoveled up the fare. Poole thought the workers looked like the Army of Oz as viewed through emerald spectacles.

His attention shifted when Don Cosgrove bustled into the place, one hand raking his pompadour. He slid into Poole's booth. "Thank God I found you. You must leave word where I can reach you. I need to talk with you...away from the office. There are... things you need to know."

"You want to eat?" Poole asked.

"No. No, not now. Mr. Poole, I'm...frightened."

"Of what?"

"Of being made to seem...implicated in this. I think I'm being set up. Framed."

"Why? By whom?"

"That's what I must tell you. People have told you about my... family background. My father's position. The bank. Right? I've been with the mall since it opened—four years now. But everybody thinks I'm a spy or a flunky for my father. What in Christ's name do I have to do to prove myself? I'm thirty-five, Mr. Poole, and everyone in

Leeland calls me 'the Cosgrove kid.' As if I'm one of the Little Rascals." He picked up Poole's water glass and drained it.

"Who would want to frame you?"

"That's easy. Samsa, for a start. He thinks he *owns* this…two-bit wonderland. When the board put me in, it was over his howls and objections. And that slob Fred Toller—he could come up with this, too."

"Why should Toller want to do it?"

"If I'm out, he and Samsa have free reign. I'm the only one in management with control over key personnel and operating decisions. Besides them."

"So you *are* a watchdog for the board of directors?"

"There's Artie Bennet, the comptroller. And Muriel Grossman, personnel director. But they always defer to Samsa."

"Toller's only security chief, isn't he?"

"Yes, but that's critical in an operation of this size. If there's a crisis—like this one—Toller is a kind of…dictator."

"Well, he can't keep on killing elves, anyway. You've run out."

"You don't know about the other…incidents." Cosgrove mopped his forehead and leaned forward. "This is just another disaster. I know you'll think I'm paranoid. That's what Samsa wants. To make me out to be an incompetent, a lunatic. But things have happened."

Poole sighed. "Do you want to give me a full report?"

"Attempts to sabotage things. A dead animal in the ventilating system—in August."

"What kind of dead animal?"

"I didn't see it. Toller said it was a…what-you-call-em. Little brown, fat animals you see dead by the road."

"A groundhog?"

"Yes. Terrible, the hottest weekend of the year, right in the middle of White Sales. Ghastly stench, like a garbage dump. Ugh!"

Cosgrove found a roll of stomach tablets in his pocket and

popped one. "I thought they were called something else. When we were kids we called them...I forget."

"Woodchucks?"

"That's it! How much wood would a woodchuck chuck if a woodchuck could chuck wood? There!" For the first time, Cosgrove looked happy. Poole decided he preferred him frightened and morose. He bore a vague resemblance, in face and form, to a woodchuck.

"Could the animal have gotten into the ventilating system by itself?"

"Toller said it was impossible. Someone had wrenched off a door or grate and shoved it in. Many days dead."

"What else happened?" Poole scribbled notes.

"In October, a gang of the...mall-rats trashed the Halloween Ball at Antoinette. The most up-scale shop in the mall. An invitational costume party. They broke in and terrorized the guests."

"How is that connected?"

"Toller and the night man caught most of the gang. When the city police arrived, one of them said—hinted—they'd been *paid* to do it. But the kid wouldn't say more."

"What happened to them?"

"They only caught two. Let off with a warning. Samsa wouldn't bring a civil action—said we don't need that kind of publicity. I have to agree."

Poole scribbled and said, "What else?"

Cosgrove leaned closer and whispered, "I've had threats. Personally. I haven't told anyone here. They began just before Thanksgiving."

"What kind of threats?"

"First, telephone calls. I thought it was just a crank. A man mumbling things—filthy language, saying he'd beat me up. Then this came, last week." He handed Poole a crumpled envelope from which Poole extracted a single photocopied sheet which depicted pasted cut-out words:

get out OF THE TOWN or ITS sudden DEATH 4 U + wife & CATS

Beneath this a crude drawing of a dripping dagger and a hanging stick-figure, with an oversized noose. Rendered by a primitive draftsman. Or woman.

Cosgrove watched Poole with an expression compounded of eagerness and revulsion. Poole handed back the paper.

"Where did you receive this?"

"Under the windshield wiper of my car when I left work. They know my car. Maybe they were watching me."

"*They* who?"

"Whoever...whoever's doing this. I say *they*, because it...sounds like a gang."

"It sounds like a sicko. Is this aimed at you or the mall?"

"It's like the calls. First, the voice said things like that. But the last one was different. It said, 'You keep on at that mall, and you'll die with the rest of them.' I think those are the exact words. I was too upset to really focus. My wife has gotten calls, too, and she's not well. She can't stand this...harassment."

"What have the police done?"

"Next to nothing. They worked with the telephone company, and I gave them statements. They say it's just a prankster. A kid with a grudge. Who would have that kind of grudge against me? I don't know people who'd do...that. The things he said were...terrible. And that scrawl..."

"He? A man? A kid?"

"I don't know. It was muffled. A growl."

"The police lab couldn't track anything on the note?"

Cosgrove shook his head. "I've given up on them. I can't be sucked into a scandal. I had an orderly life, and I value order highly. Now I'm wallowing in some sort of...catastrophe. That's why these murders upset me. It's all getting more and more weird."

He stood and dabbed at his sweaty face and slicked back his hair. "I wanted you to know this is more complicated than it may seem. If you can help me, I'd be grateful. My first concern is with the mall, of course. But I have a personal stake. These things must be... connected."

Glancing around the crowded eatery, he said, "Someone has stolen...papers. Personal papers very important to me. Significant historical artifacts among them."

"What kind of papers?"

"It's complicated. They were in the family over a hundred years. Early diaries of the Lee family. The Ossianic Prophecy. I suppose they're priceless, in historical terms. And all my journals."

"Where were they?"

"In my office safe. Friday morning I found the safe open, the contents scattered on my desk. Only the personal materials were gone."

"What did the police say?"

"I've told no one. This is...unthinkable. What would anyone want with the papers? Ransom?"

Poole started to urge him to contact the police, but Cosgrove pulled another scrap of paper from his pocket. No message, but it bore another crude hanged man, in drippy purple ink.

"This was on my desk. Mr. Poole—I don't trust the Leeland police. I don't trust anyone here. There are generations of old feuds and hatreds. I talked with you, because I know TransAtlas has a lot at stake in the mall. Or AmeriMall does. And you're not connected with all the parochial bigotries here. Can you help me?"

Poole scratched an ear. "You understand I'm here on assignment. I'm not a rent-a-cop. My brief is to investigate and report back to Pittsburgh. They'll in turn deal with AmeriMall. I'm a tiny link in a big chain. I don't have authority to deal with private matters."

Cosgrove grimaced and said, "I understand. But I *know* this is all connected. I can't go into details now. I must be back in the office. Can we talk later?"

"Okay, but first—what's this Ossic thing you mentioned?"

"The Ossianic Prophecy. Part of the Lee papers. Our city's background is...fascinating. And tangled. I'll try to explain when we talk. Please believe me—this is no delusion. Someone is willing to do anything to destroy me. And the mall. You saw the murdered men." He shuddered. "Leeland's founders were men and women of vision. But they never foresaw *this* in their future." He waved a hand at the ranks of plastic booths and winking neon then snatched his hand back as if someone would see.

"Please call me when you can speak with me. I know I can help you. And...perhaps you can help me."

He bustled away. Poole collected the styrofoam detritus from his table and dropped it into the maw of a waist-high trashcan shaped like a clown with a vastly distended gullet. The grotesque figure made him recall the dead elf crumpled like a bit of debris beside a waste can.

Poole took from his wallet the photocopy of the merchandise tag found, Dr. Grimes said, in Morris Weiner's dead hand. It was just an inventory tag, computer-coded, of the sort attached to thousands of retail items in the mall. Poole moved toward the escalator—it was a tiny lead to follow. The mall crowds had thickened, and there was a scent of feral excitement in the air, an odor of the need to buy, to acquire, to possess.

* * *

In the fourth-level accounting office, a young redheaded man peered at the photocopy through thick bifocals. He and Poole sat before a rank of terminals and tape-drive units that comprised the mall's computer brain. They were in a long, aseptic tunnel of a room, overcooled, desert-dry and devoid of humanity. A plastic name-plate on the desk told Poole this was Drew Whitman, Chief Internal Auditor, LeeLand Mall.

Whitman said, "The original would be better. It's from a small venue. Probably our code, all right, but it's smudgy. I think I can trace the venue. But not the purchase itself."

He flipped open a thick green-bound ring binder. "The number might be 02232 or 02282. Let's see: 02232 is Pets Galore, and 02282 is…Handyman Harve."

Poole thanked Whitman, who gave him a watery smile and said, "I hoped we could run it through IRMA for you."

"Irma?"

"Our new system—Information Retrieval and Management Access. It's unfortunate that the manufacturers use these acronyms with anthropomorphic suggestions."

Scanning the banked machinery, Poole said, "She doesn't look like a hot Coke date. Your friend Irma, huh?"

Stiffly, Whitman said, "A finely-tuned, state-of-the-art management system, Mr. Poole."

"Thanks again. And may your relationship flourish!"

Poole rode the long escalator down again, with another view of the mall. It was like a cavernous funhouse, with a hundred twisted vistas and distorting mirrors. On level one, he found a *HAPPY HOLIDAY HANDYMAN SALE* in progress at Handyman Harve's. He walked a labyrinth of tool-decked aisles to a blank brown door labeled *OFFICE*. When he knocked, a short, bald man with a walrus mustache peered out, blinked and said, "Yes?"

"Are you…. Harve?"

"Nah. Louis Halberstam. I'm the manager, if that's what you want. There ain't a Harve. He's a whatayasay? Corporate fiction. Like Betty Crocker, see? There are a hundred and thirty-seven Handyman Harve's stores in the U.S."

Poole identified himself as an AmeriMall consultant and handed

Halberstam the photocopy. "Can you identify this tag?"

"Identify? Yah—it's one of ours."

"Can you tell me what it's for? The, er, merchandise?"

Halberstam massaged his slick scalp like Edgar Kennedy warming up for a slow burn. He said, "It's coded *household*. Let's see…" He led Poole into the office, a closet crammed with a table, a CRT and an old oak filing cabinet. Halberstam typed and watched the terminal flicking up sets of pulsing orange numerals. Then he said, "Okay—a small package of HoldFast Nylon Cord…see? Thirty feet, dayglo orange, four hundred pounds test, one-fourth-inch diameter. That do it?"

Making a note, Poole said, "Any chance you can tell me who bought it—and when?"

Halberstam studied the photocopy. "It's one of the newer tags. Probably in the last few days. Earline works the register most of the time. She's the missus. Come on."

A portly woman with a fat bun of steel-gray hair, a salmon-pink smock and a badge reading

HANDYMAN HARVE'S

1001 HOME-HELP ITEMS

EARLINE

Poole shook Earline Halberstam's moist hand, saying, "So, this is a genuine mom-and-pop operation." She had a tidy Norman Rockwell smile.

Explaining the photocopy and Poole's query, Halberstam asked, "You recollect anybody buying nylon cord recently?"

Earline knotted her face and said, "Aisle three, bin seven. I didn't fetch it for anyone. A man was looking for heavy-duty chain, but I don't remember… Oh, yeh. Just after we opened yesterday."

"Can you describe the customer?" Poole asked.

"A man—*that* I recall."

"What did he look like? Young, old, short, tall?"

"A big coat—with a hood. A parka, one of them things all pockets and belts. He had to dig around to get to his money."

"He paid cash?"

"Yep," Earline said. "Paid with a ten and got change. A dollar thirty-nine, plus six cents sales tax, one forty-five even. That makes eight fifty-five change."

"Does that help you recall him?"

"Ah, shoot, the dang register does all that. I feel useless here with the machines doing all the figuring. I just did that to show off. In the old store, we had a big nickel-plated National that made as much noise as a brass band when you rang up. *Then* you had to know how to make change. No…I just…I can see his hand."

"What kind of hand?"

"Hmmm. Funny. It's a dark hand. Dark."

"You mean a black man?"

"Oh, no—just dark…hairy. A lot of black hairs."

Earline looked wistful. "Hands is about all I see of customers here. In the old store, you'd chat, people would want a half-pound of brads or ask what kind of wood screws to use on a job. Shoot, you didn't always sell a lot, but it wasn't this stuff wrapped up in plastic, packaged so you gotta buy a hundred brads if you want six."

Halberstam said, "See, our whole life's been hardware. Started out in her dad's store, twenty-seven years ago. Peavey's Hardware. I can still smell the old store. Smelled *good*—wax and oil and paint. It was home for us, you might say."

Earline leaned her bulk against the counter and tapped a finger on the low plastic shell of the electronic cash register. "Now, it's just totting up profits and losses for some big outfit in Boston who don't give a tinker's curse what customers want. Just move that merchandise, they say."

Halberstam said quickly, "Now, Early—Mr. Poole's with the outfit that runs the mall. Don't want to give him the wrong idea…"

"Be damned to pussyfooting around!" Earline said with a glare at Halberstam. "I don't care who knows it, Lou. It was one sad day when we moved out here and closed the Broadway store. I remember when this was all pasture and swamp and the wreck of the old brewery. They should of left it to the frogs and cows!"

As Poole left, Earline said, "My pa wouldn't of put up with this…" she gestured broadly at the harsh lights and spilling shelves, "this *chickenshit* for one second!" Lou grinned weakly at Poole.

"I think you're probably a hundred percent right, Mrs. Halberstam," Poole said, "and thanks again."

Poole steered around a woman in a fake-fur coat who fondled the tiller of a fat-wheeled sno-blower. She was like an animated emblem of winter, reminding Poole how insulated this massive building kept him. He was in an environment as self-sufficient and hermetic as a spaceship wheeling through the interstellar void.

He glanced down the long corridor out the big entrance doors: a landscape of densely ranked cars, filtered through polarized glass. The crowds in the mall were denser, the lights brighter, piped music now *accelerando*. The hall rattled to "Jingle Bells."

Across the corridor Poole saw a huge neon sign, gaudy pink and purple cursive script: *BELLY-UP.* Under it, a smaller placard: *BARSTOOLS FOR HOME AND BUSINESS.* Poole gaped. *Bar stools?* he thought. *How in God's name can you run a store that sells only bar stools?*

"The barstool market in central Illinois would be saturated in a week!" he muttered aloud.

The sno-blower woman peered at him then tugged her pseudo-fur around her and trotted away. She may have recognized the first symptoms of Mallomania seizing Richard Poole.

Then Poole heard scuffling and turned. Two men wrestled inside the entrance doors. Poole recognized the peaked cone of Buck

Buxtrider's D.I. hat. He tugged at a short, stout man.

"Simmer down, pardner," Buxtrider growled, "or I'll play the nightstick boogie on your skull."

The short man reeled at the end of the sheriff's grasp like an unstrung puppet. Buxtrider grabbed his mackinaw collar and yanked him upright. He lurched against Buxtrider, stared toward Poole and waved one hand, crying, "Lookee—my public awaiteth..."

As Poole approached, Buxtrider said, "At least Heck here didn't puke all over my unit this time."

Hector Ogden straightened in search of long-vanished dignity and opened his mouth wide enough to display a trio of ivory teeth. From this gape he projected a baritone howl of "Here comes Santy Claus, here comes Santy Claus, right down Santy Claus Lane..."

They stood like an ill-assorted triad of carolers under a banner emblazoned

ONLY ___ MORE SHOPPING DAYS

'TIL XMAS!

WELCOME TO LEELAND'S

HOLIDAY SHOPPING FANTASIA

A runty, snot-nosed boy towed by a battleship of a mother goggled at them. Poole wondered if the tyke knew this was St. Nick in the iron grasp of the law.

Good King Wenceslaus

IN THE MANAGEMENT suite anteroom, Hector Ogden lay full-length on a naugahyde-covered couch, one hand trailing on the carpet. Gregory Samsa stood by the couch, wringing his hands and glancing around. Alicine Mungo tiptoed across the room holding a large styrofoam cup that trailed vapor. They had plied Ogden with black coffee for forty-five minutes. Much of the brew had run down his mackinaw, some had pooled on the couch, and small caffeine swamps formed in the carpet. What little had gone down Heck's gullet had not dented his state of unconsciousness.

Buck Buxtrider talked quietly with Don Cosgrove across the room, and Poole slouched next to Alicine's desk. Fatigue had struck him as he helped the sheriff lug Ogden up the escalator. He envied the defrocked Santa his doze. Poole had absorbed enough cheap rye fumes from Ogden to feel giddy.

Buxtrider approached Ogden and yanked him upright. He then knelt, manfully facing the assorted fumes. Ogden's eyes opened, and he squinted at the sheriff.

"You just be a guh...a gun...a good boy for another couple weeks, an Santa'll..." His eyes and mouth closed abruptly, like a doll shutting down, and he tilted forward. Buxtrider shoved him back and called to Poole for a hand. "It'll take a solid night's sleep to sober this bum up," Buxtrider said. "Cosgrove said to bunk him in the security office. Jesus, we'll have to haul him clear through the mall and outside."

It was an Olympic trial, an anabasis, through milling mobs,

with Ogden a dead weight until he momentarily awoke and tried to sing "The Yuletide Song." Buxtrider clamped a gloved hand over his maw, right in the midst of roasting chestnuts.

They laid Ogden out on a sagging cot in a back room of the security suite. Buxtrider glared at the supine form.

"Know where I found the old bastard? *Under* his bed. He lives out in a fishing camp ten miles downriver. The stove was out, there wasn't any food in the fridge and ice had formed in the biffy. If he'd stayed there overnight, old Heck would of been a Santasicle."

"How long had he been there?"

"God knows. His truck was there, with the door open and the ignition on. Looks like he left it running—tank was bone-dry. I guess he just fell out of it and crawled inside."

"Why does the mall put up with him?"

Buck looked speculatively at Poole. "Hell—he's part of our local history. Goes a long ways back with the Cosgroves, and I guess the old man has a spark of sentiment left. He was the first Santa when the mall opened four years ago, and he's been Santa ever since. The rest of the year he's a fulltime drunk, except when he finds somebody soft enough to hire him as a yardman. Then he goes on a split shift—standing around with a shovel days and drunks at night."

Ogden wheezed stertorously, a rivulet of saliva wending from one corner of his mouth to the chrestomathy of stains on his ancient coat. He twitched in his sleep and said clearly, "No...don't!"

"What's his connection with the Cosgroves?"

"He was their gardener and chauffeur for...twenty years or so, right after he came back from the Army. Korea. He was our local war hero. Collected a Silver Star. Some hero, huh?" Buxtrider poked Ogden's chest with his nightstick, and the old man wriggled before subsiding back into troubled sleep.

"When did he leave the Cosgroves?"

"I don't know—maybe ten years ago? He must of fell off the

wagon every six months for years. Finally, the old man pitched him out. But he give him the fishing camp to live in. Used to be the Cosgroves' summer place, back in the fifties."

They left Ogden and entered Fred Toller's operations room, where Toller sat before a bank of small TV monitors, flipping switches.

"Find any clues yet, Freddie?" Buxtrider boomed.

Toller grunted. Images danced and shifted on a half-dozen screens. "Shit!" Toller said, slumping back.

"Your million-dollar spy system on the fritz?" Buxtrider asked.

Toller said, "The sumbitch blacked 'em out—six cameras!"

They watched the monitors as Toller re-ran the videotape: one by one, a series of labeled monitors winked out. One showed a hunched gray figure for a millisecond before the picture blackened.

"Sprayed the cameras with black paint," Toller said. "I can track it back and tell you to the second when they hit each station—see?" A running digital clock showed at the corner of each screen. Toller ran the tapes again.

"The last one goes out at...eleven-five-six and thirty-three. That means the mall was shut down for about six hours before they hit it. That prime asshole Randy Loggins was off sleeping or playing with himself somewheres."

"Loggins is night security man," Buxtrider explained. "What's Loggins' story?" he asked Toller.

"Story is right." Toller spat his toothpick into his palm and examined it for structural flaws. He replaced it and continued, "His *story* is that he got a call from Jinx Washburn down at Maintenance just after he came in—the heating system was shutting down. Randy says he checked all the monitors and ring-in stations and then went to see Washburn. He claims he had to help Washburn run through the trouble-shooting procedures till three o'clock. Jinx alibis him all the way. I figure those two morons were watching fuck movies on Washburn's TV. You know he's got a VCR down there, don't you? I'm gonna get *both* their asses fired!"

Poole asked, "You can trace the killer's route and times through the tapes?"

"Yeh. *If* that's the killer. Here." Toller thrust several print-out sheets into Poole's hand. "All tabulated there. I ran it off for Howells. He's off with the State Police rounding up heavy-duty clues."

"How did he break in without triggering an alarm?" Poole asked.

"Nobody broke in," Toller said. "Could of been inside already. Shit—there's a million places somebody can hide when the mall closes. You know that Rudolf the Red-Nosed Reindeer exhibit by the main doors? It's all hollow plywood bases. Howells thinks somebody hunkered in there. His forensics boys are crawling all over it now."

Toller flipped switches, and monitor No. 14 showed the exhibit. He zoomed the lens in. Men were walking around the display, inspecting larger-than-life Christmas parcels at its base.

"So—" Toller shut off the monitor. "Somebody pops out of the box, just like Christmas morning, goes down to atrium and bumps off the two midgets. Shit, that don't make any more fucking sense than Randy Loggins. What the hell were the two midgets *doing* here? Or if hot-shit from the state ME's office is right—why the hell would somebody *bring* them here?"

Poole mused, "Someone who knew he had a clear shot at knocking out the cameras. Could Loggins be in on it?"

"Yeh," Toller said. "Seems that simple, don't it? But you gotta known Loggins and Washburn to appreciate the fact that simple logic ain't enough. Loggins is only slightly dumber than my boot, and Washburn makes him look like Alfred Einstein."

Poole stared at the array of TV equipment and asked, "Isn't there a way to detect people in the building? Other than this? It sounds too easy to stow away and grab anything you want."

Toller sighed, "Every venue is protected by locked fencing and individual alarms—heat and movement, mainly. So it's not easy to get at the merchandise. We're not too worried about people roaming the corridors, except for vandalism. Since we have to deal with the mall-rats—and those little bastards might bust things up for the hell of it—we installed another system."

He pointed to a row of chromed boxes. "A general body-heat detection system. But it's only half-installed. We've got to wire in all kinds of over-rides. The animals at Pets Galore could trigger it. And we have to build in a password code system to allow dodos like Loggins and Washburn to move around without tripping it. The genius who's setting it up estimates we'll have it in place sometime before the next Ice Age."

Buxtrider donned his D.I. hat and gloves, saying, "Gotta leave you two old boys to this high-tech sleuthing. I'm off to see if the night-shift guys are checked in. Adios."

Toller watched him exit and said, "So they dumped Heck on me, and I'm supposed to babysit him, too? Jesus, they wanted to put in a lost-and-found here when the opened the mall. I suppose they'll ask me to fill in as Santa now, too, and all his goddam elves and twelve tiny reindeer. I'll get Loggins for Rudolf—screw a big red light bulb in his ass, the jerk-off!"

As Poole drifted to the door, Toller called, "You wanna know about security in this whole mess, see me, okay? Cosgrove and Samsa are busy covering their asses, and nobody's gonna pin the donkey's tail on Fred P. Toller. Whatever they say, I got this place covered. They hire somebody with more brains than Randy Loggins for a night guard, and none of this couldn't happen. You put *that* in your report, Poole!"

* * *

Poole watched snowflakes twirl through the mercury-vapor

lamp's weak beams. It illumined a painted escutcheon and the banner *PHEASANT LOT*. He looked at the acre of cars and tried to recall what he was driving.

He had rented a car at the St. Louis airport, a car with an animal name: a Ford Ferret or Chevy Civet or Dodge Donkey. Which? What color or size? All colors in the dusk and orange light were khaki. He tramped the rows until he saw a small, vaguely familiar silhouette. A sedan that seemed ludicrously undersized, with a label on the bumper reading LO-RENT U-DRIVE. His key fit the lock. He wedged his boxy frame into the small seat, feeling like circus clown No. 13 in an act disgorging dozens of pantaloons from a tiny vehicle.

Poole had grown up with Packards and De Sotos and Nashes, in memory as vast as ocean liners, festooned with useless tailfins, art-deco'd chrome slabs and dozens of gauges on radium-lit dashboards. *The bad old days,* Poole thought with a grin.

He listened to the four-cylinder engine tick like a dollar watch and felt nostalgia for the years before the Great Big *A*-rab Gasoline Ransom. He released the handbrake and nosed the car carefully across the snow-covered plain.

The highway into Leeland was an old, erratically-widened state road, largely empty now, since sane folks were home for supper. Along the highway were the ubiquitous elements of every commercial strip in the U.S.: the fast food battlefront of Hardee's, McDonald's, Arby's, Burger King, Kentucky Fried Chicken, Long John Silver's, Pizza Hut, interspersed with used-car lots draped with pennants, a semi-derelict drive-in movie, a carpet outlet advertising prices lower than Dalton, GA, a Holiday Inn glaring across no-man's-land at Howard Johnson's, several supermarkets promising the lowest prices in town, gas stations that were only pumps and plexiglas booths, with prominent posters warning CASH ONLY AFTER 6:00 P.M. and NO GASOHOL IN OUR

PREMIUM.

He spied the low, shabby outline of SleepyEye House, which must have been Leeland's first "real" motel, ca. 1950, on what had been the outskirts of the city. Now it sat among urban creep, quick-stop markets and small, decaying industries. The porta-sign before the place advertised

20 ROOMS 20

CABLE TV

ADULT MOVIES

An addendum to the old neon sign overhead read VACANCY. Poole was sure the NO had been unlit since Dwight Eisenhower was in office—The Light That Failed.

Angling the car into the slot before Unit 11, Poole felt his back twinge in protest at the cramped space. Inside, he found his room as depressing as he recalled: two double beds beaten up by professionals, a solid plastic dresser surmounted by an immense TV, a bathroom wedged into a corner, a swag-lamp of Tiffany plastic. The walls were tangerine and brown, smudged with a gray wash of age. The color TV offered only sickly green and yellow, like X-ray movies.

He sat on the bed and changed his clothes with slow-motion precision. A sign on the nightstand read *MagiFinger Relaxicizer – 25 cents. H*e fed the slot a quarter and the bed across from him belched and began to sway. It ground obscenely, emitting noises of rending materials. When Poole lay on it, the bed ground to a halt. Something beneath him hummed, clicked and issued the odor of burnt rubber.

Poole sighed and closed his eyes: If this is it, so be it. Immolated in a broken electric bed in Leeland, Illinois. He fell asleep on a tsunami of self-pity.

* * *

And woke with a snap. A fat, dying beast had camped in his mouth. Something unpleasant shrilled in his ear.

It was the telephone on the nightstand, which Poole located after only two or three scrabbling attempts. He prized his mouth open far enough to mutter, "Yeh?"

"Richard? Wilma. You said to call…"

"Hi. Yeh—I'm just…getting ready. Where do we meet?"

"The lobby of the Carnahan Hotel. Broadway and River. Can you find it? You said the best, remember? The Ribeye Room is it."

"Ten minutes."

"I've got some news, so this isn't…pure hedonism."

"Hey, I bet you're entitled to a couple of hours of hedonism." Poole thought she sounded uncomfortable. Probably not used to calling broken-down guys with jobs that sounded weird when you tried to explain them. Ah, these provincials, he thought, what do they know of the big world of international industrial security and its mind-boggling glamor and romance?

He dabbed on vile-smelling (gift) aftershave, a chemical advertised by an ex-football-pro even more battered than Poole, a man so macho he could hawk women's undergarments with impunity. His product, nevertheless, reeked like a bad summer morning's blow-off from a plant manufacturing dioxin-laced rat-killer.

Poole rammed himself into his topcoat and left the swag lamp burning, to infuse homeness into the dump. Outside, a gale blew across the Mississippi, fretted with spears of sleet. Poole fumbled his way into the Ferret, remembering why he so thoroughly detested Midwestern winters. His hands and feet died as he drove into Leeland, while the petulant heater blew an obbligato of frigid air into his face.

* * *

Downtown Leeland had perished of arteriosclerosis and

general decrepitude around 1970, Poole calculated, like the hearts of most American cities. A half-dozen blocks of the ex-center were boarded storefronts, some bearing ancient *LAST CHANCE SALE* signs. Someone had tried to create a mini-mall or pedestrian arcade effect, which had only screwed up the traffic pattern and left a forest of small skeletal trees in cement urns. The scene was powerfully melancholy—*thus perished a civilization.*

At one end of this necropolis stood the Carnahan Hotel, an eight-story brick tower with a Doric arcade around the ground floor, the kind of hostelry which once attracted the better class of commercial travelers and families motoring across the U.S. Its lights underscored the ruin around it.

Poole parked on an empty street and walked blatantly against a useless DONT WALK sign. A metal loudspeaker on a lamp pole wheezed a Christmas carol *pianissimo.* "Little Town of Bethlehem." It spoke of dark and dreaming streets, but Leeland's streets were long past dreams.

In the big red-plushed lobby of the hotel, Wilma Breithope waited in a dark green dress, hinting of parties, short to the knee and scooped low at the neck. Poole approved entirely of this non-reg packaging. Her shoulder-length blonde hair swung luxuriantly.

"We'll go straight to the Ribeye Room if you're hungry," she said.

"Hungry enough to eat a glove on the way," he said, "but let me stow my coat."

He eyed her as he returned from the check stand, and she flushed prettily, saying, "I take it you approve of my attire?"

"A thousand percent."

"You couldn't know how good it is to climb out of that Deputy Dawg outfit. It's like discovering there's a real, live woman who's been hiding inside me for eight hours."

"So, go into a line of work where you can be yourself."

A headwaiter dating from the time of the hotel's construction appeared and led them down the long, dim and largely empty dining room. He dealt them ostentatious menus encased in something like corduroy and slunk away, probably to find a mirror and practice his sneer.

Wilma settled and fluffed her hair. Poole liked the motion and its various effects on her physique. He wished he could reach across and stroke the lustrous blonde mane.

"So," he said. "You were *born* a deputy? Or shanghaied?"

"A long, dull story, Richard...I can call you Richard?"

"Sure. And *you're* just plain Wilma?"

"Yes. No nicknames attached. My father called me 'Brat,' but I can't use *that* label. He's why I joined the sheriff's office. Sort of. He was a lawyer—too good for this town. He wanted me to go into law. I was an only child, and I think he was disappointed I wasn't a son. He did come to accept the idea that maybe, just maybe, a woman could be a good lawyer."

"You went to law school?"

"No. My last year in college—Northwestern—he died. Something changed for me. I realized I had been thinking of the law because he wanted me to move into his office and keep the practice going. Suddenly, there was no practice. It was...gone."

A plump, jolly waitress materialized from the gloom, announcing that she was LuAnn. She took drink orders—a straight bourbon for Poole, a Bloody Mary for Wilma.

"To shorten my boring tale," Wilma continued, "I came back to Leeland when I graduated, ran into Bob Wheeler, thought I was in love and got married. After three years, I discovered that I had loved Bob with a desperate passion in seventh grade—and that he was still stuck at about that point. Bob had only three things on his mind: the Big Eagle Bowlarama, Wheaties for breakfast and the Cubs' standing. Everything else just...passed by.

"I did a three-year stretch in the house on Larchwood Lane, wondering what a political science honors graduate might do to affect the life of Leeland and going slightly crazy with fumes from Lemon Pledge and Windex. Then Bob came home one evening just before Thanksgiving and said he was in love with Dorothy Tallmadge—who ran the shoe-rental concession at the Bowlarama. I've known Dot since second grade. I sat there while Bob cried, and I thought. Dot's a nice, petite redhead who was on the girl's softball team and played oboe in the band. After about two minutes, I said, 'You know, Bob—I'll bet you're in love with her, all right. And I'll bet you ought to get a divorce and marry her.' It was as if someone lifted a humongous weight off me. I felt like running around the twelve-by-fourteen living room, screaming 'Free at last, free at last—thank God Almighty, free at last!'"

LuAnn appeared with drinks—a conventional bourbon glass for Poole and a gigantic schooner containing the Bloody Mary and a grove of celery, an iceberg and a lime plantation.

"Oh, goody," Wilma said, "I can get drunk and overload on vitamin C all at once."

She sipped at an edge of the bowl and Poole gargled his bourbon. The jolt of warmth revived him. Wilma peered from the celery undergrowth and said, "Then I went to law-enforcement school, found I could do that standing on my head, came back and got the job with Buck. I've been at it three years."

Poole, after lightning calculation, decided Wilma was pushing thirty. A nice age.

"Tell me about yourself, while I try to toy with this drink in a ladylike manner."

"What's to tell? You got the basic job description this morning. I come in for TransAtlas and do what they dignify as 'situation assessment'. Meaning I try to figure out what's screwed up, who screwed it up and why. Then I try to figure out what we—that's the big shots at TA—can do to straighten it out. Or somebody at TA figures we should unload the assets and recombine in some way."

"But you arrived *before* the murders."

"Pure chance. I came in because LeeLand Mall has bled red ink for eighteen months. It's the only subsidiary of AmeriMall that's in deep trouble. Our auditors howl *sell*, but my boss, Harvey Lewis, sent me in for a look-see."

LuAnn materialized and Poole deferred to Wilma over the huge menu. She ordered a Cattleman's Ribeye dinner for him and a Madame Mignon for herself.

Wilma said, "The ribeye is what this place is about."

Poole tried hard to extract glamour from his work with TransAtlas, and then dinner arrived. To his surprise, the food was excellent—the ribeye cooked exactly medium-rare, juicy *au jus*, vegetables of precise consistency. Real Midwestern Food. He belted into it, nearly injuring himself with his steak knife in his eagerness. He watched Wilma also eat with steady concentration. God, he appreciated a woman who wasn't afraid to show an appetite. *Any* appetite. Would she go in for a pie-eating contest or a spot of Indian leg-wrestling to seal his approval?

Desserts followed, as good as the main courses, and finally coffee and cognac. Poole felt surfeited and only mildly stunned by the tab LuAnn presented. He would whiz it past the TA auditor's as a business-conference supper.

As they finished the liqueurs, Wilma said, "Oh—my news. I nearly forgot. When I was checking out, Howells called. He traced the…elves. They were staying at a rooming house on River Street. The landlady is positive they left there Sunday around noon. They went with a man in a pickup truck—Howells is sure it was Heck Ogden.

He must have taken them to work at the mall. They were on duty all afternoon. Howells also got reports from the St. Louis police. In addition to being show-biz types, both elves had arrest records in the fifties for short-con and bunko activities. Not long sheets but enough to make them suspicious characters."

Poole paid with his credit card, then Wilma led him into the vaulted lobby and pointed up toward the ceiling. "You were asking about Leeland's tangled history. There it is."

An elaborate mural, a panorama in WPA fresco style ran around the upper walls. Clumps of men, women, wagons, a pitched battle with Indians, a riverboat churning across one wall, buildings under construction, a panel of women in filmy dresses performing what might be a Maypole dance.

"It's the story of the founding of Leeland in 1843, when the Lee family came down from Nauvoo. A local artist named Abel Hobart did it when the hotel was renovated in the '30s. The Lee family—Epaphimandas Lee and his wives—came from Missouri with Joseph Smith to Nauvoo, when the Mormons thought they'd found heaven on earth there. Lee had a falling-out with the saints and moved downriver here before Nauvoo went bust. He had four wives and sixteen children, all told. So he had a head-start on his own city. A few of Smith's other followers drifted down when the Mormons were run out of Nauvoo, and they had a commune going in no time. Based on Lee's ideas of Mormonism with other Utopian twists. They went in for brewing beer. That's what all those barrels are. They imported a gang of German immigrants from St. Louis, and in a few years they had a huge brewery operating. That's part of the mall design, you know—based on pictures of the old brewery, which stood out there."

Poole squinted into the shadowed height. He pointed to a corner where a group of people dispensed bananas, oranges and other fruit from a giant cornucopia. "What's that about?"

"Lee and his children got mixed up with fruitarians and developed a scheme for shipping tropical fruits North on the river.

Lee believed a fruit diet—maybe supplemented with his beer—was the key to perfect health. They tried all kinds of refrigerating and shipping schemes, then the Civil War came along and the blockade disrupted it all."

"How does this fascinating stuff connect with the present?"

"You must understand that the old-line families in Leeland trace back to this bunch of Utopians, and they're damned proud of it. Old Epaphimandas printed his own currency—based on a labor-credit idea, not on gold or silver—and ran the place as a fiefdom till he died in 1880. So, for twenty years or so, people cooked up one scheme after another to renew the Garden of Eden. Some were nudists, some were strict vegetarians, some were craftsmen. Most of our black population, such as it is, came from freed slaves shipped up before the end of the Civil War, in a plan to educate them and transplant them to Brazil to grow fruit for the town."

"So everyone in Leeland has crackpots hanging from the family tree?"

"I'm not sure they were crackpots. Some ideas make damned good sense. But there is a long tradition of wild and woolly thinking behind the city."

"And old Epi-whatsis had *four* wives? There must an army of descendants."

"Most of the Lee family picked up and went to Utah to rejoin the original Mormons in the 1890s. Only a few direct descendants stayed here. And Epaphimandas didn't push the idea of polygamy in Leeland. He was more interested in big business than big families. His statue stands in front of the courthouse. He looms there heroically, with a surveying compass in one hand and a banana in the other. Kids are always defacing it. They paint the banana yellow and put…awful graffiti on the base."

Poole laughed. "It's a lively tale."

"Stop at the city library. Ask for Ann Wilcox in the reference section. She'll put you onto the city history in a jiffy."

Poole and Wilma struggled with their coats and pushed out into the night. Snow swirled and blew in dense clouds.

"Damn!" Wilma said. "Winter for sure. I was going to ask you to my place for a nightcap. Now Buck will be on the horn calling us out for highway duty before morning."

"It's okay—I'll take a rain check. Make that snow check."

Poole clasped Wilma awkwardly in their heavy wraps and kissed her. She did not struggle or scream.

"Thanks a lot for the evening," she said. "I *needed* to show off my pretty clothes." Their faces were close, their breaths mingled in a cloud. "I'd like to…see you again."

"Tomorrow, I'm sure. Okay, I understand. We'll make a date," Poole said. "Now, get home before we're frozen to this spot."

They trotted in quick half-steps to her car, a new Japanese coupe—a Hoyota or Tonda or Subarishi. It was round and red, like a Christmas ornament, under the streetlight. Poole waited till she started it and then legged across the empty street to his own tiny car. Little snow had accumulated, but it was windblown like ice-cold shot.

In the Ferret, Poole offered a prayer to the mighty god Delco. The engine rattled like broken glass but then fired and ran cheerily. Poole drove until he saw the great purple orb that winked spasmodically on the SleepyEye House sign.

He thought it odd that the door to Unit 11 opened under his glove, recalling he had left a light on as he saw the darkness inside, thrust one foot into the room and was struck by a heavy body. A coarse gloved hand covered his mouth. He was twisted inward and downward, out of cold and into darkness.

He never totally lost consciousness, although something blunt and hard whacked the base of his neck. As he thrashed, hot, sour breath rolled on his face. Then he was parceled, his arms and legs pinioned. He was dragged, his head colliding painfully with an immovable object. Finally, he was propped in a sitting posture.

Poole could see vaguely. He was blindfolded, but there was a tiny slit under the bandage. When he tested his bonds, he found himself tied tightly around the middle, hands behind him, ankles clamped together. Someone leaned close.

"We know why you're here, Poole. Listen, and maybe you'll be all right." A gutteral, *sotto voce* whisper. A hand clamped on the soft bruise on his shoulder, and he writhed.

"Hurts, huh? That's just a taste."

A second voice, further away, whispered, "Leave off. Listen, Poole—you and the other cops back off. That bum Ogden done it. He killed the little guys. They had a racket goin, and he offed 'em. To… cut 'em out, see? Pass it on to the cops and the sheriff. We can find you. And other people will get hurt, too."

The presence backed away. Poole could see through his slit—work shoes, jeans, a leather work glove. The two voices whispered, but he could not interpret the susurrus.

A heavy hand fell on his chest. "You're lucky, pal. We're gonna let you live. But wind up your business and fuck off—hear? Get out of Leeland now."

He was tipped over, his head jouncing on the thin carpet. There was a blast of chill as the door opened and closed. He felt exhausted and ill. He could sleep. But he sighed and rolled around, testing his bonds. He sat, after an elaborate series of wriggles and kicks.

"Oh, terrific," he said, his own voice startling him. "Now you can pretend you're sitting on the floor by choice!"

Poole's hands were tight behind him, arms and feet firmly clamped. He bounced and wiggled, wincing at a symphony of pains in his neck and head. He expanded his chest and arms, wishing he had persevered in the Charles Atlas course back in…oh, 1950. If he had grown magnificent biceps, triceps and delts, he could burst his bonds with a few deep breaths and a stern application of Dynamic Tension. Youth is wasted on the young.

After geological ages passed, Poole was sure his arms and ankles were freer. After a few more millennia, his left hand came loose. He worked it, against jolts of lightning-like pain in his shoulder, till he gripped the tough, thin cord around him. He pulled, tugged and sawed until the left arm was entirely free. Then he stripped off the blindfold.

He was wound in neon-orange nylon cord. He clawed at knots. Eventually, he freed his body and feet. He staggered upright, tested his arms and legs and stripped off his topcoat, which looked as if it had housed a free-for-all for berserk wolverines.

The room had been ransacked. Clothing and papers littered the floor. His suit hung in the open rack, slashed to tatters. The desk telephone lay in the corner, torn cord trailing. On the big mirror over the dresser-desk a heavy hand had scrawled in grease pencil:

GO HOME FOR XMAS OR DIE HERE.

* * *

Poole tried to restore the room to semi-chaos then walked to the office, an annex at the end of the ranked rooms. Behind the desk sat a short, bald man, his skull shaped like a bullet, eyes startlingly magnified by thick glasses. When Poole entered, this clerk was picking absently at a tuft of white hair springing from his right ear. A slick-paper magazine lay open before him to a centerfold photograph—an enormously magnified view of a female sexual organ. He flipped the magazine shut and regarded Poole without expression.

"Mr. SleepyEye?" Poole said.

"I'm only on nights. Larry Starr. I come on at eleven."

"I'm Poole—Unit Eleven. Did you see anyone leave my room last night—late?"

"Nah. I don't generally stand outside in blizzards to watch the rooms."

"Two goons were waiting for me when I got back, around midnight."

Larry Starr squinted, a startling effect behind the milky lenses. "They give you one swell shiner," he said.

Poole touched his left cheek and winced. "They tied me up and worked me over. They also trashed my belongings and your room. The telephone is busted."

Larry's face lit up—at last, an exciting night on the job! "No shit! Hey, I'm sorry, but we don't take no responsibility."

Poole sighed and walked back into the ambiguous dawn, full of skirling, hissing snow. Only thin snow on the asphalt lot and a puddle turned to black ice. No footprints or tire tracks in that. Poole limped back to the office and begged use of the phone. Larry Starr watched as if he performed magical or pornographic acts.

The sheriff's number yielded a gruff, sleepy voice: "Sheriff ain't in. Breithope neither. Probably be back around ten. They pulled double shifts yesterday."

Poole hung up and called the city police. Len Howells was not yet on duty, so Poole dictated his report of the crime to a less-than-awed desk officer. He promised speedy (if unspecified) action.

Poole's trusty K-Mart special digital watch told him it was 3:18 a.m., 12-2. He lay on his bed, after shucking his necktie and shoes.

One wink, he promised himself, one taste of actual sleepy-bye at SleepyEye. When he woke, his watch read 9:04 a.m., 12-2. Daylight as thin as workhouse gruel pierced the window of his room. He sat up and tested the soft spots on his body and face. It had been a reasonably expert beating by someone who still valued old-fashioned pride of workmanship.

Sorting his clothes, he salvaged a shirt and trousers not hopelessly mauled. Pre-Christmas sales at LeeLand Mall would replace the rest. He could gain a consumer's-eye view of the mall and with some creative reporting list the clothing as "unexpected business expenses"—his No. 1 loophole in his report forms.

When he stepped from his room, Poole found changed weather: the wind had slackened, and heavy, wet snow fell in fat flakes like offerings in a mute tickertape parade. More inches of snow lay mounded. The sky beyond the flakes was iron-gray.

Poole cautiously followed the highway to the mall, inching behind an orange plow-truck as it scraped a lane. The mall reared up, as he reached it, like an apparition from "The Rime of the Ancient Mariner"—a ghost-steamer aground on the frozen Mississippi shore.

The vast asphalt lot was only a third full, and drifts formed over it. Poole parked in QUAIL LOT and entered the building. Just outside the main doors stood a Salvation Army lassie, huddled into a cape and bonnet, and a ruddy-cheeked boy who played "What Child Is This?" expertly on a silver cornet.

Inside the doors, the electronic music blared out a break-dance version of "I Saw Mommy Kissing Santa Claus." Poole grimaced at the harsh contrast and hurried through the building to the Maintenance-Security annex. Fred Toller's office was empty, as was the cubicle where they had parked Heck Ogden. Poole found a phone and called Samsa.

"Oh, Mr. Poole," cooed Alicine. "Mr. Samsa's gone to lunch now. But he's been trying to reach you. I don't know where Fred is if he's not there. I'll try his pager." In a hiatus, piped music hit Poole from the phone. He longed for ear-plugs. Alicine clicked back, "I don't get a response. Maybe he's out of the mall—out of range."

Poole waited in Toller's swivel chair, surveying the bank of TV monitors, which showed a jigsaw of blurred scenes. He stood and buttoned his coat, when Fred Toller staggered in, splashed with snow, trouser legs wet-dark. He said, "That silly old fart run off, Poole. I think he made a hole in the river."

While Toller made frantic phone calls, Poole found a Mr. Coffee in the corner and handed the security chief a steaming cup. Toller sucked at it, grimaced and said, "Thanks. It's the thought that counts. Loggins makes this stuff at night. He's the only human being I know who can totally ruin machine coffee."

"How did Ogden get away?"

"How the hell else? I come in and pumped coffee and juice into Ogden. Heck said he was comin around. Samsa called for me to fill him in. They'd put Randy Loggins onto the day shift, so I left Loggins here to watch Good St. Nick. When I get back, both Loggins and Ogden are gone. I found Loggins out running around in the snow in his shirtsleeves. We tracked Ogden toward the river, but it's all jack-swamp the other side of the trees. Loggins is still out there trying to find his ass with both hands."

"Did you talk with Ogden at all?"

"He was mumbling and drooling when I left. I don't know if he even understands the little guys are dead. Where the fuck have *you* been?"

Poole pulled a length of the orange cord from his pocket. "I was tied up. Some delegates from your chamber of commerce visited and left calling cards and a puzzle to solve."

"Jeez—they played hell with your face, too."

"Yeh. But, look—they trussed me up with this stuff. The same cord the elves were strangled with. Coincidence?"

"Poole, you can buy that everywhere. Every farmer and home owner in PawPaw County's got some around."

Toller finished the coffee and rose, stamping his feet. "I'm gonna catch frostbite out of this mess. Come on, let's see if the sheriff's boys are here."

As they exited the building, a maroon-and-white cruiser slewed up the access road, fright-lights winking. It stopped, and Sheriff Buxtrider and Deputy Breithope spilled out, swaddled in down parkas. Toller windmilled his arms. As the river wind accelerated, snow flew in small cyclonic clouds.

Buxtrider surveyed the scene and Wilma gave Poole a private smile from within the cave of her parka hood. The sheriff shook his head and yelled over the wind, "You can't see ten yards. If he's been wandering out here an hour, old Heck'll be an ice cube when we find him. He's got 90-proof blood, but it's damn cold."

They slogged across the parking lot and into uneven ground. Poole's shoes and socks were soaked, his feet numb. He wheezed and tried to keep up. They passed through a gap in the tall poplar windbreak and entered a landscape of reeds and marsh, spits of land surrounded by ice-covered rivulets and tongues of shallow water, wind-whipped into frozen ripples.

"Watch it!" Buxtrider bawled. "Some of this is deep holes."

Ice-coated reeds and briars bowed in gothic arches. Scrub trees were crushed into heaps of snow and rime. The wind lifted thick curtains of snow from the ground and shook them. The cold pierced like arrows.

Buxtrider waved his arms and called them together. His voice exploded from a cloud of vapor: "If we split up, we'll lose each other. We're going to have to send back for more help or wait for this wind to taper off. Wilma—hike back and call in. See if we can pull in some night people. Shit! This is going to take too long."

Wilma turned to Poole. "You're not dressed warmly enough. Come on back with me. You'll freeze out here."

Poole shook his head. "I'll hang on a bit. Maybe we'll hit his trail."

"You can't see anything to follow—it's all blown away."

Poole raised a hand and screened his eyes. "He saw an indistinct shape upriver in the shifting scrims of white.

"Wait!" he yelled. "Over there." He pulled Wilma's arm, and they slid forward, lurching on frozen mud and drifts, colliding and slithering as they struggled ahead. The wind shifted, and Poole glimpsed a row of rotted fence posts strung with sagging barbed wire.

"What is it?" Wilma shouted. "What did you see?"

'I don't know—something by the fence." Poole's legs were weighted with snow and ice, and he reeled as he tried to walk. Then he banged sharply into a solid object—one of the old locust fence-posts. He clung to it. Then he saw a dark object on the snow.

"Here!" A man in a khaki coat and uniform trousers lay doubled over the barbed wire, snow and ice blown onto him like thick white paint. String brown hair trailed the ground. He and Wilma tugged him upright.

"Randy Loggins," Wilma said. "We've got to haul him back—he's unconscious. Or dead."

"Which way?" Poole shouted. They peered around, and Poole saw a tall shape. "There—the tree line." The sheriff and Toller seemed to have vanished totally in the fierce snow-squall.

Poole and Wilma staggered and slid with the dead weight between them, their breath bursting out in head-haloing clouds. As they left the river flat, the wind slowed. They floundered in softer snow around the mall but finally dragged Loggins into the Maintenance-Security annex and dropped him on the couch.

Wilma phoned for an ambulance while Poole stripped Loggins' sodden coat and shook snow off him. His eyes were shut, his face a leaden gray.

Wilma said, "They said the wind chill factor on the river is fifty below. How long has he been out there?"

Poole said, "Get blankets, coats, anything to pile on him. He's a block of ice."

He listened at Loggins' chest. Dark blood was crusted in the long, tangled hair.

"He's hurt," Poole said. "His head. Is there a doctor in the mall?"

Wilma called Samsa's office. Poole stripped off his own soggy shoes and socks. Toller and Buxtrider arrived, just ahead of a doctor who had been paged. Wilma and the sheriff went back out to find the officers arriving to search for Ogden. Poole watched as the doctor examined Loggins.

"Nasty," he finally muttered. "Maybe a severe concussion on top of hypothermia. Where's the ambulance?"

"Not dead?" Poole said.

"A pulse, but very weak. His body temperature's way down."

In minutes, the young doctor followed the paramedics as Loggins was strapped to a Gurney and hoicked into the ambulance. Poole watched out the window as the vehicle skidded and wallowed away. Then Fred Toller came from his office, his frost-burnt face even brighter scarlet. He spat, "Shit fire and save matches! That goddam fool…"

He sighed and sat on the couch, mucky water streaming from boots and pants cuffs. He tore off his coat and threw his bright-red deer-hunter's cap across the room. "I hate this," he finally said. "That imbecile Samsa tells me to get this under control. Loggins is half-dead, and our prize Santa won't surface till the spring thaw. What the hell is going on?"

"Was Loggins carrying his pistol?" Poole asked.

"Yeh, I guess so. I keep telling the idiot not to load it. He's supposed to carry it on his rounds, though."

"The holster was empty when we found him. It may be out there in the snow, with his hat and gloves."

Toller stared blankly.

"If you go out there where we found him on the fence line, you may find the gun. Maybe he lost it. Maybe somebody took it. Maybe they hit him with it."

"They?"

"Ogden. Someone."

Toller stared at Poole and then picked up the phone. As he dialed, he said, "It's time you met people who can fill you in on life at LeeLand Mall. You talk with Cosgrove and Samsa, you'll believe this is all one big, happy business."

Toller spoke: "Hey, Alicine, sweetheart—do a favor and run down Ziggy and Heinie and Doreen Nugent. Oh, and send Pruitt, too. He's down in S-L with those guys fixing the pipes. Thanks, honey. Yeh, send 'em all to my office. I'm giving Poole a post-grad course in mall life…"

He sat back and stripped off his boots. "Now, you'll meet the citizens here. The mall is like a city, see, and you need to shake hands with plain folks."

"Do you think Heck Ogden's dead?"

"I don't know. Tough as an old boot, Hector. A real old-time river-rat. You live on that river half a century, and you can survive damn near anything. But it's *cold* out there. I'll tell you, though—I wouldn't take bets Heck was dead. If he didn't fall in the river, he could of made it anywhere down the flats."

Toller leaned back and scanned the TV monitors. "Look at that. All those people in a damn hurry to buy happiness. God bless us, every one."

Rudolf The Red Knows Rain, Dear

THE FOUR PEOPLE sitting across from Poole in Toller's office exuded distinctive aromas. Ziggy and Heinie—or Sigmund and Heinrich, as they preferred—were kids Poole had spotted in the mall. They wore jackets of slick black plasti-leather be-studded and be-zippered, with jeans and clunky motorcycle boots. Ziggy's dull blond hair was shaved short, and Heinrich wore a dark-red pileum with a Lascar's pigtail. Both were prime candidates for intensive acne-therapy.

They were sixteen or seventeen, Poole guessed, but their fixed sneers made them look older and duller. They slumped on a couch, their feet on a scarred coffee table.

Next to them in a plastic chair Doreen Nugent hunched, a tiny woman with coal-black hair tucked under a greasy blue bandana. She hugged a tattered plastic raincoat around her, with one hand vigilantly on a bulging shopping bag she towed like a dory. She might be anywhere between forty and seventy, Poole thought.

Next to Doreen, in another plastic chair, was an old man—Pruitt Bastin, a shriveled, light-skinned black man in oversized gray overalls generously stained with grease. He rubbed a hand in his short, steel-gray hair and blinked like a marmoset behind steel-rimmed glasses.

Poole and Toller faced them like interrogators or seminar leaders. Styrofoam coffee cups strewed the table, but no one acted as if this were a friendly kaffe klatsche. "Yeh," Toller said, "Ziggy and Heinie are your *bona fide* average mall-rats. Right, fellas?"

Ziggy glared, recrossed his arms and looked at Doreen. Wrinkling his stubby nose, he said, "Christ, you look worse than ever, Granny. Smell ripe, too. When you gonna give up and die?"

Drawing herself up, Doreen looked pointedly away from Ziggy.

"Why do I gotta sit here, Mr. Toller?" she whined. "I ain't done nothing."

Heinie fidgeted and pulled a fat felt-tipped pen from his pocket, examined it and thrust it back.

"One of your artistic implements, Heinie?" Toller asked. "These young gents think they're geniuses, see? Write the most godawful scrawls everywhere if you don't watch them."

Heinrich sneered and flounced his mane. He also wore heavy silver earrings, Poole noted. Heinie stared at the floor and mumbled, "You got no right to hassle us."

"Hassling? Who's hassling?" Toller was blithefully cheery. "We haven't had a nice chat in…oh, weeks. We're very interested now in people who go around with spray paints, see? Somebody, Sunday night, spray-painted a half-dozen security cameras. You two are hotshot wall artists, so I figured you could tell us who done it."

Ziggy said, "You ain't gonna drag us in on some bullshit charge, Freddie. You know goddam well we weren't here after closing."

Pruitt Bastin shifted and rubbed his hands. "Mr. Tow—I gotta get back to them pipes. You know I don't like to leave them plumbers alone. Play hell with the whole heat system if I don't keep a eagle eye on 'em. Can't figure how them valves got so screwed up and messed around. That Jinx Washburn, he hadn't ought to fool with 'em. A…*night* man, anyhow!"

Toller said to Poole, "Pruitt thinks this is *his* mall, see? He worked at the brewery here, back in the Stone Age, and he believes Mr. Samsa built this place just to bless Pruitt's golden years."

Toller smiled unpleasantly at Bastin and then at Doreen. "And our little Doreen is resident bag-lady-hostess. No matter how many times you run her out, she's back mingling with the gentry and stinking the place up. Maybe she was here early Monday morning when the little fellas were croaked."

She shook her head violently, dabbing a grimed finger at her eye. "I went into town on the bus. I gotta be at the shelter by nine o'clock or they lock me out. I ain't gonna be on the streets in this weather."

Toller sighed and stretched. "So—none of you knows anything or saw anything Sunday night? You're pure innocents who wouldn't even *think* about murder and bad stuff." He kicked at the coffee-table, knocking the boys' boots off and creating a drizzle of coffee. "Don't kid a kidder. Mr. Poole here is a high-powered investigator from back East. He'll put your miserable asses in jail forever unless I tell him you're nice folks. Got it?"

Toller sighed again. "Doreen—you and Pruitt can take off. We'll talk with these nice lads a moment more, though."

As the two oldsters shuffled away, Toller said, "You boys are on thin ice. I've talked with your parents—such as they are—and asked the cops to keep an eye on you. Next, I make it my personal mission to harass you. You don't want that."

Ziggy sneered at the nearest wall; Heinie stared at his bootcaps.

"I find any of your so-called graffiti around here, I'll bust you for vandalism. I see you here in school hours, I'll drag your butts to the high school myself. Got it?"

Toller extracted a toothpick from his shirt pocket and poked it into his mouth. He folded his hands on his potbelly and stared contentedly at the two. Then he said, "You hear anything about who killed the, er, elves, you talk to me. Or we'll see how juvie court handles accessory and obstructing charges. I can always arrange to find pot or crack in your pockets."

The two shifted, with a low clank of chains and medallions.

"Okay. Get the fuck out. Go home."

They shambled away, trying to swagger, muttering.

Toller said, "Cockroaches. You gotta swat at "em every once in a while or they get bold."

"Sigmund and Heinrich?" Poole said, bemused.

"Shit. Who knows why they call themselves that? Here." Toller handed index cards to Poole. One was headed ZIGGY and read *Wilson James (17), 2231 Riverview Terrace*, with a summary of James's parental situation and school record (both dismal). The other read HEINRICH, followed by *Chance Cosgrove Brewster (18), 113 Norton Avenue*, with another tedious resumé.

Poole said, "Chance *Cosgrove* Brewster?"

"You got it, sport. He is Dandy Don's nephew. Which makes him even more a pain in the rump than he makes himself. I have little prayer-meetings with Cosgrove once a month to tell him how his zoomy sister's angel-child is doing. Enough to make a goat puke."

"How about Ziggy?"

"James is just a draggle-assed poor kid. His old man cut out years ago, and Thelma James has struggled as a waitress at the Steamboat Tap, maybe picking up nickels hustling on the side. I can't blame him—he's got diddly-squat to look forward to. But little Heinrich has a nice home and a bundle of bucks swaddling him."

"Why the, er, Teutonic monikers?"

"The silly little bastards think that makes them big time Nazis. Who knows? A whole mob of mall-rats wear those loony haircuts and shitty clothes and think they're tough guys. Here—their girlfriends."

Toller dealt Poole two more index cards, these bearing small, smudgy photos as well as typed data. The first card showed a thin-faced girl with soulful eyes and dark, stringy hair. It read TOTTY —*Caroline Hawes (14), 101 N. 1st Avenue*, followed by a profile. The

54

second card showed a moon-faced, curly-topped girl with giant eyeglasses. Her card read LOLA—*Robin Jowett (13), 44 Saylor Street,* and a briefer resumé.

"I was expecting maybe Brunnhilde or Gertrude," Poole said. "They're awfully young."

"These kids are *born* old. You first see them, you think they're grade-schoolers out playing dress-up. You talk to them, you know they'd cut your liver out any dark night if they got a chance. And not blink. The girls scare me more than the guys."

"Where did these pictures come from?"

Toller snorted. "Would you believe they *gave* them to me? Took them down at the Photo-Mat. Said they wanted nice pictures for their files. Jesus. You can't guess what goes on inside their heads. If anything."

"Where are they from?"

"You want high-powered sociology, or what? They're just kids from pretty average Leeland families. Christ knows why their folks let them spend ninety percent of their time here. Probably a hell of a lot better than having them at home. If you think they come from disadvantaged families or high-crime-risk groups, forget it. They're just nasty little imps who get a charge out of being public nuisances. They graduate from small-change shoplifting to hanging out full time, badgering other kids, scrawling graffiti, scaring shoppers. Little Lola's another 'privileged' kid—her old lady's related to the Lees. But who isn't?"

"You really think they could have killed the elves?"

"The cops shook them down. They take them seriously enough, but God knows. It's a sicko idea. But they can be sicko kids. Maybe it was a fun thing to do. Maybe they were charged up on crack or speed."

"You *know* they use drugs?"

"What's to know? The stuff floats everywhere. It's a billion-to-one shot those four haven't snorted or shot up anything they could find. You hand them rabbit turds and tell them it's a cool high, they'd scoff them down and go wild."

Toller dialed his phone. "Hey, Alicine-babe—what you hear up yonder?" He frowned and nodded, waggling his toothpick.

"Yeh. Okay. Tell his highness I'm on my way. But there's nobody minding the store here." He hung up and groaned.

Poole said, "I'll hang around here and cover, if that'll help."

"Thanks. Samsa's been breathing fire all day. Or as close as he gets— pissing and moaning. If the sheriff's guys come in, call me, huh?"

Poole sat before the tall array of monitors, letting the shifting vignettes of commerce mesmerize him. It was hard to recall that a winter storm howled beyond the insulated walls and tiers of tinsel. He heard a carol simpering in the background.

* * *

Wilma Breithope entered with several other deputies an hour later, the group chilled and wind-rumpled. Buxtrider made phone calls, sitting behind Toller's desk, drumming his fingers. Lighting a rope-like and rancid cigar, he regarded Poole blankly.

"No damn luck. Weather bureau says we've got a thirty-six-hour blow. We won't be able to get a search team up and down the river till tomorrow. Which means Heck's a goner, one way or the other."

Wilma stood fluffing her hair. She smiled at Poole. With her cold-burnished cheeks and golden hair, she could model for a Christmas cherub.

Buxtrider scowled at her and said, "Hey, Deputy—go on back to the office and warm up. You can relieve Ernie on the dispatch desk the rest of the afternoon."

"I don't need favors."

"No favor. I'm taking this operation home, and I want somebody on the radio besides that bonehead. There'll be a slew of emergency calls, and you can coordinate with the State Police. Okay?"

Buxtrider winked covertly at Poole and crushed his noxious stogy. He stood and stretched his big frame. "I'm gonna hit the pancake house and stoke up on the way in."

The sheriff and three deputies clattered out, while Wilma lingered to say to Poole, "I get to be Little Miss Telephone while the big, strong men go out for a bean-feed. That's terrific with me. They need time to grab-ass around, and I don't want to be in sight then."

"Surely," Poole said, "they wouldn't pass a chance to grab your comely ass?"

"Easy, boy," she said. "Besides, it's probably frozen off." She glanced down the back of her parka.

"I think old Buck means well," Poole said. "Call me tonight, and we'll find a better place than the pancake house."

"Mmm. I was hoping you'd say that. You're on. We'll ignore the hell out of this weather. I'll call after six unless we get into a swivet at the office."

At three in the afternoon, Poole found the parking lot was virtually empty except for ranges of snow pummeled by a yellow front-loader. Heavy flakes spun lazily down. Poole scooped ineffectually at the rime caked on the Ferret, gave up and drove it slowly into town still laden with snow.

A few cars crept ahead of him. He entered the center of town and parked before the looming courthouse. Across from this gothic pile was another opulent Victorian building spiked with crenellations, spires and turrets, the Leeland Public Library.

Poole slithered and skidded up the snowy steps and charged into the building, nearly bowling over a small brunette inside the big doors.

"Oh," she gasped, "I was just coming to see if we should close-up. Most of the staff are on their way home."

"Excuse my clumsiness," Poole said, reluctantly releasing her. She was small and trimly packaged, with prominent curves under a tweed skirt and bulky sweater. Her brown eyes were steady under dark bangs. *What a look!* Poole thought.

"Can't you stay open a bit? I braved this storm for information —local history. I hear you're the authority on Leeland."

"Well…" She broke eye-contact and glanced out at the white gale.

"I'll bet you're Ann Wilcox."

"Yes. And not precisely *the* authority."

She smiled. "Very well. No more soft soap. But I must close the library soon, if I want to get home."

She led Poole through an empty reading room, past the main desk and through big, carved doors. The library exuded a remarkable scent, evoking in Poole memories of cutting high school to sit reading in the public library, behavior inexplicable to himself at sixteen. He preferred to be regarded as a truant to explaining to Mr. Bartholomew the principal that he loved passing whole days with old books.

He watched Ann Wilcox's sensuous motion—much woman in small wrapping. She smiled over her shoulder and led him to a long table in the special collections room. "What brings you here? You're not from Leeland, are you?"

"No, no. Visiting for a few days. But I'm fascinated with your early history—the Lees, the Mormons and all that. Can you give me a kind of basic outline to read?"

"There are several popular histories, but they're stuffed with legends and wild inaccuracies. Best starting places are a couple of scholarly histories of western Illinois, then work up to Aunt Mary's tome."

"Aunt Mary?"

"Mary Lee Llewelyn—my great-aunt, actually. She spent forty years on her book, which she thought would be a sensational best-seller. She called it *Saints and Sinners by the River,* and she dreamed of selling the movie rights. She's a sucker for *Gone with the Wind*, and she waited years for a million-dollar offer. The book sold about two thousand copies, all told. Ah, here it is."

She added a fat book from the shelf to the two she had gathered. She set them on the table by a big bronze lamp with a green-tinted shade.

"You speak of her in past and present tenses."

"She inhabits both. She's ninety-one…ah, ninety-two. For the last ten years she's been in Sunnyside Home, and she wanders in and out of the present. I remember her when she was younger and very lively. I grew up with her and never realized she was old till I was leaving for college and a friend mentioned that Mary had turned eighty. I was shocked and angered."

"Angered?"

She flipped through a book to locate a place. When she looked up, Poole saw that her eyes were like Emily Dickinson's—"a little sherry at the bottom of the glass," a red-brown.

"Yes. It seemed supremely unfair that Mary should be old and wise and seem young and happy. I was full of my own self-importance and grownup-ness, and I was sure going to college was the most important act a human being could accomplish. I also felt angry that she was so old she might die before I came home. I was quite piqued with God for arranging things as they are."

Picking up a second book, she flushed. "I'm prattling, Mr.—?"

"Poole. Call me Richard."

"It's an occupational hazard for reference librarians. We're cooped up with books all day. They're hardly mute, but when a live human arrives with a question, you can't shut us up."

"I don't mind listening to you."

"Well. What in particular do you want to know about our history? Can I save you time by locating specific topics?"

"The Lee family, I guess. And all their Utopian ideas."

She moved to another shelf and found an even larger book. "All right—chapters four and five here, in *Seekers for a City*. Mr. Pullman was biased against some of the founders, but he sketches a good background for their ideas."

Poole was a sucker for slightly pedantic women. If Ann Wilcox had donned a gown and mortarboard, he would have crept on hands and knees across the oak flooring to her.

She slid the book onto the table and smiled. "Call if you need help. But I'll have to shoo you away soon." The high windows around them were blanked white with snow.

Poole watched her exit appreciatively. He turned to the books, now less inviting than they might have been. Perhaps Ann Wilcox would just recite Leeland's checkered history for him, in some comfortable, warm place—by a fireplace on a wool rug, with hot toddies all around. He shoved the idea away, opened a big green-bound book and began to read.

* * *

Leeland's tangled history pulled Poole from the snowbound present to a past crammed with volcanic change and violence. Epaphimandas Lee, as a young man, met a strange prophet named Joseph Smith in the Burned-Over District of New York State. Lee was both fascinated with and repelled by Smith and his odd preachings. The fourth son of a failed grain-merchant from Yonkers, a remote cousin of Mother Anne Lee who founded the Shaker movement, Lee had an apparent genetic attraction to powerful, quirky ideas. And a strong will to believe. He followed Smith, left him, then rejoined the Mormons in their trek to Far West, the Missouri mission they had planted.

When Smith commanded polygamy, Epaphimandas took four wives, two of them widows with five children between them. Lee settled in Nauvoo, on the Illinois bank of the Mississippi, with the Mormons, and worked on the new city of God Smith mandated.

But Lee lost some of his faith in the charismatic prophet of the Angel Moroni. Lee was an autodidact, with the strong need for self-assurance of such men, who read widely in the Utopian socialists. He was as intrigued by secular schemes for the perfection of humanity as in Smith's theological zeal. Restless and ambitious, Lee made enemies among the Mormons and few friends among the anti-Mormons who observed the growth of Nauvoo with horror. They felt subverted, overshadowed by the streams of pro-Smith pioneers who made Nauvoo the second-largest city in the new state of Illinois.

Smith inspired hatred and violence across the nation, and, in 1845, Nauvoo was ravaged by vigilante terrorism and Smith murdered in jail. But Epaphimandas Lee, with shrewd foresight, had in 1843 packed his swelling family into wagons and shifted downriver to the tiny steamboat landing where he founded a town. Lee carried with him an encyclopedia of radical notions to try on a blank wilderness. A few ex-Mormon families followed, and in a decade other westering souls gathered, including the band of Hessian brewers, assorted Moravian craftsmen hankering for ideas more salutary than the stuffy Whiggism of the East and dozens of unaffiliated yeomen abandoning scanty Ohio or Pennsylvania farmsteads for prairie adventure.

Refugees from failed communes—Fourierists, Fruitarians, ex-Harmonists, lapsed Shakers—were magnetically drawn to Leeland (as the town was christened by one of Lee's assertive wives). Riverboat traffic brought migrants from the Deep South as slavery ground itself into ruin, and bewildered European immigrants were dropped at Leeland by land-company sharpers. In 1851, a boatload of manumitted or abducted slaves arrived. (Lee persistently called them Ethopians, in accordance with his notion about the *real* Lost Tribes of Israel.)

Leelanders discovered during the boom years after the Civil War that Making Heaven on Earth was not inconsistent with the older

American dream of Making Money Hand Over Fist.

The Hessian brewmasters kegged and bottled Wurtzheimer Brau as fast as yeast, malt and hops could work.

E.P. Lee Shipping & Transport proliferated wagons, boxcars and steam packets.

A sawmill and tannery poured forth endless board feet of lumber and noxious streams of yellow-green effluents. Bales of bison hides were heaped on the wharves.

Three grain elevators were built, wondrous towers on the flat prairie, dwarfing the church steeples of the town.

A three-story brick factory, one city block square, housed a weaving enterprise devoted to the manufacture of undergarments, male and female, each after its kind.

A tribe of Amish craftsmen from Eastern Pennsylvania built sturdy buggies and wagons adapted to hard use on the prairie.

The town formed a volunteer fire brigade, a salaried constabulary and a silver cornet band. There was talk of a free militia company and an opera house.

Riverboat sharpers and roustabouts found the three grog shops on the waterfront congenial places in which to lose their money, their virtue (if any) and their senses.

Epaphimandas Lee, having invested over seven decades on earth, looked at his creation and found it not-so-hot. Three of his wives had departed when neighbors protested the heathenish notion of polygamy as an evil legacy from the bad old days of the Big Mormon Threat. His children were scattered by war, economic depression and ill luck, although he heard by post of grandchildren arriving in squadrons.

In 1880, Lee decided to close his enterprises, liquidate his assets—capital and spiritual—and find a new Garden of Eden in the West, as Brigham Young and Joseph Smith's other theological heirs had done. The nation was obsessed with expansionism, frontier settlement and genteel piracy. The White House was occupied by a nonentity whose very name citizens could not recall, while pirates and pork-barrel princelings manipulated the nation's money supply and destiny.

As he gathered his harvest, Lee discovered that the Merchants Bank of Leeland (Ebenezer Nathaniel Cosgrove, President) in fact owned most of Lee's worldly chattels. He had signed papers and closed deals without bothering to read contracts. He believed Leeland was a congregation of brothers and sisters with all things held in common, with the Holy Spirit the only power-broker.

Ebenezer Cosgrove was an ambitious young man who held to the letter, not the spirit, of U.S. banking regulations. He read the motto on his money—*E. pluribus unum*—with grave approbation. He, E.N. Cosgrove, was the *unum* of *unums,* and those who banked with him were the inconsequential *pluribuses* from which he was made. It was as simple a proposition as $2 + 2 = 4$, and Cosgrove was exasperated when the mangy old prophet Epaphimandas Lee would come in of an afternoon to wrangle endlessly about rights and properties.

Cosgrove came by his resonant name as many of his generation did: the children of Leeland's first generation were named for giant figures from *Exodus* and *Genesis,* heroes of Yaweh's Golden Age. Snot-nosed schoolchildren in knee-worn knickers or gingham aprons answered to Ezekial and Zebediah and Meshach and Rachel and Ruth and Hagar and Sarah and Elijah and Amos and (even) Jezebel, Uriah or Ahab. Roll-call in Sunday School was like a serious exegetical reading of the begats.

Epaphimandas Lee knew, deep in his heart, that his apparent bankruptcy was a mere misunderstanding, a superficial error of materialist capitalism to be rectified in the fullness of time. But he was nothing if not stubborn, so he harangued Eb Cosgrove, Mayor Zachariah Bates and anyone else handy. He packed essentials into an Amish-built prairie schooner as big as Noah's lifeboat, gathered his remaining wife and two children (Buz and Abednego) to travel west, ignoring the possibilities of rail and river transport.

He went one last time to the Merchants Bank to expend sweet reason on that officious puppy Cosgrove. As a clincher, he carried a .44-caliber Colt's revolver. When the old prophet burst into the bank president's office, white beard a defiant flag (not of truce) and six-shot syllogism in his left hand, a newly-hired bank guard sounded the alarm. He had been reading a dime-novel romance on the road agent Jesse James and his band of untamed, ungalvanized ex-Confederates who lurked in terrible force across the river. He thought he was thwarting a daring daylight bank robbery.

In the melee, Lee's pistol discharged, and Ebenezer Cosgrove, the youngest bank president in Illinois, was flung arse-over-tipple backward across his mahogany desk. The bank guard, Clevis Ogden, subdued the ancient warrior by bashing Lee over the head with his .41-caliber Colt's pistol. He simultaneously shouted, "Help! Robbery! The bloody James gang!" and fired his revolver, the ball passing through the window of Cosgrove's office and striking Obadiah Simpson, farrier, in the left buttock while he crouched over his anvil, shaping a red-hot horseshoe.

A volunteer fire-brigadesman heard the commotion and rang the bronze fire-bell recently donated by Ebenezer Cosgrove.

Wamba Bastin, major and organizer of the PawPaw Zouave Rifles, dashed from his home, where he had just sat down to a cold collation, with his Henry rifle in his hand.

Mary Magdalene Breaux, an octoroon prostitute, rolled off her client in the back room above the Two Deuces on the waterfront, hearing shots and recalling the principal reason she left New Orleans one step ahead of the constabulary. She found the four-shot Derringer pistol in her shoe beside the bed and crouched next to her Jordan (French porcelain decorated with choice scenes from the legend of Leda and the Swan), ready to defend herself to the last bullet.

The town pharmacist, Ivanhoe Bastin (his father was addicted to the Waverly Novels), spilled a mixture of laudanum-based whooping cough nostrum on the floor, as a bullet from his brother's Henry rifle shattered the window.

The shot occurred when Wamba, seriously short-sighted, saw a figure running toward the bank, heard a shout of "Help! Robbery! The bloody James gang!" and reacted with myopic but spontaneous conviction.

Three horses broke from Simpson's livery stable and galloped around the bank. The butt-shot blacksmith called weakly after them and collapsed into his quenching trough.

The battle lasted several minutes and involved most of Leeland's citizenry. There were two other casualties besides Cosgrove, Lee and Simpson: one of Simpson's stable boys, kicked by a runaway horse as he tried to snaffle it, and Wamba Bastin, knocked down by Franklin Quinn, owner of the Two Deuces and Leeland's foremost pimp, who was told by Mary Magdalene Breaux that the joint was being robbed. Quinn erupted from his saloon-cum-bagnio and cold-cocked Bastin with a presentation bung-starter left him by the Wurtzheimer Brau salesman.

Lingering a few days in a semi-comatose state, the founder of Leeland finally expired of his head wound. Ebenezer Cosgrove preceded him to that bourne from which no traveler, etc., by a day. Their funerals were elaborate, lengthy and dramatic. Enduring feuds and hatreds were kindled among the survivors, including second-generation Lees back from the West for the obsequies.

Poole was immersed in the saga, flipping from book to book and scribbling notes, when Ann Wilcox coughed discreetly from the doorway. She repeated the signal, and Poole awoke from his vision.

"Mr. Poole? I really must close up now. I'll set your books aside, if you'll come back after this dreadful storm."

Poole shook himself. His digital watch read 4:54 p.m., 12-2. He looked at Ann Wilcox and decided he was in love yet again.

"Thanks. I'll be back—but I can't promise it'll be tomorrow."

"That's all right. I can fetch the books again, if you ask for me. Is there anything special I can locate in the meantime?"

"No, no. It's all so…intriguing. Oh—I would like some, er, genealogical information. On the Lees, the Cosgroves and the Bastins."

"Easy enough. You're shaking my family tree. Wilcox is my married name. I was born a Lee, related to plenty of Cosgroves and a shirt-tail bunch of Bastins."

"Fine." Poole thought, *Married? How married? Wherefore married?* "I appreciate your help."

They stood for a moment at the main doors as Poole buttoned his topcoat. Gravid snowflakes still whirled onto empty streets, stoplights cycled futilely and the streetlamps bled weak beams.

Poole descended the steps carefully, soaking shoes and pants cuffs again. He decided to add boots, gloves and a stout winter coat to his tab. *Ah, well—do your Christmas shopping early. From Richard to Richard. Merry Christmas.* He pondered gloomily that he had few people to send gifts. Cold fell on him like tangible melancholy and soddened his soul.

* * *

Salvaging scraps from his ruined wardrobe, Poole dressed and examined himself in the mirror. He saw a squarish man obviously crashing headlong into his mid-forties, with fine brown hair that was thin on top, deep-set blue eyes in a rough, asymmetrical face. A lot of *character* there, Poole thought of his countenance. Meaning that assorted scars and irregularities didn't amount to outright disfigurement. He looked like a jock who had only narrowly evaded pneumatic obesity—which was true.

Several women had told him he had a "kind" face. *But* what *kind?*

The telephone was still unrepaired, so Poole trekked to the office. On duty now was a short, chubby boy—good material for a junior-high football water-boy. He chewed bubblegum enthusiastically while surveying a magazine, evidently the one Larry Starr was memorizing. Perhaps SleepyEye House clerks were required to study pornography so as to identify it if a traveler appeared with a suitcase-load.

The boy shunted the magazine under the counter, stared at Poole and slowly inflated a balloon of bubblegum the size of a infant's head. His beady brown eyes regarded Poole around the perimeter of the giant bubble.

"If I can interrupt your practice, I'd like to use the phone."

The bubble collapsed on itself, and a film of pink stuff retracted into the boy's mouth like a creature in an especially repulsive sci-fi movie invading an earthling. The boy smacked his lips and enunciated, "You stayin here?"

"Unit Eleven. Poole."

Blinking, the boy said, "Ain't got no pool. Pa started to put one in, but they built the slag warehouse back of us, and that fucked up the view, see?"

"My *name* is Poole. With an E. And what's yours?"

The boy flipped through a packet of index cards bound with a knotted rubber band, the latest innovation in information storage and retrieval. He frowned and moved his lips slightly as he read one card.

"Okay. I'm only on duty afternoons, when Pa has to be down at the factory. My name is—" and he made a face like a crazed Oriental —" Elbert. Albert. Ain't that a bitch? But everybody calls me Coz. Or Cap."

"I'll bet Coz is short for Cosgrove," Poole said, thinking, Ah, you sly dog! What a wizard of the inductive method!

Munching his pink cud, Elbert said, "Nah. Short for Cosmo. After Captain Cosmo, see? I used to run around with a towel tied to my neck and tell people I was Captain Cosmo. When I was a kid."

"And your, er, real last name?"

"Bastin. Everybody misspells it. B-A-S-T-I-N."

Great, Poole thought, now we can spell each other's names.

"The phone?" Poole prompted.

"Yeh. If it's long distance, it'll go on your room tab. How'd your phone get busted?"

"A long story. If you see Larry Starr, he'll relate the details."

Poole pinched the receiver on his shoulder and found a number in his notes. Elbert Bastin watched him dial as if he performed an astonishing feat of legerdemain. Turning his back, Poole stared out at snow howling horizontally past the window.

He got a harried clerk and a burst of static. After a moment of negotiation, the line clattered tinnily and Len Howells' voice came on: "Yeh. Howells. What's up, Poole?"

"I wanted to find out where you and the ME stand. Anything new on the, er, little people and Ogden?"

"This storm has screwed everything. I talked with our ace cadaver-cutter this morning, and he's sending a report. I'm monitoring the sheriff's fools when they bother to call in. That's about it."

"I've got questions and a few items to report."

"Like what? Your night visitors? The night-shift boys left me a copy of their paperwork on that."

"I'm digging at relationships, and I need somebody to fill me in on Leeland's family feuds."

"I go off here in an hour unless the Chief decides we're all hanging around because of the goddam blizzard."

"I'm tied up tonight. Could I meet you first thing tomorrow?"

Poole noted his appointment, listened politely to Howells' litany of weather-related maledictions and rang off. As he turned to replace the receiver, he stared directly into Elbert Bastin's small and glittering eye.

"You with the cops?"

"Not with," Poole said. "Just gathering, um, data. Don't eavesdrop, sonny—it's a lousy habit."

Elbert collapsed into a rump-sprung swivel chair and sneered at Poole. "You think there's anything better to do here? What a boring-ass place!"

"Okay. I've got a mission for you, and it's important."

"Yeh? What?" Elbert looked skeptical but intrigued and even missed a beat on his gum chewing for a nanosecond.

"I'm expecting a call from an associate—it's vital information. You hike down to Unit Eleven and fetch me when it comes in, and there's a tip in it for you. It's from a woman—one of my...agents."

Elbert struggled with the will to believe vs. adolescent doubt, formed another crazed-Chinese face and said, "Aw—you're shittin me!"

"I never joke about my work."

In his room, Poole sat on the edge of his bed and scanned his hasty library notes. He looked for logic in dead elves and AWOL Santas.

Twenty minutes later, Elbert pounded on the door, just as Poole had decided to pack it all in and drive the Ferret south till he hit a palmy beach. He dodged out into the storm and to the office. The macroscopic gynecological study was open on the counter next to the phone. Elbert split his concentration between it and Poole's conversation with Wilma Breithope.

Poole arranged to meet Wilma at the hotel, and she promised to drive him to a riverside restaurant which was open, she swore, despite the blizzard. He asked for fifteen minutes.

Elbert watched as Poole slid a dollar to him. Then he blew a bubble the size of slow-pitch softball, sneering as he retracted the gum. Poole added a one. Elbert snapped off a small bubble. Sighing, Poole took back the ones and laid down a five. Elbert inserted this in the magazine as a bookmark.

"You on duty tomorrow?"

"Yeh, after school most days. Till supper time."

"Terrific. We'll talk then. I want to find out about the kids who hang out at the mall."

Elbert whistled. "You gonna bust the old mall-rats. Jeez, I'd like to see that!"

Poole put a finger to his lips. "Keep it all to yourself, Cap. It's a highly confidential operation, see?"

Elbert smiled in a sinister way. "Gotcha. Hey—this could be cool!"

"Remember, no blabbing. You could get in a real jam with the cops."

Poole returned to his room, bundled into his coat, checked his pockets for notes and papers, then trekked to the Ferret. He scraped at it again, wishing for a blowtorch. As he scrubbed at the rear window, Poole noticed a scrap of red cloth hanging from the trunk. The cloth looked like wool, a knit strip. He found the correct key and opened the stiff lock.

Crammed into the small compartment was a big man Poole had never seen. He was wedged into a fetal position, face-up, arms crossed on his breast. A long red wool scarf trailed from his neck. He was dressed in a heavy, greenish down jacket and rubber boots. He wore no hat or gloves. His eyes were open, his mouth twisted in a contorted pout. He also wore a small, neat hole in his forehead above his left eye. He was as dead as Christmas Past.

The weak trunk light showed Poole these details, but he needed more. He went to the office and got a flashlight from Elbert.

"Cap, you call the police. Right now."

"How come? What you up to?"

"Call the police, ask for Detective Howells. If you don't get him, ask for anyone in Homicide. Tell them…look, there's somebody who's been killed out here. Just get the damn cops."

Elbert's mouth fell open, revealing a cache of pink gum. Then he enunciated, "Jesus Cah-rist!"

Poole shoved the phone at him and returned to the Ferret.

The flashlight revealed more of the grisly tableau. The man had thin, gray hair, a big gold wristwatch, dentures and little else to identify him. Poole did not want to dislodge the corpse to check pockets. The hole in the man's blue-gray forehead was tidy but disconcerting, like a mystical third eye glaring up at Poole.

As he was about to step back, Elbert arrived, wheezing and blowing frost. "I got them, Mr. Poole, I got them! They said a car was coming. They thought I was shittin 'em at first, but I said…"

He looked over Poole's shoulder into the flashlight's beam. Then he staggered a few steps backward, slipped on a patch of black ice and sat down hard. He stared up at Poole. Then he wailed: "Jesus, you crazy fucker—you killed Captain Cosmo!"

While the words rattled in Poole's ears, Elbert Bastin leaned forward and threw up in his own lap. The snowstorm was abating, Poole noticed, as he listened to a siren howling in the distance.

Xmas Crazee Daze

WHIRLIGIG LIGHTS FROM an ambulance, a sheriff's cruiser and a police car threw clashing blades of red, white and blue around the parking lot of the SleepyEye House Motel. Lurid highlights splashed the uniformed figures milling around Poole's rented car. He stood facing Detective Len Howells, whose features were alternately deep red then purple. The effect made Poole slightly queasy.

The local coroner, a lanky youngster with a Will Rogers shock of blond hair over one eye, joined them, rubbing his bare hands briskly and blowing a plume of breath. He gestured with a thumb over his shoulder, saying, "Now, that's what I call a frozen stiff."

Howells dropped his cigarette butt and ground it into the snow with an elegant shoe, growling, "I've had it to here with mortuary humor, Stevens. Cut the crap and tell us what you can before the big cheese from the state office arrives to slow everything to a crawl."

Stevens shrugged and grinned. "Okay—just trying to lighten the mood. Not a lot to tell, anyhow. Decedent plugged in the head with a medium-caliber weapon from fairly short range. Period. Unless something shows when we get him straightened and undressed. No marks I could see indicating other violence. I guess whatever kills you is enough, huh?"

"You said frozen," Poole said. "You mean that literally?"

"Ah, he's into rigor mortis, been there awhile. It's gonna screw

72

up estimates on time of death."

"How long?" Howells said.

"The temperature's been well below freezing for a couple of days. Add in wind chill factor on that car trunk, you can freeze even a big guy pretty quickly. We'll have to wait for the P.M. to see how the tissues look."

Howells grunted. Stevens glanced over his shoulder and said, "Ah—they've yanked him out. Better ride back in the wagon with the boys."

He departed jauntily. Howells stared morosely at Poole. He said, "You've either got worse luck than me or you're in some shit up to your ears. When did you last look in the trunk?"

Poole said, "Never. I've only got a flight bag and a suit hanger. I threw them in the back seat at the airport. I never would have looked in the trunk if I hadn't seen the piece of scarf sticking out. I couldn't see that the snow on the trunk had been disturbed, either."

"Yeh. So you could of been hauling Captain fucking Cosmo around for three days, huh? You think the car people put him there? Or he was hard up for a ride and thought it beat hitching? Now I've gotta put a trace on him. One frigging Santa Claus I *can't* find, and one frigging superhero I don't *wanta* find! Maybe it's some kind of trade." With a valedictory glare, Howells walked away from Poole toward a pair of uniformed officers examining the car.

Poole hurried to the motel office, his fingers and toes tingling with preliminary signals of frostbite. Inside, he found Wilma Breithope and a uniformed city policewoman with Elbert Bastin. Elbert sat on the battered plastic couch by the desk, flanked by two dumpy adults who could have been cloned as living bookends. They were minatory warnings of Elbert's future state, given his genetic code. The man sat back, hands knitted on his potbelly, looking both frightened and furious. The woman clung to Elbert and sniveled. Elbert radiated excitement. He had at last become the center of his universe.

"…and then, and then," he blurted to Wilma, "I looked down and saw the dead guy. I mean Captain Cosmo. Jesus, did he look dead! I never seen him before, except on TV, but I knew it was him. He was lookin up at me like he does at the end of the program." Elbert stopped and looked pensive. "But he won't be lookin at nobody anymore. Maybe somebody ought to…say something."

Wilma peered at him. "Say something?"

"Yeh. I mean some kind of thing about him being dead. Jeez, I wish I could remember 'Thanatopsis.' We had to memorize it for Mrs. Hamm. What a bitch!"

Mr. Bastin stirred. "You watch your goddam mouth!" he growled.

"I don't mean her. I mean trying to memorize all that…stuff. But it would come in real handy now."

The policewoman, a chunky redhead with a spray of attractive freckles on her cheeks, said in a school-teacherly voice, "Now, Elbert, I want you to tell us again what you and Mr. Poole said before we arrived. Just so we've got it right."

Elbert squirmed and grinned like a gopher. "Okay." He recited without too much dramatic license, Poole decided.

As he ended, Mrs. Bastin blew her nose into a wad of tissue and sighed, "I don't want Elbert getting in no trouble. I always told him to stay out of trouble. I didn't even like him to watch that TV guy…"

The policewoman efficiently bundled the Bastins away, making small, reassuring statements. As they exited, Elbert leered over her shoulder at Poole and squeaked, "If you done it, I hope they give you the death penalty!"

Poole sighed and sat heavily on the vacated couch. Wilma said, "Some supper date, sport. What do you do for an encore?"

"Sorry. The coroner says he was long dead and frozen. This time of year, he could have stayed there till your spring thaw. I wish I'd delivered him back to Lo-Rent and let the St. Louis cops have a whack at it all. Who the hell is—was—Captain Cosmo, anyhow?"

"I forgot—you're an outlander and wouldn't know. He was another local hero. Harry Nugent. He started out here in radio years ago, then he went to St. Louis and eventually hit what passes for the big time. He was the, um, host of a kid's program called Captain Cosmo's Universe. Every kid in town has watched it. I even dimly remember it, and I must have been in high school when it started. Now, get this—it turns out that Nugent was also the sole owner and proprietor of the agency that rented the mall their elves. Howells just passed on that tidbit. He'd been trying to call him for a couple of days. Then he gets the squeal on this and nearly passes out when he finds you've got the guy in your trunk. Small world, hey?"

"Nugent? Don't tell me he's connected with the mall's bag lady?"

"You got it. Or not-connected, I guess. Doreen was married to him back in prehistoric times. He dumped her at some point, and I think she's kept the name just to aggravate him ever since."

"Good God! Everybody here is related by blood or marriage, and someone's killing off comic-book characters. Does that make any damn sense to you?"

"No, but we'd better start finding people who think it *does* make sense. If someone planted Nugent in your car, they must be trying to send someone a message—presumably you."

"Those goons said they could find me. You think they left Nugent then? Why? If it's a frame-up, it's stupid. If they're trying to scare me, they're picking very weird methods."

"Perhaps it's all of the above." Wilma looked meditative. "Look —this evening is shot with all this fun. We'll have to go out to Astin Lee's restaurant tomorrow night, if you're still up for it."

"By all means. Astin Lee?"

"I'll fill you in when we go to The Happy Landing. That's his place. Believe me, you'll enjoy it. And maybe we'll find answers to some questions."

Wilma left as Howells entered the office. He rubbed at his face to restore feeling and said, "Okay, Poole, let's ride down to my lovely office and get your official statement on record. Then, if I'm real lucky, I'll be able to get home for a midnight supper and a few hours' sleep. If we don't get a call that somebody's kidnapped Mickey Mouse."

* * *

Poole arose with a pang of guilt. By K-Mart time it was 9:53 a.m., 12-3. When he peeked through the warped Venetian blinds, he saw a blinding white snowscape. The storm had passed on and left sculptured drifts under a bright, remote sun.

At the mall, Poole munched abstractedly on a croissant Alicine had brought him. He sat in Don Cosgrove's office, reading through a heap of files on mall employees and hoping the hot but vile coffee would jolt him wholly awake. He also awaited a return call from TransAtlas HQ with more data on LeeLand Mall's staff and financial status.

As terminal numbness settled on his brain, there was a tentative knock on the door, and Poole said, "Come."

A blue-black feather appeared around the door as it opened a few inches. Then a woman slipped after the feather, which waved on a small hat, a kind of yarmulke with glitter and feathers, Poole decided. As if someone had brained a rabbi with a grackle. Under this hat was a tall, thin woman who must have been elegant and svelte in her youth. Her hair was the gray that comes from careful treatment, and surgeons' hands had smoothed the wrinkles from her face. She was carefully made up, but her pointed features looked both fragile and hard. *"Brittle" is the word,* Poole thought.

She wore a bulky, elegant fur coat, black gloves and fur-trimmed boots. She stared at Poole, who rose gallantly. Then she slipped all the way into the office and carefully closed the door.

When she turned back to Poole, she looked either frightened or determined.

"You're Richard Poole?"

He indicated a chair, she stood undecided and then sank into it. Her eyes were intense, bright and a rich brown. Poole guessed she was in her late fifties, going on forty-five. She dabbed at her nose with a tissue, shook her head as if to clear it.

"I'm Margo Cosgrove," she said. "My son said you were here, and I decided to...Mr. Poole, I need your help. I know why you're here, and Donald has told us of the...problems he's having. Charles and I are desperately concerned about all this...violence."

"Your husband?"

"Yes. He's so terribly busy with the bank, and now he's not a well man. But he has a deep concern for Donald and his future."

She paused and gnawed her lip. "We've always done everything we could," she hurried on, "to help Donald without...manipulating him. He was an adopted child, and perhaps we spoiled him. I am his step-mother, you realize. Charles' first wife died when the children were tiny, and I stepped in. Or so they must have thought. His father worked hard to see that Donald was independent and self-confident. We sent him to camps, to training courses, to the very best schools. Of course, he's always understood that the bank—all of Charles' businesses—were to be his future. Perhaps it warps a person to feel his life is...planned out."

In a long silence, she rummaged in a tiny black purse and found a silver cigarette case. From it she extracted a cigarette of ludicrous length and slimness. Poole stood and presented a flame from a desk-lighter sculpted as a sportive dolphin. She smoked in silence and then looked directly at Poole. He could see in her gaze the ghost of coquetry past. *Margo must have been a knock-out*, he thought. Then he realized uncomfortably that she would not look too old on his arm. He passed readily for forty-five going on sixty.

"I try never to interfere in business—my husband's or my son's. But I have never been a doormat or a bystander. When Charles and I married, I understood I was a partner in the Cosgrove affairs, with all the responsibilities of a partner. So…"

She faltered and stubbed out the cigarette. "I want to tell you a few things about Donald and his…problems. They may help you resolve this unpleasant business. I also want to offer my personal support and the support of the Cosgrove family."

"Mrs. Cosgrove. I'm a security investigator for TransAtlas. They write my paychecks and give me assignments. I don't work for individuals, in any fashion."

"I understand. But our family has a great deal of influence in Leeland. We can open doors and provide information. I think you would be wise to accept our assistance."

He nodded, and she looked past him. "Donald had many difficulties as a child. He was frail and introverted. We provided everything we could to give him a comfortable life. His father took him fishing and hunting. We encouraged him to socialize with… suitable companions. But in his adolescence, he had…unusual problems. Entanglements of a sexual nature. He fathered an illegitimate child. He was under treatment for obsessions. The too-expensive analyst we retained came up with theories about agoraphobia. Pyromania. But when he was at college and when he married, everything smoothed out."

"Agoraphobia? Pyromania?"

"He was fearful…timid. We had to force him to leave the house, to play outdoors. He was fascinated with fires. According to Dr. Schirmer, all this is sexually connected. I had enough explanation of Donald's behavior to last a lifetime. Suffice it to say that Charles and I feel Donald was, ah, cured of his delusions. But I am afraid the events you are investigating may…disturb him. Trigger some recurrence."

"Are you hinting that he may be…involved?"

"Of course not. But if his background is investigated, someone might draw that conclusion."

"The police know of this?"

"There is nothing on official record. But I'm afraid that in a tight community like ours, everything is known and nothing is forgotten —let alone forgiven."

"I'm not sure what you want me to do."

"Just be very careful in the conclusions you may reach, Mr. Poole. And be very careful in how you deal with Donald. I'm afraid that…"

The door opened, and Donald Cosgrove hurried in. He stopped dead when he saw his mother. Poole watched his face as an expression of raw fear was replaced with a manikin's mask of polite recognition.

"Mama! For God's sake…I told you not to bother Mr. Poole. He's a busy man, and things here are…in terrible disarray." He glanced pleadingly at Poole. "Gee, I hope Mother hasn't been boring you with family history. I'm so sorry—"

"You needn't apologize for me, Donald. Mr. Poole has been very understanding. Your father is quite concerned about your welfare. If he were in better health, he'd be here himself."

"Yeh. I'll bet he would. He's already bent my ear on the phone every day." Cosgrove collapsed loosely on his couch and dropped a thick stack of papers next to him. He swiped at his forehead with a handkerchief. "Please, Mama—listen to me. Just don't worry. Don't horn in. Everything will work out all right."

His pleading fluttered with panic, Poole decided. Cosgrove stared fixedly at his stepmother. She drew herself up and looked toward Poole.

"Mr. Poole. Thank you for your time. Remember—you can call on us at any time. We're most anxious to assist. Donald…your father would like to hear from you. You might call to cheer him up."

She left in a rustle of the heavy fur coat, trailing the razor's edge of a delicate perfume, so expensive per milligram that Poole could only imagine it as a corporate investment.

Cosgrove stared at the door, slumped further on the couch and said, "Shit! Leave it to the Wicked Witch of the Middle West to crash in and foul up the works."

Poole was embarrassed and slightly fuddled from the interview. He scooped up the papers before him. "I'll give you your office back. Alicine can track me down if the Pittsburgh call comes through."

Cosgrove sat up. "Wait a minute, Poole. Look—I know what she told you. She's got a routine she runs off about me. I want you to hear my side of the story."

"Don...I don't think I should get tangled in this family business."

"Yeh. If that's all it was, I wouldn't sweat it. Let me...okay, she told you I was...what? A firebug? A teenage delinquent? A sex pervert? I know the outline, but Mother's damned inventive with the details. Here's what happened: I fell in love with a girl when I was sixteen. I was home from prep school over Christmas, and I met Rita at a sleigh ride. I'd been cooped up at that school for three years. It was only a hair above a military academy, and I *dreamed* about seeing girls. Not about kissing them or, you know...just *seeing* them.

"So they shipped me back to school, and Rita disappeared, as far as I was concerned. Oh, I tried to get in touch with her, but I was a dumb kid, too scared to kick up a fuss. Her mother cursed me when I phoned, and her brother called me at school, said he'd kill me if I didn't stay away. I thought the cops would come for me— that it was some kind of crime. The next summer...that's when what Mama calls 'the accident' happened. The garage burned down. Big, four-car job with an apartment over it. No small deal, you see. Other kids might burn down a chicken coop, but little Donny gets to torch a place like the Taj Mahal."

"You burned it down?"

Cosgrove shuddered and wiped again at his forehead. He shook his head. "I had these...attacks. I don't know how to describe them. Like seizures, almost. I could see...flames. Smell burning, smoke. I'd had them since I was little, but I kind of ignored them. Then it was like...a command. I'd wake up at night, and I'd have to get out of bed and walk around. Something was *ordering* me to look at a fire. I got more and more screwed up. Then one hot night in July I was out on the lawn, and the garage was going up like a bonfire. I don't even remember doing it. But...it was like someone else did it. I just stood there, feeling sick, and watched it go up.

"That's when I got the treatments from old Slimey Schirmer. Three years of them. Who is it talked about 'a season in hell'? Well, that just starts to cover it. But I swear, Poole, I haven't had...problems in years. Since college. My wife...she doesn't even know about most of this. Mama makes little noises about telling Betty. If she ever did that I'd have to...kill her."

Cosgrove choked and looked at his hands. He shook himself and said dully, "That's all I can say." He sorted the papers he had scattered. "Oh...Fred Toller has rounded up the mall-rats you wanted to see. He says to come to his office this afternoon."

Poole paused at the door. "I'll keep this to myself as far as I can. But if you've got ideas that connect with this mess, you'd better come forward. With Nugent dead, we've got a sticky situation to hand. Unless we come up with Hector Ogden soon, it's going to be guessing-game time for the authorities."

As he passed Alicine's desk, piped music reverberated with "Deck the Halls." Poole felt a thousand light years from the Christmas Spirit.

* * *

Lola was dressed in baggy white pants that Poole associated

with silent-movie comics, an equally balloonish Hawaiian blouse and brown hair cut into stubby spikes and tipped with pink-and-orange neon dye. Totty wore a sack-like dress that ended in a jagged hem somewhere at mid-thigh and was belted with a broad sash or scarf of a crispy gold lame. Her blonde hair was also short and brushed up and back into a feeble duck's-ass stiffened by bear-grease or synthetic equivalent. Both smoked black cigarettes with gold tips. Despite the bizarre costumes, which made them seem standbys on a Theda Bara film, they were cherubically childish in repose. Lola had removed her sandals and inspected her toenails, which were lacquered black. Totty held a necklace of lumpy agate-like stones in her hands like a rosary or worry beads. Both affected deep boredom and/or catatonia.

"So you don't know about the murders, about the whereabouts of your pals Ziggy and Heinie or about the smash-and-grab job at Lucky Jewelers?" Fred Toller seemed at least as bored as the nymphets, as if he were reading a routine checklist of queries. He sat behind his desk, with Poole next to him in a sagging plastic chair. The girls sprawled on the office couch. Totty put down her bauble, removed a fragment of a comb from a small purse and dragged it through her stubbled pompadour.

Lola blew a series of small smoke rings, squinted through them and said, "No. No. No. No."

Alicine Mungo entered with a tray laden with coffee, assorted pastries and stacked styrofoam cups. She set them on Toller's desk, and he said, "Lissy. Stay a second. I'm going to examine these lovely damsels'…effects, and I want a female witness, so they don't squawk that I strip-searched them to cop a feel."

He rounded the desk and plucked the purse from Totty's hand. With a quick motion, he jerked a sequined shoulder-bag from Lola.

"Hey, god damn you, give it back!" Lola cried.

Toller ignored the girls and dumped the purses' contents on his desk. Totty lurched to her feet and reached, and Toller shoved her roughly. "Sit your ass down," he snarled, "or I'll have the cops haul you down to juvie again."

"Those are…private property," Totty whined.

Poole watched Toller separate heaps of detritus from the purses. He glanced at Poole and said, "See how the animals live?"

Lola's heap included a lipstick, a cheap compact, a crumpled cigarette pack, loose change and a package of condoms. "You switch to a better brand, honey?" Toller said. Totty's included a fake-snakeskin wallet, more cosmetics, a wad of dollar bills and two strips of small black-and-white photos. Toller looked at her and growled, "You still peddling pussy pix, sweetie-pie? You're gonna hit on the wrong square and get yourself strangled in an alley."

Peering at the little photos, obviously from a coin-booth mechanism, Poole saw what seemed to be fuzzily unfocused bits of a geological formation. He realized then that it was a pair of thighs and a vulvar region. The definition was so poor the shots were like fragments of a Rorschach test.

"These little slobs stand on the bench in the PhotoMat booth and hike up their skirts. Then they try to sell these to poor old creeps. A dollar a shot still the market price, ladies?"

Lola glared sullenly into a corner, and Totty squeaked, "I found them in the John. Somebody threw them on the floor."

Alicine, standing by the door, seemed torn between horror and hilarity. She refused to catch Poole's eye.

Toller opened the wallet and rummaged. In a moment, he said, "Ah…here's an intriguing memento." He shoved a rectangle of paper to Poole. "How did you get this card? Now we get to the serious stuff." It was a business card, printed in red and black in florid circus type:

Harold Mckay Nugent * Cosmo Attractions, Unlimited

Novelty Goods * Music * Entertainment * Party Planning

"The Good Times Always Flow When You Call Cosmo"

Addresses and phone numbers adorned the corners.

Totty glanced at the desk and sniffed, "I prolly just found it someplace."

"You find a whole shitload of weird things, babe," Toller said.

"Whyn't you go talk to Queen Doreen if you're interested in weird trash?" Lola snapped.

Toller glared at her. "You two cornflakes don't grasp the situation. There have been *murders* you may be tied to. You think this is just farting-around time? I can ask for charges of soliciting for prostitution, fraud, distributing pornography. And there must be enough traces of nasty drugs in these bags to add that. You think because you're underage nobody's gonna give a shit? You want to grow up fast? Okay, we'll sling you into county jail for a couple months and let the bull-dykes have you. Then you'll grow up and die!"

For the first time, the girls seemed uneasy. Toller rested one fat buttock on the edge of his desk and twiddled the card in his fingers. "Mr. Poole and me are willing to not push things real hard, if you come up with answers about this. Not the usual bullshit."

Lola looked uncertain, and Totty sank back to resume her bead-counting. Poole said, "Look, Mr. Toller's trying to restrain himself. I asked him to go easy on you, as a favor. We're trying to open up a murder investigation. We're not into persecuting minors."

He wondered if his phony good-guy voice was right. He doubted if a Mutt-and-Jeff act would work on this pair. Lola stared blankly, and Totty arched an eyebrow and giggled.

"Hey, Lola—this guy's gonna let us have an all-day sucker if we talk nice. *You* know what kinda deal that is—a blow-job in the back room, and we go home free."

Toller slammed his meaty hand on the desk. "Shit!" he

bellowed. "Call the cops, Alicine, get this scum out of here. Put 'em away for six months, and I don't have to see their asses in the mall, anyhow."

"You got no right," Lola squeaked.

"Shut up," Toller said. He removed a last black cigarette from the pack on his desk and lit it. He puffed ruminatively, expelled a cloud of smoke, hacked and crushed the cigarette in his ashtray. "Jesus," he wheezed, "it's perfume!"

"Those are Egyptian," Lola said. "My mother smokes them, and they're really expensive."

"They're pure camel-shit," Toller said, "and your old lady must of got them hooking on the waterfront."

Lola's face screwed up abruptly, and she began to cry, silently, her mouth open. Totty sat up and said, "Fuck you, Piggy!"

"Not a chance, sweetums. You two must have every disease in the world, including maggots."

Poole tried again: "Easy, Fred. I know they've got you, er, pissed off. But I think the corporation will deal lightly with them, if they cooperate."

"Yeh, that's what I'm afraid of," Toller muttered.

After a pause, Totty blurted, "Fuck it. It don't matter. Ziggy left it in his car. I found it there and picked it up. I don't know what it means. It was that old jerk he and Heinrich was messin with."

"Messing with?" Poole said.

"He was hangin around with them a couple times last week. They were talkin some kinda deal. I don't know what. Ziggy always thinks she's got a million-dollar thing going. Shit. I think it was peddling toys or something."

"Toys?" Poole stared at her.

"Yeh. I don't know anything else. They kept talkin about somebody called Gertie. But I don't know shit about it."

Toller softened. He growled, "You two little tramps get outta my mall. Stay home. Keep away from those two creeps. I'm gonna talk with the cops, and they'll wanna know what you're into. I'm gonna forget this shit now. But I'll goddam well remember it if I see you again. Got that?"

Totty soothed Lola, who had stopped crying and stared vacantly. She looked like a nine-year-old whose heart had been broken at a Halloween party. Mascara and eye-shadow bled down her face, staining her clown's visage into a German Expressionist death mask.

Toller talked with Alicine, who showed the girls out, staring at them with puzzled concern. He turned to Poole, saying, "Had enough of the freak show, sport? It turns my stomach to deal with them. Christ, they're just kids, but they're like some kind of...*animals*. How the hell do they *get* that way?"

Poole had no theodicy adequate for a reply. His mind was busy with the odd things Totty had said.

"Do you make sense of what she was saying?" Poole asked.

"I gave up trying to make sense of what they say. But we need to get to Ziggy and Heine pronto. They're into something here, and if they were with Nugent last week, the cops'll be all over them. I'm calling Buxtrider and Howells."

While Toller phoned, Poole leafed through the mall reports Cosgrove had supplied. He pursued an angle now—new franchises. He found a print-out listing venues with recent contracts. He eyed the list:

SOL'S TANNERY

HICKORY DAIQUIRI DOCK

SHOE SOUL

THE HAIREM

TINKER'S TOTTERY

LAFAYETTE ESPADRILLE

AND LITTLE FISHES

THE WISH FACTORY

NIGHTWEAR ALLEY

INTERFAITH BOOKS

A notation indicated that the stores were to open at the beginning of the last fiscal year. Poole knotted his brow. The names were like a strange code. He wished he still carried his Captain Midnight de-coder-ring and emergency whistle.

When Toller hung up the phone, Poole said, "Fred, lend me your mind. I need info on these places…"

* * *

Wilma picked Poole up in a department Land Rover, exactly right for the terrain and weather. The day had been bright, but the temperature had plunged into the teens, and a brisk wind sculpted the thick snow into exotic forms. She drove expertly on the back highway out of Leeland, running alongside the black ice of the river's verge. They plowed and slewed through drifts at curves, and Wilma said cheerfully, "Relax—I'm a trained driver, remember?"

She turned into a long, drifted lane lined by evergreen trees bowed by snow into irregular ziggurats. In the sunset, the effect was stunningly pink-tinged. Lee's Happy Landing was a low, log-and-fieldstone inn framed by spruces, deep in unsullied snow. Blue smoke flew in feathers from stone chimneys. Poole half expected Bing Crosby to saunter down the broad steps and chirp, "Welcome to Holiday Inn!"

The dining room was long and airy, with open log-beamed ceilings and an ox-deep fireplace at the far end encasing a roaring blaze. A chubby-and-dimpled waitress who identified herself as Dolores brought them hot toddies. "Compliments of Mr. Lee," she said. "Anyone who'd come out in this weather deserves the best treatment, he said."

When the food arrived, Poole was stunned. Lee's restaurant specialized in wild game, and Poole had cautiously ordered venison, while Wilma asked for pheasant. The courses were simple but excellent. Lee also sent a bottle of a new California cabernet sauvignon he wanted to test. By meal's end, after dessert—chess pie—while they contemplated wisps of vapor rising from their coffee, Poole felt recivilized, as if he had staggered from an ordeal in a wilderness to find an oasis of culture in an unexpected site.

Astin Lee, when he appeared with an open cognac bottle, was a short, trim man in his late fifties, Poole guessed, with gray flecking his black hair and toothbrush mustache. He was clad in casual clothes from Freeport, Maine, and he wore an engagingly youthful smile. Poole recalled late photos of Charlie Chaplin. Wilma introduced them, and Lee slid into a chair, offering small snifters of his brandy.

"Marvelous food," Poole said, "in an elegant setting."

Lee said, "Thanks. It's been a struggle to keep it going. But twenty years ago, I decided if I must sweat for a living, I'd do it the way *I* want. When my wife and I built the place, we had visions of getting rich and retiring to Rio de Janiero. Now I find I don't really want to be anywhere but here, so I please myself first. That seems to work for the customers, too."

"So your wife is a partner in the place?" Poole asked.

"*Was* a partner. Brenda died four years ago. Liver cancer."

"Oh. Sorry."

"She had a good life here for almost fifteen years. It was her money that got us underway, and she enjoyed every minute of the place. It's another reason I can't walk away from it."

Wilma said, "Mr. Lee, Richard is investigating the crimes at the mall. I spoke to you briefly on the phone yesterday. Have you thought of anything in your family background—or in the connections with the Bastins and Cosgroves—to…explain it all?"

Lee sighed and stroked his mustache. Then he said, "I can make a lot of guesses about ancient history, but that's just denatured gossip. The family connections are twisty in the extreme. My grandfather, Erasmus Lee, was the last of Epaphimandas' brood. He was born in…let's see, 1864. He rebuilt the family fortunes with a lot of, well, 'sharp practices' would be charitable as a description. But that was during the time of the Robber Barons, so I suppose everyone said it was business as usual. He formed a bank in competition with the Cosgroves, took over the wagon factory, bought out the knitting mill. When he died in 1930, he'd seen the wagon factory become an auto plant—he built the Leeland Flyer here—and everything humming along. He also saw Black Thursday, when the family money all disappeared in Wall Street's puff of smoke.

"His son Elphas—my father—came along in 1899. There were three other children, two boys and a girl. One of the boys died of TB, the other was killed in a hunting accident in his early twenties. The daughter, Elaine, married a Bastin. That was Albert—Bertie. Elphas was the youngest. Everything in the family seems to work backward, you see. He was sent off to the best schools, traveled in Europe and came back from Harvard Business School ready to be a proper captain of commerce. He got here in time for the crash. But he'd fallen in love with a pretty hometown girl, and they were married in September. They were back from a cruise a week before the market collapsed. Elphas had to go to work like any honest man, and his new bride—Ruth Cosgrove that was—stayed home to have little me."

Lee paused and decanted more brandy for them. He stared at the cordovan-colored liquor for a second and then continued.

"The Cosgroves were an insulated family—their money was in a lot of safe places. They weathered the Depression quite nicely, thank you. The Leeland Merchants Bank was one of the few sturdy banks of the era. It achieved history—or notoriety—by defying FDR. Old Maurice kept it open during the official bank holiday. He was reported as saying, 'No goddam jumped-up East Coast political hack's going to tell me how and when to run my bank.'"

"I came along in 1930, and my father and mother struggled to hang onto things for a decade. They had Cosgrove support, of course, but it was gall and wormwood for my father to accept that. He hung onto some properties, but the industries were kaput. When the war came along, he was rescued. The old wagon works made PT boats, and the underwear factory was rehabbed to make uniforms. War *is* good business, as they say. Everything was on its way to restoration as far as my father was concerned. He collected his government awards and E-for-Excellence flags and even contemplated a dollar-a-year job in Washington as an economic advisor.

"Then Fortuna's wheel ground around. FDR died, peace struck and the bottom fell out of the economy. The plants shut, after a few stabs at conversion. My father was infatuated with the plans for the Tucker car and put schemes afoot to get the Leeland works going as an assembly plant. He hobnobbed with Howard Hughes on a few visionary proposals. It must be genetic, you know—if someone comes down the pike with a harebrained idea tinged with social utility, some Lee will grab the bait and go. Father's last venture was in building pre-assembled houses, to cure the housing shortage and put those deserving GIs into dream homes. Some cockamamy design by a disciple of Bucky Fuller—a sphere or tesseract or something. He was scouring for financing when he had his stroke. A year later, he was dead, and I spent ten years sorting out the reams of worthless paper from his imaginary kingdom."

Poole felt bloated and drunk. The cozy fire, soft lights and comfortable chair had dimmed his reason. Lee poured another finger of the excellent cognac, and Poole gave up any attempt to clear his head. They sipped silently, then Poole said, "What about all the Bastin-Cosgrove connections?"

"Ah—there you strike swampy terrain. The Bastins arrived in, er, waves. Ripples, perhaps. They came along about the time Epaphimandas' commune was disintegrating. A tinker from somewhere South—Calvin Bastin. He had a huge family, and they married everyone in sight. You know about the...bar sinister? That is, there's a tribe of black Bastins as well. Their pedigrees have been matters of dispute and outright feuding. Some of Epaphimandas' Ethiopians got the name, in whatever manner. The lilywhite Bastins explain it as servitude, the blacks say it was simon-pure miscegenation. But for seventy-five years, it was worth your life here to get them mixed up. The, um, Caucasian Bastins went to the trouble of a bit of French pronunciation for awhile in the twenties— Bas-teen, you see. That was a bit much even for Leelanders, so it faded quietly years ago. But it's a touchy notion, still.

"Somewhere along the line, one Abraham Bastin got wealthy— during the Spanish-American War. The family story is that he was a doctor combating Yellow Jack. Everyone else says he sold patent medicines of high proof and low curative powers. Anyhow, the pharmaceutical company got its start there. His daughter Jessica married a Cosgrove. Their son Elijah married a shirt-tail Lee. A couple other Bastins and Cosgroves got intertwined in the thirties. So the town has become a kind of Irish stew—except we're not Irish."

Poole said, "Some questions off the track: what do you know of Don Cosgrove's adolescence? He mentioned a...girl friend named Rita."

Lee smiled. "Ah, the most recent semi-private Cosgrove scandal. You've been talking with him or with his battle-ax mother, no? That was Rita Bastin, oddly enough. From the Ogden-Bastin branch. That's yet another tale. Don and Rita must be something like fourth cousins two-and-a-half times removed, I suppose. If I walk down the street and address everyone I see as 'cousin,' I won't be far off the mark. Ditto for Donald. Nobody gives a hoot in hell for that nonsense anymore. Except for Mrs. Charles Cosgrove. She had a dozen demons when she found out. It was all *very* odd, since Donald was adopted, but…in any event, Donnie packed off to school. Much consternation. Granted, he was too young to be a responsible husband and father, but I'm not sure that ever changed.

"The tragedy of his young life, I'd guess. He's certainly remained frozen in time. But the Cosgroves will have their way, and I'm sure they, er, settled with the Bastins. Rita's father got a tidy sinecure with a Cosgrove-controlled firm in Seattle and took Rita with him. End of juicy romance for all the disappointed denizens of Leeland."

"Okay. What about Harry Nugent? What's his story?" Poole thought Lee looked uncomfortable for the first time. He twirled his snifter and looked sharply at Poole.

"You must know all the nonsense about Nugent's radio and TV careers. Dear old Captain Cosmo. He's a sad case, though. I haven't thought much about Harry recently. It's a little close to home. You see, he was a partner of sorts with my father. In the early fifties, when things were taking their last nose-dive. Another venture Father was drawn into was the radio station—WLEE. Yes, that's an indicator—a vanity thing, I think. He and Nugent took over the old station, which was petering out. Nugent could talk a great story, and as I said, our family is bonkers on uplifting ideas which just may turn a buck.

"My father was the major investor, but Nugent put money into the scheme, too. They built up the equipment, sorted out the staff. Nugent went on the air—he'd been a linchpin in the local little-theater bunch, so he thought he'd gone to heaven. Ten thousand watts of power, an audience he predicted in the hundreds of thousands. You can see the twist coming, of course. They bought a nifty radio station at precisely the instant TV exploded. Neither Father nor Nugent evidently gave it a thought.

"When Father died, the station was running in red ink, and it went into receivership. Nugent thought he'd been swindled. He lost whatever he'd invested, a media group from Chicago took over the operation, and a young man arrived talking up something he called rhythm and blues. Harry Nugent couldn't read the handwriting on the wall if it was ten feet tall. So, he drifted off to St. Louis and got what I assume to be the best revenge. I used to hear from him every few years—nothing nice, you know—but I haven't kept track of him since Brenda died. I've really become a recluse, I suppose. But I think I've earned a little garden-tending, like Candide."

Wilma looked at Poole and then said, "So you haven't heard that Cap...Harry Nugent is dead?"

Lee's polite smile faded. "What? When?"

"We're not precisely sure. But we know how—he was shot to death."

"My God! Another murder. Here?"

"Perhaps. The body was here. We're trying to find out where he was killed."

Lee set his glass on the table and stared blankly at it. Then he looked up at Poole and Wilma and said, "I'm sorry. I'm...stunned. It's a real shock. I can't say I was ever fond of Harry, but he was about the last direct tie to my father. And I've always felt troubled that the Lee family may have harmed him. Oh, all the legal and financial transactions were proper and above-board. But he was a... vulnerable man. I think he swam way over his head."

"He hasn't contacted you for...money?" Poole asked.

"As I say, it's been at least four years since I heard from Harry. And if you're hinting at blackmail, I haven't had the means to pay extortion even if I wanted to. But...well, he got a raw deal from the Lees, all without malice. I think he once said, 'You got my money and you got my girl. All I have left is my name.'"

"His girl?" Poole said.

Lee gazed at the tablecloth and said softly, "Yes. He was engaged to Brenda before I…came along. He never forgave me for that. That's why my last contact with him ended when Brenda died. I saw him at the funeral for the last time. I think he blamed me somehow for her death. At least he was in no forgiving mood. He was genuinely grief-stricken. He said an odd thing. 'You stole her twice,' he said. Curious. I still remember. You'd think time would erase such pains, but it doesn't."

* * *

When Wilma delivered Poole back to SleepyEye House, they sat for a moment in the Land Rover. He felt overstuffed, woozy from brandy and totally confused. The motor ticked over and the heater blew intermittent bursts of hot air around their feet. Wilma was pensive. Poole sighed and glanced at her. She smiled, he scooted closer and took her in his arms. The bulk of their winter coats made him think briefly of Eskimos and improbable courtship procedures. The kiss was warm and deep, adding to the tranquilizing effects of the evening,

Wilma pulled away and said throatily, "Richard—I've got to go home tonight. It's midnight, and the dispatcher will be right on my case at six."

Poole nodded and squeezed her. There was a curvaceous woman somewhere under that lumpy carapace of nylon, down and wool. "Okay," he said. "But we've got to steal a minute sometime."

She pulled a mock-pout. "A minute? I'm not sure what you have in mind."

Poole grinned. "Mere figure of speech. I hope. No, a day or two would be a much better idea. World enough and time…"

Feeling like a seventeen-year-old after a heavy date, Poole watched the big boxy vehicle lumber off on the frozen, rutted snow. As he fumbled with his room key and the sticky latch on Unit Eleven, he

94

heard a scuffing noise behind him. He whirled in a half-crouch, trying to recall up the reflexive self-defense posture he had been taught twenty years earlier.

A figure hunched in shadow two doors away. "Who's that?" Poole called. A thin shadow-man straightened and stepped forward.

A squeaky voice emerged in a whisper: "Mister…I gotta talk to you…please."

Swathed in a lumpy, worn duffel coat, her feet in cracked, sodden sneakers, Lola Jowett stepped forward. In the vague light from the SleepyEye House sign, Poole saw she was wan with cold, hunkered into herself. He opened his door and flicked on the light. She stepped cautiously through the doorway, looking fixedly only at him.

"You gotta help me, please," she sniffed. "Everything's gone rotten. I'm so scared…"

Let It Snow, Let It Snow!

POOLE PURCHASED ACIDIC coffee from the vending machine in the SleepyEye office, and Lola gulped it, holding the steaming plastic cup against her duffel coat, as if to absorb its warmth inside and outside. She sat on the edge of the bed, still shuddering with chill. It took twenty minutes for her to calm and speak coherently.

"They was talking about killing," she said finally. Her voice was so pale and weak Poole had to strain to hear her words. "Ziggy and Heinie met this guy out back of the mall."

"What guy? Who?"

"I never saw his face. I didn't want to get too close. But I heard them talk about somebody who got killed. And somebody else who…would. Ziggy kept saying, 'We'll get him…'"

Lola stared vacantly at Poole. Her lips moved, but no sound emerged. She rocked her head, and a single tear ran from the corner of her right eye, a jewel shaken loose from a setting.

"I don't wanna…get involved with murder. When Heinie saw me, he asked what I heard. I told him nothin—but he don't believe me."

"Lola," Poole said patiently, "try to remember anything about the man. Where was he?"

"He was in a van. A black one. Or maybe dark blue. It was too dark to see good. Last night."

"What time? Where?"

"I don't know—late. After the mall closed. Totty went home, and I was looking for a ride. I saw Ziggy and Heinie go across the parking lot, and the van rolled up. They stood and talked to the guy through the window. I mean, he didn't get out."

"Only one person in the van?"

"I don't know, mister. I couldn't see much." She sucked at the rancid coffee. Then she found a bit of crumpled tissue in her pocket and dabbed at her smudged face. "I must look terrible," she mumbled.

"What else did they say? Try to remember anything you heard."

"I don't know. Then Heinie saw me. I started to walk up, but they were talkin funny, so I stopped and stood by one of them big trash bins. I was scared to go and scared to leave. I tried to sneak away, but…" She snuffled and wiped at her nosed with her sleeve. "So I couldn't go home. I wandered around, then I come here. I heard that snotty Lissy Mungo say you were stayin here."

"Ah," Poole said. "You mean this *just* happened? Tonight?"

"Yeh. Didn't I say?" She stared around the room as if she had never seen such opulence. "This is a nice place," she said emptily.

"Lola, you've got to think if there was anyone or anything else mentioned. *Who* did they talk about?"

She gazed blankly at Poole, and for a second he wondered if she had fallen into deep shock. Her eyes were as flat as chipped obsidian. Then she smiled seraphically, an eighth-grader again.

"Oh, I know a lot of stuff. Everybody thinks I'm just a dumb kid, but I know what's goin down. They were talkin about Gertie."

"Gertie?" Poole tried to shift his mind's stripped gears. He had heard—what? Who had mentioned Gertie? Lola smiled again, and thin giggle escaped.

"They had Gertie in the van. That's what Heinie said. Then Ziggy took a box out of the back."

"A box? How big?"

Lola shrugged, frowned and made a vague two-handed gesture. About two feet by a foot or so, Poole decided.

"A small box. What was in it?"

"I don't know. That's when I got scared. Heinie said, real tough, 'We'll kill that fucker.' I took off."

She stood and looked uncertainly around. The dregs of her coffee dribbled down her duffel coat, joining the map of stains mottling it.

"I gotta go. I gotta get…home."

"Wait a minute," Poole caught her sleeve. "You may be in real danger…"

"Shit!" she pulled away, backed around the bed. "My ma'll put me in danger if she gets up and I'm not there."

"Look, I'll get a policewoman to drive you home. Or Wilma Breithope."

"No!" Lola moved to the door. "You'll get me in more trouble. If anybody finds out I seen you… You just stop Ziggy and Heinie from hurtin anybody."

Poole lunged, but she twisted the knob and rushed out. By the time he reached the door, she was halfway across the parking lot, her legs flashing as she ran. Then she plunged into shadow and re-appeared across the highway, dashing through a pond of sickly orange light. Too fatigued to decide, Poole stared. The raw wind bit into him, and he shut the door and staggered to his bed. *It will have to wait*, he thought, bending to strip off a shoe. He fell asleep across the counterpane, one shoe still on.

* * *

Poole woke to a senseless pounding, like a distant steam drill. It was Larry Starr, hunched into an old mackinaw jacket and thumping a mittened fist on his door. He peered owlishly up when Poole opened the door, saying, "Got a call from that Howells cop. Says you need to get right to his office. Hope they get your phone back in. I ain't signed on as no messenger-boy."

"Have a nice day!" Poole bawled at Starr's back as he stumped to the office. He looked at his watch, trying to keep his head out of the raw morning light. It was 7:07 a.m., 12-4. As he stared, the :07 turned to :08. Time flies when you're having fun.

"Jesus, you look like something the cat puked up!" was Howells' greeting. Howells was as immaculate as ever. Poole wondered if he kept a super-discreet valet tucked in his office closet to effect speedy repairs on his costume and person between bouts of work.

Howells flipped a sheaf of paper across his desk and then slid a cup of coffee after it. "Get the joe into your system while you catch up on this data."

The top document was Marty Grimes' super-exhaustive post-mortem report on the elves. Under it was a letter on stationery from the Leeland Merchants Bank, signed in a rococo flourish by Charles E. Cosgrove. Below that a sheet of photocopied notes by police officers.

Poole sipped the scalding coffee and scanned the paper, while Howells rocked back in his chair. "We got a call last night…early this morning. Somebody saying they had Greg Samsa. And we found the murder weapon in a dumpster back of the mall."

Poole tapped the photocopy. "You found a .38 revolver. And —?"

"It matches with the slug from inside good old Captain Cosmo's cranium. It was issued eight months ago as part of his working gear to one Randall Hogan Loggins. Ain't *that* a pisser?"

"Er, somebody *has* Samsa?" Poole scrubbed his knuckles on his forehead, where something like an ice-cream headache was building.

Howells donned half-glasses and peered at his notepad. "The desk got a call at…one-seventeen. Anonymous caller, muffled voice—all on tape. Voice says, 'We got Samsa, and we'll keep him till you cops clear out of the mall.' *Click*. That's it. Verbatim."

"I don't suppose you can use voice-prints?" Poole said feebly.

"If we were Dick Tracy or Buck Rogers, we could. Shit. You see what's happening? Now I'll have the FBI on our asses. Those super-dicks *will* futz with all that high-tech crap! Even if it doesn't work. We'll be up to our asses in crew-cuts and creeps in white coats. Jesus, we gotta find a string we can pull here!"

Howells removed his glasses and pitched them into his desk drawer. He pinched the end of his aquiline schnozz. "So," he sighed, "some wise-ass wants us to think he's a bad-ass kidnapper. It's probably a crank call. Even if we can't find Samsa. What do *you* see in this mess?"

"You don't think Loggins could be involved?"

"Randy Loggins isn't smart enough to be a wrong guy. Nobody else is dumb enough to hire him as a tool, and he sure as hell couldn't think any of this up himself. Nah, it's all bullshit. Somebody took Loggins' weapon and used it. He's still lying in County General listening to the little birdies inside his head, but the docs think he'll be coherent today. So I get to have a nifty interview with him. But...Samsa *is* missing. He lives with his sister on Fairlawn Drive, and we checked. She's having kittens now. He never showed up after the mall closed last night."

Howells tapped a ballpoint pen on his blotter arhythmically. Poole finished the coffee. "You think this may be a smokescreen by Samsa?" Poole asked.

"It's perfect, isn't it? If it weren't so ham-fisted. I've seen more than one big shot try an arranged snatch or beating or 'attempted murder' if he's in a squeeze. But this has *klutz* written all over it in capital letters. Even an absolute beginner would do a better job."

Poole described Lola Jowett's visit, and Howells scribbled notes. "Why the hell didn't you call in?" he asked.

"Sorry. I plain crapped out. I still feel like a blivet that fell off a truck."

"Okay. I have a couple men tracking down Heinie and Ziggy. We'll add little Lola and Totty to the list. What the hell is this 'Gertie' business?"

Poole scratched his head. "A German poet? A street in Chicago? No—the locals call that '*go-thee.*' *Gertrude?* Who?"

They regarded each other blankly. Howells shrugged and said, "When we get our hands on the right combination of wrong guys, we'll sweat it out."

Poole examined the Cosgrove letter, two terse paragraphs in bankerly prose, addressed to the chief of police, abjuring law-enforcement agencies to lay off C. Cosgrove's son and heir. It attempted majesty and achieved peevishness. Poole described his interview with Margo Cosgrove. Howells nodded and said, "That's the family style. All the finesse of a rabid hound."

"You think they're crying wolf? It's tantamount to tying a tin can to Don's tail."

Howells shook his head. "Nah. The Cosgrove manner. After four or five generations of hollering Hop Frog, you get used to wading in with your farm boots flying. The old man's on his way out, and he's finally realizing Don may not be cut from Cosgrove cloth. But their mixing in adds another layer of chaos."

Howells scribbled another note and said, "How'd you like to meet the great banker? I'm going to see him, and you can tag along."

Poole started to answer, when a desk officer entered, handing Howells a note. He scanned it and swore. "Come on," he said to Poole. "Another bit of business. The sheriff's department got a call from Astin Lee. He's located Heck Ogden."

* * *

Howells drove an unmarked car, a large, maroon late-model sedan, rapidly out of town. The streets were clear, at least scraped, but the country roads were drifted and icy. The car slewed and slithered on corners and dips in the old highway, and Howells concentrated on controlling it.

They wallowed up the lane to Lee's Happy Landing and nosed in behind a tan sheriff's car. As Poole and Howells got out, Astin Lee appeared on the inn's long veranda, bundled in an old parka and carrying a lever-action rifle. He waved and called, "Out back, gents. Ah, welcome again, Mr. Poole. Miss Breithope and a cohort are negotiating a truce, I hope."

Howells showed Lee his badge and replaced it, producing a snub-nosed revolver and arching an eye at Lee's rifle. "Who's shooting whom?" he asked.

Lee shrugged. "I'm trying my level best not to shoot anyone. But I dragged this out after the old fool started taking pot-shots."

"What happened?" Poole asked.

"My baker, Hans Koopman, came in about three this morning to start work. He's been snowed in town the last two days, but he managed to get out here. He was in the kitchen firing up the ovens, when he heard someone trying to get into the storage pantry around back. There's an outside delivery door. Hans thought I was up and about, and he came in from the kitchen in time to see Heck Ogden breaking a window. Hans is high-strung—it's endemic in bakers. He waved a cleaver or carving knife or other implement at Ogden, who responded by shooting at him. That woke me from pleasant dreams.

"I came down to find my baker—who, believe me, is rarer than gold and impossible to replace—running through the snow, waving a knife and shouting naughtinesses in double Dutch. He had run Heck out back to a shed—where I keep garden tools. Heck was whooping like Chief Blackhawk on the warpath and intermittently shooting his popgun. That's when I decided to send for the law rather than imitate Lee's Last Stand."

Lee led them down the wrap-around porch and stopped at the

rear corner. "I wouldn't advise sticking your head too far out. Heck is about a hundred yards down toward the river. Our stalwart sheriff's people are down in the back of my kitchen."

Howells stepped out and hunkered behind a rusticated post. Poole peeped around the corner. A rude board-and-batten shed squatted under a heavy load of pristine snow, drifted up to its single window. Footprints were poked blackly into the snow around the shed's door. A mechanical voice coughed once and uttered in stentorian tones, "Come on, Ogden. Cut it out. We just want to talk to you. Throw out the gun and come on out."

The stark black-and-white landscape reinforced Poole's feeling that he had walked into reel two of an old B gangster movie. He expected Ogden to retort, "Come'n get me, coppers! Y'll never take Johnny Gunsel alive!" Instead there was only silence punctuated by howls of wind from the river.

Howells dodged back to Lee and Poole. "I'm going down to see the deputies," he said. "Poole—you hang on and watch. Be sure Ogden doesn't sneak out the back of that shack. Lee—come on along. Maybe you can help talk the old weasel out."

Poole hunkered in the corner. Nothing moved in the landscape but a solitary crow, which circled and then settled in a tall, skeletal tree next to Ogden's lair. Then the shed door edged open. A squat figure in a dark coat crept out into the deep drifts. Ogden held an automatic pistol loosely in his left hand.

"Hey, put the gun down, Heck!" Poole recognized Wilma's voice.

Ogden straightened, looked around as if disoriented then plodded forward in a bear-like shuffle.

Another voice shouted, "Throw it down, Ogden. Now!"

Ogden lumbered on in an unwavering straight-ahead charge.

Without thinking, Poole stood and vaulted the porch railing, dropping six or eight feet into thick snow. He landed heavily on a slope and slid, feet splayed in an awkward, ski-less *schloss*, powdered snow flying in a wake. As he plowed to a halt in a drift, he saw over his shoulder Ogden turning slowly toward him. He seemed astonished at the sight of a burly stranger falling (evidently) from the gray sky.

Poole waved and attempted to shout but found his impact had knocked his wind away. He was mute. Ogden faltered toward him, as if deflected. Then he slowly raised the pistol, now in his right hand. "Another goddam meddler," he said.

The end of the pistol looked as huge as the bore of a field-piece to Poole from the cushion of snow. A dark figure emerged from the inn's back door and loped down the bank.

With a sharp *ping!* a wreath of blue smoke blossomed from the pistol's maw. *Like a conjuring trick,* Poole observed inanely. Ogden frowned and aimed again. Then the rushing figure plowed a wave of snow and collided with Ogden, flinging him sideways. The pistol spun in a parabola and disappeared into the snow.

Poole staggered upright, heaving snow from himself. He limped a half-dozen yards to find Wilma Breithope dragging Ogden to his feet. A hatless deputy with the face of a depraved choirboy skidded down the slope, pointing his service revolver at Poole.

"You!" he shrieked, "Get your hands up!"

"Jesus, Ralph—are you losing your mind?" Wilma said.

Wilma, Howells and the deputy bundled Ogden into the kitchen of the inn, while Poole limped behind. As they sat Ogden down at a vast chopping-block table, hands manacled behind him, Howells surveyed Poole and said, "I'd only give you a three on that ski-jump technique, Claude."

Wilma turned and snapped, "What kind of dumb kamikaze stunt was that, Richard? Do you have a death-wish?"

"I wanted to distract him," Poole said.

"Hey—a feat worthy of our dear, departed Captain Cosmo!" Howells said.

Ogden wheezed, "I need a drink. I think I froze my ass plumb off."

"You're damn lucky you didn't get your worthless ass *shot* off, "Howells said. "Where you been holed up, Og?"

"Don't you *Og* me, you slick piece of catshit! I recall when your daddy run the fruit stand at Twelfth and Broadway."

Howells flushed and grinned, "And I remember when you were too fucking soused to steal an apple off the stand without getting caught. But we're not here to stroll down memory lane. We're here to find out what runs through that sewer in your head and ask ourselves why we shouldn't charge Leeland's great war hero with murder, extortion and aggravated assault. Maybe even malicious mopery."

Wilma raised a hand. "Mr. Ogden. You're into a batch of serious trouble. But we don't want to throw you in jail. You can help us, if you tell us what's been going on at the mall."

Ogden looked around at the law's minions fencing him. "I don't know jackshit," he said dully. "Who'd tell a broken-down soak anything?"

"You know the elves are dead?" Poole asked. Ogden peered blearily. A tear formed on one red eye-rim and coursed down a crack in Ogden's old face.

"Yeh. I know. Shit—I…those guys were my *friends*. They didn't treat me like a stinking drunk. And they didn't think I was a… freak. Maybe because they got that treatment all their lives. They were square guys."

Howells lit a cigarette and slid the pack to Ogden. He stared and said, "How 'bout a drink instead?"

Astin Lee stepped forward with a bottle of bar rye. He glanced questioningly at Howells, who shrugged.

Wilma took the bottle and poured a finger into a tumbler, setting it before Ogden, who lurched in Pavlovian reflex against his gyves. Wilma lifted the glass and he drank it down, collapsing back with a sigh.

"God. Damn," he said. "I ain't never gonna be warm again. I kept remembering Inchon, and the frigging dead gooks heaped up in the snow. That's why I got the gun. I was sure I'd hear them fucking bugles again, and they'd come out of the snow after me." He shivered.

"You were talking about the elves," Wilma prodded.

"They had names," Ogden snarled. "Don't call them fucking elves. You think they was *born* in funny costumes? Mo and Jake—real Christians. God damn!" He shook his head fiercely. "I was gonna arrest who killed them, and…" He slumped. "And bullshit. I can't even take care of myself. Some fancy lady cop takes my gun away." More tears blurred the incised grooves of his face.

"Mr. Ogden?" Wilma leaned to him, her voice soothing. "We'll take care of that. That's why we're here. If you'll help us find who killed…Jake and Mo. Now, when did you see them last? Didn't you take them to the mall Sunday?"

Ogden shook his head. "I don't…let's see, Sunday. Yeh, I picked them up. But we didn't go to the mall. Old Samsa was raising hell about their costumes. He said the agency stuff was crappy, so he got new ones. He told me to take Mo and Jake to the Cosgrove place, to try them on. I thought it was all chickenshit, worrying about that stuff on a Sunday. But he's the big cheese, ain't he?"

"Samsa called you?" Wilma asked.

"Yeh, in the afternoon. I guess. I don't keep good track of time no more."

"You're *sure* it was Samsa?"

"Yeh. Yeh…I guess. I mean, he *said* it was Samsa. That prissy voice."

"So—you drove the…Jake and Mo to the Cosgrove house?" Howells asked.

"Sure. After we knocked off work, I took them in my truck.

106

We…had a few drinks."

"You took them into the Cosgrove house?" Wilma asked.

"No. Let 'em out by the drive."

"So," Wilma pressed, "you don't *know* that they went into the house?"

"Well…shit, no. I just drove off. Jesus—I drove off an left them, and somebody…" He hunched his head to hide the flow of tears. He said in a low voice, "Some big war hero, huh? Sitting and blubbering about…"

Wilma patted his shoulder. Ogden looked up, trying to grin lopsidedly, out of a mask of stubble, grime and patchy wind-burnt skin. He looked like The Last of the Frontiersmen, prepared for a taxidermic exhibition.

"I guess I screwed it all up, like everything else," he said. "All my life, it's been somebody saying 'Let's put the weight on dumb old Heck Ogden. He's just another fucking useless river-rat.'"

* * *

Poole rode with Wilma and Deputy Ralph Lightman. The deputy was in the back seat with Ogden, watching him narrowly, while Poole was in front with Wilma. The sun was bright and even, and the snow shimmered like an illusion, a vanilla-frosting fantasy, all around.

"We'll get a complete statement at the office," Wilma said. "With patience, we may coax some real facts from Heck. He's going to need sleep and food and time to fight off the DTs, I guess. But I think he's straight, under all that grunge and those years of bottle-fighting. If he knows anything, he'll tell us."

Poole glanced back. Ogden had slumped into a fetal heap and slept profoundly. Howells had left the inn for the County Hospital, to see Randy Loggins. Poole was unsure which way to jump. He pondered the Cosgrove family and Ogden.

"Wilma, if you'll drop me at the cop shop, I'm going on a little fishing expedition."

"Okay, but don't go jumping off buildings again. I almost had a kitten when I saw you rolling in the snow. And Sleeping Beauty there really was trying to put a hole through you."

"Thanks for the concern—I need a fulltime keeper." The Ferret started, after mild complaints, and Poole elected a frontal assault—a visit to the Cosgrove manse. He could shake things up, and maybe, a huge clue would roll out at his feet, or he could trace the footprints of a gigantic hound in the snow.

He steered the Ferret around a bank of plow-thrown snow and got his first glimpse of the baronial palace, a long brick-and-stone house framed between eagle-capped gateposts, rambling off into low wings, surrounded by great blue spruces and ancient oaks, lawns now like bob-sled runs. He pulled into a circle before a wide veranda under whiter Corinthian pillars. A giant holly wreath hung on the front door, and enough Christmas lights dangled on the boughs of the evergreens to illuminate a modest city. A life-size crèche stood in the lawn, framed by cadres of shepherds, wise men, sheep and camels. It looked like gridlock at Bethlehem. Some minion had cleared this Cosgrove artifact of vulgar snow.

Poole found a knocker at least at least as big as Jacob Marley's head and let it clonk on the broad oak door. After vague internal echoes, the door swung open and a thin blonde woman with dishwater complexion stared out.

"Yeh? You from the insurance people?" She had a hoarse voice.

"No. I'd like to speak with Mr. or Mrs. Cosgrove. My name is Richard Poole."

"Yes? Do you have an...appointment?" Poole saw that she held loosely in her left hand an old-timey martini glass, one of those shaped like a birdbath. It was, fortunately, empty as she waggled it.

"No. I spoke with Mrs. Cosgrove recently, and I have some... information."

"Oh, wow. Golf pro? Tennis? Or you just selling encyclopedias?" She wore an unpleasant leer.

Poole produced his wallet, trying to decide which meaningless TransAtlas card he could flash, when Margo Cosgrove appeared and pulled the door wider, using a small cross-body block to nudge the younger woman aside.

"Lainey. Go see about lunch. I'll take care of Mr. Poole."

"Yes'm—just betcha you will." She threw Poole a wide-angle sneer.

"Come in. I was just thinking I should call you. I do have this…psychic talent. Little good that it does me."

Margo Cosgrove wore a fluffy lemon-yellow angora sweater and plaid flannel slacks. Her steely hair was tangled, and she was bare of makeup, looking as if she had gained a decade in days. To point up her psychic understanding, she dabbed a hand at her cheek and frowned, saying, "It's quite naughty of you to drop in and catch me at my very worst."

Poole began a demurrer, but she cut in, "And you *must* overlook my daughter's frightful behavior. Lainey is having…difficulties. So she terrorizes everyone else. She's had thirty-odd years to practice, so the difficult is now easy for her."

"Your daughter?"

"Please *don't* say I couldn't be the mother of a full-grown woman. I'm depressed enough as it is. Donald and Elaine are Charles' children by his first wife, but I am quite aged enough to pass for Elaine's biological mother."

Poole had followed her down a nearly endless entry hall, past rows of severe oil portraits, bits of dysfunctional Victorian furniture and ranks of brass or crystal gewgaws, to a wide doorway into the living room. Poole started at a standing figure which he then recognized as a small black bear, taxidermically mounted upright, standing like a butler or guardsman, just inside the archway, paws out to hold a small silver salver. Elaine Cosgrove had left her martini glass on the tray, which transformed the bear into an insolently grinning waiter about to shuffle to the bar for another round.

"Charles' idea of a mild decorating joke," Margo said, sweeping the glass up, "and my daughter's idea of another way to annoy me. She's well along to a postgraduate degree in alcoholism."

"A hunting trophy of your husband's?" Poole asked.

"Au contraire. I shot it with a forty-four caliber express rifle in the Tetons, in 1949. Charles couldn't, as they say, hit a bull's ass with a banjo if the bull was tethered."

"You've always hunted?"

"I was brought up to hunt, fish, shoot, swear, ride a wild horse and in every other way be a perfect lady. A might huntress. A sharp-shootress."

Poole decided both Cosgrove women had been bashing the martini-shaker, which stood like a silver idol on a kidney-shaped coffee table only slightly smaller than a pocket battleship, before a long leather couch. Margo took one end of the couch, plumping a heap of pillows, and Poole took the other end. If there had been a net they could have played seated-position badminton. She lit another of her long, black, aromatic cigarettes.

"Now," she said through a small blue cloud, "that we have the social crap out of the way, I'll tell you my dream if you tell me yours."

"I have questions. No dreams, not even a second-hand guess. But I keep tripping over stray notions about the Cosgrove family, when I'm trying to find out mundane things like who wants to murder elves and Santa Clauses."

"Tell me what you know, and I'll do my best to answer your questions."

"Yeh, and I bet you have a nifty bridge out back to sell me. Or a solid-gold brick, huh?"

"Oh, you suspect I'm dupis…du…duplicitous. How ungallant!"

"Let us—as you said—thrust the crap aside. I can tell you things that won't interfere with the police investigations, but I'm not here as a courier—or to satisfy your curiosity."

"A shame. I'll bet you could be…satisfying. If you tried."

A sharp honk of laughter erupted. Elaine Cosgrove stood in the open doorway to the kitchen, a new glass in her hand, raised in salute.

"Hooray, Margo!" she brayed. "Let me toast your ever-subtle entendres."

Margo ground her cigarette in a flower-shaped silver ashtray. "You hardly need an excuse to drink, do you, my dear? Or to eavesdrop."

Elaine wiped at her lank, pale hair and leaned heavily on the doorframe, grinning like a feeding shark.

"If I needed excuses, you'd kindly provide them, wouldn't you? That's what I remember best, Margo dearest, about the long years. You were always there to explain how and why poor little Lainey wasn't up to scratch. Or to put the fix in for Donnie when he got in trouble. As to eavesdropping—I'd be a damn fool not to keep years open and watch my back. You've been a good teacher in the basic survival skills. Red in tooth and claw—we Cosgroves don't need nail polish and lipstick. Fresh human blood…"

Elaine laughed dippily, the sound shading into a squall. Margo glanced at Poole and shook her head.

"Would you *please* let me talk with Mr. Poole? A day without your histrionics would be like a century of international peace."

Elaine smirked, waggling her glass. "A thousand pardons, your highness. I'll creep back into the scullery and scull away. Cheers, Mr. Poole. Keep your guard up."

Elaine lurched away. Margo stared wearily into space, slumped and looking further aged.

"That girl has worn her father out. Broke his heart. And I swore she'd never wear me down, but I don't know. It's harder every day to go on. And we worry so about Donald."

"Elaine—your step-daughter—lives with you?"

"Now she does. After two marriages. Innumerable attempts to set up what she calls *careers*. Schools. Tutors. Lessons. God—my life is a roadmap of places I've dragged them to, the people I've badgered and cajoled, creeping letters I wrote, loathsome headmasters and proctors I sucked up to, just to keep them both going."

She stood and walked agitatedly along the wide marble hearth. The mantel above was crowded with small pictures and trophies. Margo paused to stare at the glittering phalanx of memories. She flicked her hand at them.

"That's what we garnered—two dozen silver-plate pots. Tennis, rowing, shooting, riding. And we end with a daughter who can't stay married, who's drinking herself to the bottom of a gin vat, and a son who can't even decide what color tie to wear every morning. And they are, my God, *my* son and daughter! I've...earned them with thirty years' hard labor. Maybe, God help me, I *deserve* them."

She plopped awkwardly onto a large leather poufe." She seemed for a second to revert to the untamed tomboy ready to scrap.

"Listen," Poole said, "I didn't come here to umpire your family battles. Your son is in the midst of a sticky situation, and I think you can help me. And that I can help him. We tracked down Heck Ogden, more or less intact."

Margo looked up. "Is he, by God? Another refugee from reality, saved to drink again. You don't credit anything that rum-soaked crook utters, do you? Charles sacked him for his random gossip, and Hector hasn't improved with age."

"I talked with Don, too, about his...difficult adolescence. I understand Heck Ogden was in your employ most of that time."

"When he wasn't lying in a gutter."

"Has Ogden ever attempted...blackmail?"

Margo stood and shook her head fiercely, hands on hips. "Neither Charles nor I would have tolerated it. You know a little of the Cosgrove family's place in this town's history. We have a reputation for toughness that isn't phony. Heck styles himself a fighter, but he was a little lamb when he worked for us. He kept his macho-man act for the beer joints. He had a sinecure with Charles, and he wasn't about to kill the golden goose."

"And after you let him go? No attempts at revenge or retribution?"

"That worm is incapable of turning."

Spots of high color, passion telltales, rose in her cheeks, and Poole decided he liked her in this natural state, with the varnish cracked.

"Why would someone want to see your son implicated in murder and fraud, along with Greg Samsa? Who would do that?"

"Anyone who could profit from discrediting the mall and the bank. Anyone who wanted to buy properties cheap or gain control of the corporation."

"You think this is all about money? That's all?"

She laughed harshly.

"That's sufficient, isn't it?" Poole rose. "I'd like your help, Mrs. Cosgrove. Is there a chance I could talk with Mr. Cosgrove? Perhaps he has ideas..."

"Charles is sedated. The doctor was here less than an hour ago. In any case, he would be...less than helpful. His mind and memory are not trustworthy."

Margo looked worn, cornered. She clenched and unclenched her hands. Poole nodded and gathered his coat and hat.

"I can find my way out," he said. "If you can shed any light..."

She nodded, her face bleak and impassive.

Poole walked down the long hallway. As he opened the door and glanced back, he saw her standing in the archway, the upright bear next to her like a leering familiar, a hairy demon whispering in her ear, its paws extended as if about to give her a shove.

Poole started the Ferret and sat staring at the sprawl of the Cosgrove mansion in its Christmas-card perfection. He looked at the immaculately arranged crèche before it, thinking, *Happy families are all alike.*

***

Poole drove to the mall with only half his mind on the light traffic venturing on half-cleared streets. He parked and entered the vast complex, his ears assaulted as he stepped from the whining wind into "It's Beginning to Look a Lot Like Christmas." In the atrium, the Santa Claus exhibit was cordoned off with maroon velvet swags, but a pair of clowns in red-and-white polka-dotted outfits juggled and joked, and a lissome young woman in a green body stocking demonstrated a food processor that looked as cumbersome and complex as an Atlas rocket.

Up in the administrative aerie, Poole greeted Alicine Mungo, who handed him a scrawled note. It urged him to call Howells' office, which he did, and the switchboard officer patched him into the squad-car radio system. He got a scratchy connection with Len Howells.

"Hey there," Howells said. "I've been to see Randy Loggins, and now we're in the middle of a situation. You know where Don Cosgrove's home is? Ironworks Pike?"

"My next stop."

"Can you gather up Don and bring him? I've been trying to track him down. I think we have Ziggy and Heinie cornered. On his land. Someone at the gate will direct you."

"Ziggy and Heinie? What's happening?"

"No time for a field-briefing, Poole. Just get out here—with

Cosgrove, if you can."

When he asked for Don Cosgrove, Alicine looked distinctly unhappy. "Gee, Mr. Poole, I can't locate him. He came in early and said he didn't want to be disturbed. When I went to his office awhile ago, he was gone. Must of sneaked out when I was on break. I been paging him for an hour."

"What about Toller?"

"He's looking for Mr. Cosgrove. What's going on? I'm really getting worried. Somebody said Mr. Samsa was missing, too. I mean... kidnapped?" Her voice rose hysterically.

"You just man—er, *woman* your desk, Lissy. Somebody's got to hold the fort. Right?"

She stared earnestly at Poole. "This is real creepy. People are scared to come out here now. You think somebody might do something...crazy here?"

Poole edged away. "Nobody's going to come through the offices looting, raping and pillaging. Listen, you may be the key to keeping the place going. Hang in there."

She made a sniveling sound at Poole's back.

Out in the security offices, a pimply-faced young man in a new, ill-fitted khaki uniform stared at the TV monitors. He held a polished nightstick in his hands like a wand of office and glared at Poole.

"Mr. Toller took off about an hour ago," he mumbled. "You with the cops or the sheriff?"

Poole left a scribbled note for Toller. The young man took the paper gingerly, regarding it with deep suspicion.

"I just started here," he said, "and nobody has told me dick about any of this. I'm supposed to be on a training program, and the only thing I got so far is this dildo and three hours of TV-watching. I was better off on food stamps."

Poole cut back through the mall. The atrium clowns were gone, and the jolly green nymph looked frayed at the edges as she started through her food-processor pitch again. A half-dozen people stood around her, eyeing her and the machine with equal indifference. He headed out into the parking area, angling toward GROUSE LOT, in a light spatter of tiny snowflakes blown sharply on the wind. The sky was lowering and gray, the temperature plummeting.

He followed Alicine's directions, turning from the interstate highway on an access road only vaguely scraped by snowplows. It twisted past new suburban developments, sprawling estates with pretzeline road systems, and into open country. He passed several old farms, their decay softened by the snow, and saw a pair of tall gateposts at the roadside, an echo of Charles Cosgrove's imperial entryway. A city patrol car was angled at the gate, and a uniformed officer huddled in its lee. When Poole identified himself, the man puffed vapor and pointed down the drive.

"Howells said he'd flag you before you get to the house. Hey—can you see if anybody in there has hot coffee? I'm about to freeze my buns off here."

Poole rolled up the serpentine drive, less efficiently cleared than that at the big Cosgrove manse. The house too was smaller, a low cedar-and-stone prairie house with a three-car garage appended like an afterthought to one end. The building seemed to crouch or cower on a flat hilltop obviously once a farmstead for a sprawling corn fiefdom. A grove of old beech and poplar windbreak trees stood deferentially to one side of the house. Poole imagined that a patent mechanical windmill once loomed on the rise, pumping water to a cattle tank or turning a little generator.

Before he could swing up the final gradient to the house, Poole saw Howells' unmarked car under a gnarled oak, and Howells stepped around its bow, waving Poole in. He let the Ferret coast into the thick snow at the shoulder.

As Poole extricated himself from the car, Howells leaned over and barked, "No sign of Donnie-lad? Shit. We've got the barn down behind the house staked out, and we think we've boxed our bad boys in there. We found Greg Samsa's van across the place on a back road, and we tracked at least three people across the field. C'mon."

Howells moved briskly around the hill, slogging into the fresh snow unconcernedly. Poole followed, feeling his shoes soak and his pants legs wick up cold and wet. *Boots, boots, boots,* he thought. When they reached a low stand of evergreens domed with snow, Howells slowed and held up a hand. He pointed around the shrubbery.

The hill dropped into a shallow bowl which cradled a small barn-like building of stone and rustic-red clapboard. Howells pointed toward it.

"Donnie's imaginary kingdom," he said. "He has a toy-train setup in there you'd have to see to believe. I guess he comes home after a tough day at the office, puts on a pillow-ticking engineer's cap and drives his little choo-choos till he's knocked out."

Poole peered across the drifts. The building was a toytown version of the archetypal American dairy barn, complete with miniature silo. Its cheery barn red was trimmed with white on lattice-like battens. The slope, the miniaturization and the blank snow made it seem an optical illusion, a mirage, of indeterminate size and scale.

"I put two SWAT fellas down behind the bushes. And another one in that greenhouse." He waved at a small conservatory whose windows were opaque with frost, a hundred feet behind the barnlet. "The windows are so frigging small in that barn that you can't see into it. I just hope no one was looking when our boys went in."

The fine snow blew in a vague, dancing curtain of white. The light was dull. Poole hoped poor visibility was on their side.

"You don't *know* who's in there?" he asked Howells. The

detective shrugged and tucked his Chesterfield collar around his neck.

"Nope. Three men is a guess from the tracks. And this was on the floor of Samsa's van."

He held out a smudged shred of paper. On it was the same drippy hanged-man emblem Poole had seen, with a scrawl below it: WE'VE GOT HIM WI. Poole stared.

"Any idea what it means?"

Howells said, "Looks like somebody started to write a note and stopped, huh?"

"Why are they here?" Poole asked.

"Take a guess. That's why I hoped you'd have Don along. Or at least locate him."

"You think Don's in there? He was at the mall up to a couple hours ago."

"Right. No, I don't think he's in there. But I wonder if he knows who is—and why."

Two uniformed men appeared behind them, hopping in low strides. One wore a baseball cap emblazoned LEELAND * SWAT and carried a radio. The other held a stubby-barreled Browning shotgun at port arms.

The SWAT officer said, "Mrs. Cosgrove's okay. We got the doctor in, and Doris is holding her hand. When she stopped with the hysterics, she says she doesn't have a clue about it. I put Jenkins into the back bay window to cover the east side."

Howells nodded. "We've either got a Mexican standoff here or a sack of horseshit. I'm going to find out which. Tell the boys to stand by. I'm going to walk down there."

The SWAT officer started to reply, but Howells held up a hand. "Hey, I'm not doing a John Wayne number. I'm just cold and tired and hungry. Enough of this crap. I'm going to that dip in the path and hail them. If somebody shoots, I can flop down out of the way. I think. But keep it cool. Tell your guys not to shoot without your direct order. And for Christ's sake, don't plug me in the back. Poole —sit there and think up a sure-fire negotiating ploy you can use if this fizzles."

Howells walked around the evergreens. When he had slogged a dozen yards, he was already half-shrouded by whipping snow. He stopped, and Poole heard him call out, but his words were snatched by the wind.

He stepped further, while the SWAT man muttered into his radio. Howells stopped and half-turned toward them.

"God damn it!" he shouted, "Fire! The place is burning."

Poole stood for a better view. A plume of black smoke erupted from the fake silo, like a head of steam from a riverboat's stack. Thinner gray smoke leaked from a rear window, and then a pall burst from the front door as it swung open. Len Howells jumped side-ways. A figure materialized from the gray smoke, dodged a few steps then leapt back into obscurity. The SWAT man bawled into his radio, "Watch it! Hold your fire!"

But there was already a series of heavy concussions, gunshots that seemed to make ripples in the thick air. A man in a deerstalker's camouflage suit stood behind a clump of iced bushes working a pump gun. A plume of red lept from the barrel, and blue smoke whipped around the man's head. Howells, Poole saw, thrashed on his belly behind a cusp of drifted snow. The little red barn was nearly engulfed in smoke, and Poole smelled the acrid tang of destruction. Two policemen charged down the hillside.

Poole turned toward the house on the hill and lumbered up the crusted slope, lurching and skidding. Another man in mottled camouflage burst from the deck-level door on the house, a scoped rifle in his hands.

"Hey, you! Call the fire department!" Poole shouted.

The man pointed the long gun at Poole and said, "Freeze,

asshole! And hit the ground. Now!"

It would not be at all hard to freeze, Poole thought, as he sank prayer-like to his knees in the wet, clinging cold.

Buy Now, Pay Later

GUNFIRE RATTLED FOR minutes. A siren howled, and eventually a phosphorus-yellow pumper truck wallowed around the house. Poole's captor released him from gunpoint. The mini-blizzard mixed with pungent smoke and bits of flying ash. When Poole could shake the cold from his feet and stagger down the hill, he saw that the toy barn was nearly leveled, a tower of thick smoke pouring up from stone foundations. Squads of police in winter gear trampled the snow. Len Howells stood in the lee of the greenhouse with a SWAT officer whose face and hands were blackened and greasy. This man held firmly onto a hunched figure half-swathed in an old blue poncho.

It was Ziggy, Poole saw, when the boy twisted to scowl up at him. His forehead was creased with a raw, bloody gash, his hands pinioned behind him in cuffs.

"I think we got 'em all out," the SWAT officer said to Howells. "The other two went in the ambulance."

"In what shape?" Howells asked.

"The older guy was out cold, the other kid ate a lot of smoke and was puking up his guts. The medics didn't waste any time, just grabbed 'em and ran. Sergeant Hoskins went in the ambulance."

"I want a report from him when they reach County General," Howells said. He stared at Ziggy, who crouched and writhed in the cape like Quasimodo in the hands of his tormentors.

"How did the fire start?" Howells asked him.

121

"How the fuck do I know? I thought you pigs did it. Some kinda smoke bomb?"

"Who were the other two?" Poole interjected. The SWAT officer looked annoyed.

"Heinie and Samsa," Howells said. He returned to Ziggy. "Who else was with you?"

Ziggy shook his head. Howells grabbed a fistful of poncho and shook him.

"You play games now, kid, and your ass is in jail forever. I'm gonna start filing murder charges, and every one will have your name on it."

Ziggy whipped his head again. Fresh blood trickled from the lip of the ugly wound. He grimaced out of the smoke stains like an imp peering upward from hellfire. "Get fucked," he whispered.

Howells told the SWAT officer, "Take him away, Mirandize him, get him looked at by the medics, then get him delivered to my office."

Poole watched the squad of firemen lurching around the smoldering ruins. Sheet ice from the hoses covered the ground and looped in rococo buttresses from the standing foundation stones. Several policemen probed gingerly at the smoking mass with long poles. Howells spoke into a radio. He seemed as tidy as ever after the fracas.

As Poole stared at the melancholy landscape of devastation, Wilma Breithope joined him. She shook her head and whistled. "It's worse than I thought. When the call came in on the radio, I thought it was a routine fire-call. Then we got gunfire reports, too, and I was in the cruiser, so I pushed on over. Do you know you're totally covered in soot?"

Poole dabbed at his face and grinned. "A minor inconvenience, after being frozen and nearly shot." He tried to summarize the Battle of Cosgrove's Barn for her.

As he finished, Poole saw Sheriff Buxtrider's burly figure emerge from behind the pumper. He spoke animatedly with the fire chief, gesturing at the ruins.

"What on earth is Buck doing here?" Wilma wondered aloud. "I called in when I was on the way, and he was at the office. He must of burned up the roads getting here."

Wilma moved toward her boss, and Poole followed. Buxtrider ended his colloquy and hailed Wilma, "Deputy, I need you to cover back at the office. There was a big pile-up on the interstate, and I had to put the other cars on it. Lightman's on the radio, but I don't trust that luncher."

"I didn't know we were called in here," Wilma said.

"Now, honey, don't let's us have a big argument. I make the final calls on jurisdiction. You hightail it back before Lightman gets his thumb plugged into the radio and short-circuits his IQ."

Wilma started to speak, caught herself, shrugged and nodded to Poole as she trudged away. Buxtrider started to turn away, and Poole said, "Are you trying to see your department gets its hand on a piece of this pie?"

Buxtrider stopped. "No pie here, Toole, unless it's under those cinders. Not even Eskimo pie. I'm minding my business as a peace officer of PawPaw County, and I suggest you don't get in my way."

"Did the city police call for assistance?"

Buxtrider gave Poole a brief high-voltage glare and moved off. The sheriff picked his way around banked snow and ice at the base of the burned building, hunched in his sheepskin jacket, his Drill Instructor hat pulled down, like an outrider in an old cowboy flick surveying the scene of an Indian massacre.

Poole felt the long-term chill right to the base of his soul. He began to shudder and decided this was nature's way of telling him she was about to deliver a solid case of pneumonia if he didn't use his head. He threaded his way through the gangs of uniformed men and women arriving on the scene, found the Ferret half-bogged in the snow, managed to rock it loose and reverse it down the driveway. As he passed through the tall gates, he saw the same shivering cop on duty, hopping feebly from foot to foot and beating his mittened hands on his jacket. Poole wished he could magically deliver him hot coffee and an electric foot-warmer.

* * *

As he drove, Poole tried to collect himself. *Where next? Who next?* He considered holing up in the library, admiring Ann Wilcox and plowing through more of Leeland's history. It would be hours before he could break Howells loose from his work to find out about Randy Loggins, Ziggy, Heinie and Samsa. He could sit around County General and try to weasel information from the staff. He could try the mall again, to see if Toller had surfaced. Or Donald Cosgrove.

He found himself pushing the Ferret briskly at 60 mph and slowed, feeling the little car express an urge to perform ice-dance figures. On an impulse, he turned back toward Leeland, passing a lot full of evergreen trees heaped and bundled like teepees. The trees displayed, Poole saw, were of every rainbow hue except green: pink, azure, puce, chartreuse, even black, sprayed with gooey flocking like prismatic marshmallow. A huge banner billowed in the gale, lettered in red and green:

* ACRES OF XMAS *

THE 3 WISE MEN WILL NOT BE UNDERSOLD

Poole turned onto Fairlane Drive again, into the whitened quiet purchased by Leeland's Oldest Money. He passed the eagle gates and followed the meandering street. It wound around the estate, and Poole found he could look down across the grounds, surveying the whole little empire.

He parked the Ferret and walked along the low stone wall that marked the outer boundary of Cosgrovia. The big house and its outbuildings looked as diminutive as Don Cosgrove's playhouse. Through the bare trees, Poole viewed the estate as if it were a black and white topographic map. He was not sure why he skulked like a poacher contemplating a raid. It seemed like a good idea.

As he watched the house, a figure emerged from a back door, a woman bundled in a long, dark coat. She moved quickly down a cleared walk to a long Tudor outbuilding that might have been meant to be a stable. Poole waited. After a few minutes, the figure re-emerged and moved briskly back to the house. Nothing else moved in the landscape.

Impulsively, Poole vaulted the wall and walked down the gentle slope toward the house. As he approached, he saw that the Tudor building, with its half-timbers and schlocky cupola, was a long garage with five bays. A garret-like half-story ran above. Poole found a glazed door on the side and peered in: a narrow staircase slanting up into dimness.

He tried the door and found it unlatched. He glanced back at the house. Nothing moved. He stepped in and moved quietly upward toward a solid door at the top of the stairs. He tried this door, and it too opened. He cracked it and squinted in. A square anteroom, littered with tools, boxes and game paraphernalia—a croquet set in a wooden case, a volleyball net folded in a corner like a shroud, a long workbench on which lay fishing tackle, rods, a baseball glove. Across the room another solid door. He felt trapped in Bluebeard's Castle—so many doors to open unbidden. What lurked behind the next—or last—door?

Poole crossed the room, returning the stare of a ten-point-buck's-head on the wall, a dismal trophy flocked with dust and shriveled with age. He tried the door, which pulled open. Inside was a studio livingroom cluttered with cast-off art deco furniture. Sitting in an old easy chair was Don Cosgrove, wrapped in a faded flannel robe, his hair uncombed, unslicked. He gripped the armrests like a man about to be executed or a white-knuckle flier hearing the pilot announce take-off. He faced Poole, staring uncomprehendingly.

Poole stepped into the room, and Don shook his head slightly, as if to clear it. He croaked, "Poole? They sent you?"

"Nobody sent me. But I've been trying to find you all day."

"They won't hurt me, will they? Don't let them hurt me." Poole stood before Cosgrove. His eyes were unfocused, bloodshot. The robe was several sizes too small, its mock-Navajo pattern faded almost to oblivion. Cosgrove released his grip on the chair and raised one hand to his pudgy face, touching it as if to reassure himself of his corporeal solidity.

"They said they'd kill me if I didn't do it. Just ask Lainey—she knows. She's in it, too, all the way. Take her. Leave me alone. She's always been a worthless bitch. I tried to do everything they said. That lousy Chance…he's *crazy*, and Lainey would do anything to protect him."

Poole sat on the edge of a sprung sofa-bed. The room smelled of damp, mildew and dead air, an ancient sepulcher reopened. Cosgrove babbled in a reedy voice.

"My father would do anything for her. And Chance. My God, the money he's pissed away on them! And that bitch Margo's even worse. It's not fair, damn it."

Cosgrove ran down, like an old gramophone at the end of its spring. He held up a hand, which trembled like a small animal writhing for freedom.

"All my life, somebody's been chasing me. That was a dream, Poole. Yes! I woke up from it and heard the fire engines. I can't turn and look, you see. Something keeps me from turning my head, but I know they're right behind me. Feet pounding, breath wheezing. God—it's huge, whatever it is. Like a steam engine. And then I woke up and there were fire engines everywhere, all that red and gold in the dark. And smoke I could taste."

Poole tried to follow the spilling words. He patted Don's arm. Cosgrove shrank away.

"My father sent you, you bastard! He'd do anything Lainey and Margo asked. They won't let me see him, you know. I'd just upset him, they say. My own father! Oh, he calls on the phone. Yes sir, every day. But...how do I know it's him? His voice has changed. It's...old and shriveled. They have these machines now, you know. How do I know I'm not talking to an answering machine?" He coughed and then laughed caustically. "Oh no—*I'm* the answering machine! Yessir, no sir, three bags full sir. *That's* the answer they want. But they won't let me *see* him. It would make all the difference in the world..."

He stopped and looked down the front of his robe, tracing the faded pattern with a finger. He frowned as if amazed at the sight.

"My sick robe," he said. "The one *she* always put me in when I was...bad. I spent half my childhood in it. Do you know that poem, 'The Land of Counterpane?' She'd come and read it to me. I learned it by heart, even though I hated the damn thing. I mean, she was really good at *pretending* to be my mother. That must have been a hard job. I'll give her credit. I'm not a small person. Well...I am a small person. See? I'm growing into my robe." He held up a sleeve. "Give them a few months working on me, and I'll grow right backward through it. They'll have little Donnie back in diapers. In my playpen. Crawl right back into the womb. But whose?"

He stared listlessly around the room. The thin light from the windows made him seem sunken into himself. Poole tried to soothe.

"Who are the people who threaten you, Don? I understand about your mother—Margo—and Lainey. But who else? Who did you think sent me?"

Cosgrove smiled craftily. "This is a test, right? You want me to say certain things you can report back. Let's see…if I tell you names, you'll mark down that I'm a tattletale, a snitch. Right? If I don't, you'll put down that I'm crazy, deluded. Can't remember names. Temporary amnesia, created by acute anxiety. Oh, I got *good* at taking those tests. Minnesota Multiphasic Personality Inventory. See? You won't box me in. I can slide right *through* those boxes. Just lines on paper, you know. But there are *other kinds of boxes, my friend*. This room is a box. It's impossible to walk through the walls. I've tried. My office is another box. The whole goddam mall is a big, big box. That policeman said the elves came out of boxes. Amazing. They just popped up, probably on springs." He smiled bitterly. "And you see what good it did them? They're still dead, aren't they? I'd have heard if they came back to life."

Poole nodded wisely, trying to seem a master of nondirective interrogation. "I agree," he said. "But who were the people who frightened you?"

"No, no, no," Cosgrove said, "you won't put me off that easily. I've got to tell you—the *womb* is a box, too! See? They made a big mistake in ever letting me out. Oh, they can push me back inside, if they really want to. Brute force. They fold up your arms and legs and cram you in. God, I'll bet that hurts!"

Poole felt himself losing it, patience evaporating. He tried to keep sweet reason in his voice. "Forget the boxes a second, Don. You've got important things to tell me."

Cosgrove lurched upright and stared around. He shuffled forward, and Poole saw his feet were stuffed into old, cracked leather slippers of the same scale and vintage as the robe. He crossed the room and opened a big square pine chest. It was stenciled in faded enamel with clown-faces and stylized flowers, a child's toy chest. Cosgrove knelt and rummaged in the chest, emerging with a long cardboard box.

"You don't know anything, Poole. You listen to what people tell you, as if the *words* were important." He clasped the box against him. "So I'll have to *show* you. Then you'll know. Your *eyes* will know."

With an odd ceremonial solemnity, Cosgrove handed Poole the carton, a plain manila cardboard container about a foot and a half long by six inches by eight inches. It was unmarked except for a faint stencil in pink stamp-pad ink: PRODUCT OF LATIN AMERICA. It was not heavy.

When Poole lifted the top off the box, the sight almost caused him to drop it. Inside, nestled in a bed of crumpled tissue, was what seemed to be a grotesque fetus, a wizened homunculus folded in on itself like Don Cosgrove's bad dream, staring up with a wicked grin and bright shoe-button eyes.

"Jesus Christ on a pogo stick!" Poole breathed.

Cosgrove emitted a cracked cackle, a victory-whoop, "I got you, you smug bastard!" Poole lifted the curious doll from its nest. It was a soft toy, almost a sculpture, in lizard-green, representing an old woman in caricature, a tiny twisted gnome of a green woman in a patched dress, with a shark's-mouth grin, stringy carrot-red hair, talon-like fingers, wide lemur's eyes. Its expression was one of triumphant male violence, mirroring Don Cosgrove. He, too, seemed about to crow, "Got you, you smug bastard!"

Poole examined this totem. It wore a dress with rough patches, and under the dress, ballooning Victorian bloomers. On one arm hung a bulging shopping bag and on the feet were perfectly detailed replicas of worn running shoes. It was an awful travesty of a bag lady, metamorphosed from an object of pathos to one of fear and terror.

A lozenge-shaped label dangled like an amulet from the neck, and Poole read its printed text:

* * GROTTIE GERTIE * *

BEWARE! You have just taken into custody one of the most dangerous characters in the Universe! Gertie only seems to be a harmless Derelict. But she is Armed and Dangerous! Examine her shopping bag. Find the secret pockets where she carries her Special Weapons. She blends into her Surroundings as a social Outcast but Gertie is a highly trained Urban Terrorist! Don't turn your back on Gertie! She spreads Disease in a fiendish program of Biological Warfare. She is a Master of self-defense and Killing Arts. HANDLE WITH CARE!!!

On the obverse of the label was another smudgy text:

COLLECT KRAZED KILLER KIDS—SEND FOR ARREST WARRANTS!

Stevie McSnott—con artist and pervert

Sarah Sicklee—a Terminal Gal

Percy Pewkes—the World's Most Revolting Snob

Limping LuLu—she'll pick your Pocket!

Ferdie Floo—one cough and you're dead, MacCatalog and official Arrest Warrants from:

DaisyChain Imports Inc. * 1124 Industrial Blvd. *St. Vitus, LA.

"Good God!" Poole muttered. He stared at the fetish. Holding it made his hands itch, so he lowered the carcass and slipped the lid on the carton. His impulse was to take the bundle to the garden and bury it.

Cosgrove, seated again in the old chair, grinned in a mirror of Gertie's lupine expression. "Welcome to the zoo," he whispered.

"What on earth *is* it?" Poole asked.

He had met Gertie, he realized. What did that mean?

"Only the toy sensation of the Christmas, season. Or so I am told. Retails at thirty-four ninety-five. Christmas pre-sale price twenty-nine ninety-nine. Wholesale price, special to me, you understand, ten bucks flat, if I buy the whole line in bulk lots of at least five hundred per model. That's five grand per model, thirty grand for a shipment. Two hundred percent markup."

Cosgrove smiled thinly and tapped his fingers on the chair arm.

"Of course, I'm not a merchandiser, am I? If I merely funnel the deal into toy concessions, it's not quite so rich. So—I could merchandise them directly through big displays in the atrium. SantaLand. You get the idea. Maybe hire some little people to hawk them. Mount a campaign. Exclusive regional rights, see—none of the toy franchises will have them. Simple and sure. Right?"

Poole nodded, and Cosgrove frowned, saying, "Wrong. It stinks. It's a rig—come-on. Nobody does business that way."

At a slight noise, Poole and Cosgrove turned. Margo Cosgrove stood in the doorway in a long blue coat, her hair under a loose scarf. She cradled a short rifle across her bosom; Poole recognized it as a .30-caliber M1A1 carbine.

She smiled and said, "Why, Mr. Poole, it was nice of you to return so soon. But I wish you had come to our front door. Don needs his rest and quiet, and I fear you're bothering him."

* * *

She hustled them down the stairs and back to the big house. They entered a back door and descended to the cellars. Margo Cosgrove gently herded Poole to a room crowded with old office furniture and stacked cardboard boxes. An overhead fluorescent fixture but no window.

"This is Charles' home office," she said cheerily. "He likes to come down and play overseer, managing our household books and so on. A harmless pastime. I'm the head accountant and auditor here. But it has the virtue of a strong-room door—to keep out thieves, moth and rust. It will also keep you securely in."

Margo held up a dainty hand, the other securely on the carbine, a finger inside the trigger guard. "Oh, it's not durance vile, exactly. Just a breathing space for me, so I don't have to divide my attention and wonder where you'll pop up next. A bit of time for a quiet talk with my son."

Don stood behind his stepmother, shifting fretfully from slipper to slipper. He looked like an outsized urchin deprived of his prize teddy bear. "Mother," he said, "Mother…"

"Not now," she said, without looking. "Not yet, sweetheart."

"Bye for now," she said with a smile, closing the heavy door with a solid thump. A key turned, a deadbolt shot home.

Poole surveyed the room, a narrow space eight feet wide by twenty long. An old partners desk in the middle. Walls lined with floor-to-ceiling shelves. A dusty swivel chair, an old mimeograph machine under a hood, an L.C. Smith typewriter like an organ console. Ranks of boxes and files, sprinkled with the dust of inattention. The fluorescent fixture shed a dull, uniform greenness.

Poole examined the room carefully, checking desk drawers, peering at shelves, baseboards, the heaped boxes. Fifteen minutes' search convinced him he was in a seamless space. The door was metal painted to resemble oak, unyielding to shoulder or fist, hinges concealed in the wall. The handle turned but a bolt froze the door.

A phone jack in the baseboard skirting—but no phone. A ventilation grille in the end wall, sighing brackish air. Less than a foot square. He had once read that a man could crawl through any space larger than his head, but he knew this for a base canard. Houdini might be able to do it, but he was dead, and no wonder.

Poole sat in the swivel chair. He could pretend he was a captain of industry and while away the hours building an empire of imagination. He found pencil stubs in the desk: he could indict his autobiography, or a journal, or a novel onto the whitewashed walls. Some of the world's great literature, he recalled, was written in prison

—Don Quixote, Pilgrim's Progress, The Gulag Archipelago. He remembered that Tom Sawyer insisted Nigger Jim write a work of pathos while awaiting deliverance. But he had always hated Tom Sawyer, a snotty little prick who should have been thrashed and sentenced to life in Dotheboys Hall.

He could write coded notes and slip them out by a clever ruse, when his warders brought food and interrogation. Always provided things went on that long. Or they could come in and bolt an iron mask him over his head and keep him in Chateau Deaf for thirty years.

"I am the *real* Dauphin," Poole muttered.

They. He realized he was thinking like Don Cosgrove. When you are locked up, the whole world is a conspiracy, every man's (and woman's) hand raised against you. Life is nasty, brutish and short. *Gloom.* He drew a frowny-face on the wall with a pencil stub. *Take that!*

"Even paranoids have real enemies," he said. The sound of his voice was a teeny comfort. He saw a motion out of the corner of his eye.

A biggish black cockroach scooted like a mechanical toy across the linoleum floor. Oh, boy, Poole thought, the Roachman of Leeland. I could tame him and have a friend to talk to. Me and Mehitabel. Teach him—it—to fetch and carry. Have him (it) bring friends to form a labor force and dig our way out, in a few eons.

He stamped his foot, and the hexapodal arthropod raced to the end wall, scampered up the baseboard, scaled the wall in even strides and disappeared into a crack where the ceiling joined the wall. Poole sat for a moment, depressed that he was poor company for even a lowly bug.

A faint idea shimmered. He dragged the swivel chair to the wall and blocked its casters with a file. He stood gingerly on it, bringing his head to the low ceiling. The room, he realized, had a false ceiling laid in under the rafters. He poked it. It was as hard as...sheetrock. He wound up and delivered a short jab. It dented. He jabbed again, and his fist penetrated. It also hurt like hell. A few minutes searching yielded proto-tools: a thin sheet metal paperknife wedged back of a desk drawer, emblazoned

LEELAND SEED & FEED CO. * 1907–57

A HALF-CENTURY OF SERVICE

TO SOUTH-CENTRAL ILLINOIS.

God bless advertising giveaways! He also found a ballpoint pen long dead, a 1937 buffalo nickel, a small pot-metal box, evidently a portmanteau paperweight/paperclip-arsenal, a styrofoam coffee cup and two more pencil stubs, one with red lead.

He surveyed these implements, thinking that if he were Robinson Crusoe, Thomas Alva Edison or Tom Swift, he could build from them a nuclear-powered escape auger and drill his way straight to freedom through the concrete-block walls. If he were James Bond, he could fabricate a crude pistol which would propel unerringly lethal pencil stubs. If he were not a patent idiot, he could figure out what to do with this trove of technological detritus. He wished he had spent boyhood hours reading *Popular Mechanics.*

He pocketed the things, noting that he had in his pockets more potential tools—a hardly-utilitarian fingernail-snipper-cum-keychain-fob, a handful of coins, another defunct ballpoint pen.

Eschewing finesse, he stood again on the chair and bashed the ceiling with his fist, now handkerchief-wrapped. Overhead punching was heavy work, but he managed to open a hole bigger than his head, showering himself with debris and gypsum dust. He hoped there was no asbestos inlaid or in fifty more years he'd be dead. He grasped the ragged edges and yanked, putting a hundred and eighty pounds of his dead weight into it.

A great raw chunk of sheetrock ripped loose. He stared into a cavity backed by oak and pine rafters. *Now what?* he asked. He could keep going straight up, try to rip or chew his way through the rafters, sub-flooring and flooring, to emerge like Mole Man in the comix in the Cosgrove parlor—or whatever was up there. He could go sideways: he peered into the gap. The cement-block walls went right up to the flooring. *To hell with it!*

Tired of standing tipsily on the chair, Poole sat and surveyed the damage. His impotence irritated him. His best was to rip up sheetrock. *Take that, you tyrant! Shit.*

The solid side wall was (presumably) the house's foundation, several feet thick. The back wall ditto. The further side wall, with the ventilation duct, was inside the basement and new. Ditto the wall containing the vault door. He thought about drawing a plan of the cell for prolonged study. If the walls went right up to the floor-or-ceiling, he was screwed, with little point in wasting energy in dismantling the false (i.e., sheetrock) ceiling.

"Think, shithead!" he said aloud.

He found a matchbook from the Carnahan Hotel in his pocket, mounted the chair again, struck one and peered back into the cavity. Old wiring in metal-flex conduits, a small length of furnace ducting, dust, dirt, despair. The match flickered out, after frying his fingertips.

A horizontal space or layer about two feet thick between rafters and lowered ceiling. He could crawl up and hide, so his jailers, upon entering, would see an empty room and decide (a) he was Jesus Christ and had pulled the old empty-tomb gambit again; (b) he had vanished into thin air by exerting secret powers learned in the Orient; (c) they were going mad and should turn themselves in to an appropriate mental-health officer. They would—in any event—run away crying havoc, while he could slip down and find egress via the left-open door. He had seen it work dozens of times for everyone from Lash LaRue to Abbott and Costello.

He wondered what Margo Cosgrove was doing. Lining up her family and plugging them full of carbine slugs? Calling in a squad of Chicago goons to do same? Convening whatever confederates fit in this ungodly Chinese puzzle of a case? Undoubtedly the latter. She would be finding out that Heinie—aka Chance—her...what was it? step-grandson?—was jugged for arson, mayhem, resisting arrest, kidnapping, extortion, theft, murder, etc. Or she would be contacting...who? Or whom?

Poole squinted into the crawlspace. A small heating duct ran across the area, terminating in an upward bend at the wall. A floor vent, doubtless, in whatever room was above.

A stupid idea struck Poole with the force of divine revelation. He could reach this duct at arm's length and found in its side a small, square indentation—a sheet metal knockout placed for the use of the sheet metal worker installing said ducting, to allow vent or branch openings. He pressed on the square. He pounded it. Eventually, he bent it inward till it popped loose. He had made a square opening, about six inches on a side. If he could reduce himself to the size of his pal Archy, he could scamper into the duct and run all over the frigging house. He hummed "We Shall Meet Then in That Upper Room."

Working with blind concentration, Poole gathered the handful of pencil stubs, a sheaf of ledger sheets from a file box, the styrofoam cup and his handkerchief. With the paperknife as tool-of-all-work, he poked the rubbish into the duct, around the corner of his opening toward the upper vent. He struck another match and started a ledger sheet ablaze, noting idly its heading: HOUSEHOLD INVENTORY—JUNE, 1951. He reached his improvised torch into the duct and prayed to Zeus that the debris would burn, hopefully with many fumes. He was rewarded with a puff of black and acrid smoke in his face. A draft ran in the duct, all right. He saw orange flames, more smoke billowing. He clambered down, found a ledger book, clambered up and clamped it over the opening.

Poole was sure, surveying his mental schematic of the house and its probable system of hot-air ducts, that he was sending at least a minor cloud of noxious fumes to some overhead room. He remembered Don Cosgrove's history of fire-buggery, or at least putative pyromania, and the family's sensitivity thereto. With his free hand, he whanged the metal paperknife on the duct, bellowing "Fire! Fire!" at the rafters.

He paused and waited, smelling a stench of scorching. The magnificent stupidity of kindling a ceiling fire while locked inviolably in a tiny room struck him. If this didn't work, he would be reduced to a fritter in a welter of paper-ash and charred office furniture. The pathos of this idea enraged him, and he resumed his sheet metal percussion and *fortissimo* shouting.

When he paused again to listen for the pounding of feet and the wholesale panic he presumed to have instilled in the household over him, Poole heard a light voice say, "For goodness sake!"

He looked down to see Margo Cosgrove, out of her coat and into an elaborately embroidered silk dressing gown, with her trusty carbine pointing accusingly at him. She stood inside the opened door and wore a quizzical expression.

"Why, Mr. Poole," she chirped, "what on earth are you doing up there?"

Glumly, Poole answered, "Ralph Waldo, what are you doing down there?"

***

Margo motioned Poole down from his chair and prodded him out of the room. Wisps of brackish gray smoke curled around the hole yawning in the ceiling. Poole marched ahead of her, and as they approached the back stairs, a lumpy figure descended, a man in lime-green trousers and a splashy neo-Hawaiian shirt, as if abruptly debouched from a South Seas tour.

It was Fred Toller, who goggled and said, "Miz Cosgrove? What you folks up to?"

"It's very tiresome, Mr. Toller," she said. "Would you be an angel and fetch a fire extinguisher? There's one on the wall at the top of the stairs. Take it back to the office and put out a fire in the ceiling."

Toller nodded and trotted back up. He reappeared hugging a red amphora. As he passed, he winked at Poole and said, "Brother, you surely know how to get into all sorts of mischief!"

Margo escorted Poole upstairs and down a passageway from the kitchen to a formal dining room dominated by a long hunt table. Sitting at the head of the table, with papers scattered around him, was Sheriff Buxtrider. He still wore his sheepherder's coat, but his D.I. hat sat in the middle of the table like a lumpy epergne. He looked up as Poole entered.

"Mrs. Cosgrove...Toole," he said. "It's hard to get a bit of brainwork done here with all this hullabaloo."

"Mr. Poole was naughty," Margo said cheerily. "He played with matches and made a mess."

"Sounds like someone else we know."

"I think Mr. Poole listened to old gossip and tried to be clever."

Buxtrider frowned and tapped a pencil against his enviable chin-cleft. "We need to find out what it is you know, Toole, and why you're dabbling in this business."

Margo pointed the carbine toward a chair at the table. Poole wondered if she had been a schoolmarm with a pointer-fetish.

Buxtrider scowled. "Good grief, Margo—I know you're a dead shot and all, but don't brandish that thing."

She tittered. "It's not loaded, Buck. Heavens, I wouldn't keep a loaded gun in the house with Donald on the premises. But I had informed Mr. Poole of my expert marksmanship earlier, and his imagination did the rest."

She propped the short gun in a brass umbrella stand. Then she carried a tray laden with a silver service to the table.

Buxtrider nodded to Poole and said, "I really want to know what in blazes you're up to. I need to hear a half-dozen solid reasons why I shouldn't haul you in on conspiracy charges."

Poole snorted, "That's hot, Bucko! Here I am, grabbed by a gaggle of ace conspirators, and you want to charge *me* with conspiracy? I don't think *you* want to put *me* on trial."

Buxtrider grinned evenly. Poole wondered if his orthodontic perfection was a perk of office. The sheriff shook his head and clucked, "Toole, you're a wizard at getting a grip on the wrong end of a slippery stick. Mrs. Cosgrove called me as a friend of the family, because she just apprehended an intruder in her garage. Since she don't need a lot more publicity about her step-son's delusions and, ah, eccentric behavior, I run on over to handle it all quietly."

Fred Toller entered from the kitchen, holding a jelly-donut captive. He nodded over it to Buck and Margo.

"All took care of," he said. "Just junk in the heating pipes. No problem."

Margo said, "Mr. Toller, we're about to have a civilized tea. You're welcome to your, er, pastry, of course—but I have a nice preparation here."

Toller glanced regretfully at his donut, then parked it on the sideboard. "Sure thing," he mumbled.

Margo poured from the Revere pot into a set of delicate Limoges cups. She regarded Poole thoughtfully across The Smoking Tide.

"I think we must take Mr. Poole into our confidence," she said. "There's little point in assuming we can circumvent or bluff him. I'll credit you for resourcefulness, Mr. Poole, even if you have confused yourself and created a muddle."

Toller nodded and grinned over his eggshell-thin teacup. "You don't mind diving headfirst into cowflop, do you, son? If I rushed around like you, I'd of collected a double hernia and a purple heart."

Margo gently presented Poole with a teacup. Its aromatic fumes were soothing. Lethe? He felt exhausted and wished Margo would tell him a nice bedtime story and tuck him into a trundle bed so he could visit the Land of Counterpane for about seventy-two hours.

"I don't know," Buxtrider ruminated. "We don't need this more complicated than it is. We don't *need* a corporate snoop in the picture."

Poole felt this a churlish application of the principle of Occam's Razor. Toller winked across his teacup.

"Mr. Poole can be of great benefit," Margo said. "He can advise us on the, ah, legality of our enterprise. I mean in terms of corporate law, business acumen, and so on."

"Look," Buxtrider said. He held a tiny petit-four in a big mitt. This business has been balled up a hundred years. This nerd has no big news for us."

Nerd? Poole thought. *He thinks I'm a nerd?*

"Er, what is this subject?" Poole asked. "Is there an agenda here, or is this a word game? Botticelli? Charades?"

Margo scrutinized him. "This is a *most* serious issue, Mr. Poole. My... associates don't fully trust you. I'll take a chance. Do you see these papers? They may resolve this...unpleasant business. But family interests are at stake, some obligations that go back to my great-grandfather. Oh yes, I'm a Lee that far back, too."

"To hell with that, Margo," Buxtrider said, inhaling the eensy pastry in one gulp. "I'm not about to scuttle a career. I don't give a... damn about the past, but I'm sweating bullets about the future!"

"Chalk up a point for Bucky," Toller said, tossing back his oolong as if it were a shot of Old Red-Eye bar-blend. "We all hope to see him mayor of our fair city, then on to Springfield, hey?"

"This," Margo riffled the sheaved papers, "is the past, and we must unravel it before you leap onto the fast track, Sheriff."

Poole examined the papers. They were frayed and yellow, bound with scraps of ribbon, splotched with ancient stains and seals. Margo untied a bit of string and straightened the documents. Then she rose to answer the dull thump of the front-door knocker.

Poole stared at Buxtrider, who casually ingested another little goody. "Shoot," the sheriff muttered. "Not enough in one of these things to tickle your gums." Toller looked around and then passed a nickel-plated hipflask to Buxtrider.

"Put a squirt in your tea," he whispered, "and it won't rot your gullet on the way down. Pass it to friend Poole, too. I think we'll all need fortifying."

Buxtrider tipped a dollop into his cup. He handed the flask to Poole, who rose and grasped it. As he did, he grabbed the sheriff's wrist and wrenched him hard into the edge of the table. Poole let Buxtrider yank backward, and the pull skidded Poole on his belly across the polished walnut table. He surfed into Buxtrider, threw an arm around his neck, and the two men collapsed backward over Buxtrider's chair, which splintered under their weight. The old wood snapped like ancient bones. Poole's hand fell on a teacup, crushing its eggshell delicacy.

"Jee-zus!" Toller howled, while Buxtrider gargled, "God dam! Led go!" as Poole tightened the half-nelson.

With his right hand, Poole found Buxtrider's gunbelt and holster, tugging the .357 Magnum revolver free. Buxtrider rolled his mass onto Poole. He worked the four-inch barrel to the sheriff's temple.

Which was when Fred Toller planted a 10 EEE Thom-McCann walking shoe on Poole's hand, grinding hand and pistol into broadloom. Toller stooped and yanked the heavy revolver from Poole's grasp.

Toller backed away, and Poole dragged himself up, leaving Buxtrider coughing and gagging on the floor. He rolled over and glared at Poole, face red as boiled ham. "You fucking lunatic!" he finally gasped. "You're due to get yourself killed."

"Boys!" Margo Cosgrove called from the doorway. She stamped a foot pettishly. "Stop this instant! Oh—you've destroyed one of Aunt Maude's anniversary chairs!"

Margo was trailed by Ann Wilcox, who stared wonderingly at the scattered furniture and papers then unwound her coaching scarf and pulled off a green car coat. She knelt and collected the papers tenderly, glancing at Poole.

"I missed all the fun. Now I understand why your face was so battered the other day, Mr. Poole. I thought you'd had an accident, but I see it's part of your sport."

Fred Toller examined the big handgun and then gingerly handed it to Buxtrider, who was massaging his neck and muttering, "I get first dibs on giving this dumb bozo a hiding."

Margo said, "Now, Buck—a mere misunderstanding. We should have brought Mr. Poole into the picture sooner. The poor man is as deluded as my son now. Everyone, please sit down and be halfway civilized for an instant. We're all here, so we can begin our meeting."

Margo pointed and led Poole firmly to an end chair. Buxtrider limped by and sat well down the other side. Toller collected and stacked papers. Ann Wilcox donned half-glasses and sat before the mass of documents.

"Now that you're here, you may guide us, dear," Margo said to Ann Wilcox, who glanced at Poole and said, "Sit quietly and listen, and we'll answer every question, Mr. Poole."

Fred Toller, as he passed the Jacobean sideboard, on his way to a chair, palmed his jelly-donut. He saw Poole's reproving glance, put a finger to his lips and winked again.

God Rest Ye Merry

THE GROUP SHUFFLED papers around the table, with Ann Wilcox as proctor and amanuensis. They tried to decipher blotted scrawls and unravel lengthy screeds in scratchy, alien writing. Poole was fascinated by this word-horde but baffled by it. One manuscript sprawled in faded sepia ink, traced in a fine copperplate hand, over several heavy yellowed sheets. Under a title inscribed with a rococo flourish SO SPEAKETH OSSIAN, Poole read:

O sing not of ancient Days and tribal lays but sing instead electric Muse of What Will Be, sing of the Rising Glory of Columbia.

And OSSIAN Son of Fingal left rude endeavors in the Caledonian wilds to travel on wings of wind to the West many days journeying on the whale road to seek a Destiny as yet unglimpsed in life of battles and drinking deep draughts of Royal Mead. A Ship like a gracious Swan carried him with his Warriors unafraid past Ice arid Dragons of the deeps to the untrimmed shores of a new Land.

Sing of what Will Be, the tale to come of the place once found later lost by OSSIAN and his Nation!

In this rough Land the heros band met Wild Men who spake unto them through an Angel who led men both bronze and red to Places Unseen by Human eyes. Mounden earth made unto mountains the Angel with magick means discovered. In bowels of Earth OSSIAN saw layed bare eldritch eons of this old New World and all the men were sore afraid.

Leader of the redden band, Chief Pompanatus spake to OSSIAN through Angel's tongue which maketh all mens language level.

Saying This sheweth Ancient Days and we by Arts of Faith sailed on wings of wind through whale road deeps to come. Treasures in the maw of Earth were multitude—of Afric artifice etched with letters and signs of People Ethiope. Cunning pictures wrought as to move and speak disporteth themselves by the Angels tongue who gave unto the Men spectackles which maketh them see and hear in their minds tongues and knowings. Moving Signs enacted ancient days of the trials and anabastick travailing of the Ethiopes. Who by burdensome and affrighting struggle sailed reeden boats across shoreless Seas and up Great Father River.

The Black Race found sweet Ships Haven to the North where grew great Sycamoores and where Father River was many cubits wide. The River sleepeth cried Chief Pomapanatus in this place. The Angel closed the Mouths of Earth by directing so with Golden wand. He transporteth red men and bronze by Wings of wind to the place they had seen and set hem on rivers banks to see in their own Eyes and minds this Chosen Place.

Beasts prowled and rough winds blew but the Angel made them Pacifick with his wand saying This Place will henceforth be the New Garden to which wendeth all Races of Men to find plentitude and Peace. And struck the Earth with golden wand again—from which springeth fecundities of Vegetative Matter of all manner and Kind— melons maze berrys fruits of Trees wheat and oats food for men and Beasts. Hills were made flat and rough places plane and roadways for Men and wagons appeareth with houses of habitation and Commerce sprung as from the black Soil.

O sing of the Vision of OSSIAN with his pale band on the rivers side beholding his Destiny and the Fate of his peoples people in years yet unfolded from the brooding Wings of Time.

Here appeareth iron Waggons of tremendous girth shaking the

144

Earth with smoken thunderings and Boats that with Firey Wings gliden the face of the River. And other wagons that moveth with silent Magick with no steeds to pull them and in blue skies waggons that flew by unapparent means. All bearing in their inwards multitudes of people of every Kind and stamp to settle by the Rivers edge. People who spake to one another by means of Voices in the Air and saw Visions flickering on the Walls of each Dwelling so that all knew Language and Knowledge at Once as if the very Angel dwelt in every breast.

And Chief Pompanatus uttereth the cry LEE! to the Winds which made OSSIANs band cower in fear. But smileth Angel on the Word and with Wand unfolden more of Years Uncome.

All men standeth unbidden for goods which fell from a gapping CornuCopia into waiting hands, all manner of domestick chattels fell ripened fruits into hands unstained by gold or Moneys dross. Easy labors brought pleasant Rewards and dreams unriven by Despair. All men worketh and liveth in close Harmony. No strife riseth from outward lineaments of coloring. And as ripples radiate in glorious halo'd Circles from a stone dropped into still waters So from this Place went unseen radiants of Good-will and Angelic harmonious Love which tamed the broad Land from Coast to Coast.

And OSSIANs band stood amaz'd at evidences of Love that subdued the Wild Land and made men cleave to Peace and Plenty, that banished strife of Gain and reburied Gold into the bowels of Earth from which 'it was digged. And Chief Pompanatus leaned on his Warrior Bow and wept as in forgiveness.

Ethiopes children and the brood of OSSIAN played in primal innocency with tribes of Pompanatus. In the East as far as a white domed city the Perpetual Peace encircl'd. No more War of weapons and of Commerce marred the Land.

And OSSIAN saw the River sleep in peace beside the City.

The manuscript ended here, near the bottom of a sheet, and Poole wondered if this was the end or merely a hiatus. Clipped to the bundle was another single sheet of paper, also yellow and dog-eared, but covered with faded typewriting.

A sheet of letterhead stationery with an emblem in blue at the top—a crown pierced by a cross, surrounded by cursive type:

St Oleg College

Normal, Illinois

The letter was dated October 12, 1925, addressed to Miss Mary Lee, 112 Broadway, Leeland, Illinois. Poole read it:

> *Dear Miss Lee:*
>
> *I have examined the photostats of the document we discussed and have taken the liberty of sharing them with a distinguished colleague, Professor Thomas Chatterton of McGill University. Our conclusions are virtually identical. The work is, first, not of ancient pedigree but a modern forgery or invention. Setting aside the mystical (and perhaps deranged) ideas of the piece, it is fabricated of various crude pseudo-antique phrases (many derived from Biblical cadences) and shows no real understanding of Medieval philology.*
>
> *The Great Cham himself said "Any man could write such stuff if he would but* abandon *his mind to it." I suggest this is the present case. Linguistic analysis is unnecessary to isolate innumerable solecisms impossible for a writer of early English. This effusion resembles neither Medieval writing nor James MacPherson's "Ossian" productions. MacPherson's own work was, as Doctor Johnson satisfactorily demonstrated, a puerile forgery, an idea of more interest perhaps to alienists than to philologists.*
>
> *I am sorry to destroy any illusions about the provenance of the writing. My busy schedule here will not permit me the luxury of a journey to see you in your charming home, but if you could arrange to come to campus, I will gladly discuss the manuscript with you. I suggest you examine it closely for watermarks or other*

evidence for dating the copy. It is a fascinating farrago of language and ideas, but alas! not an ancient or historically significant document.

Yours respectfully,

William R. Sutton, D.D., Ph.D.

Godwulf Professor of Anglo-Saxon

When Poole set the letter down and rubbed at his forehead, Ann Wilcox leaned toward him and said, "An odd bit of rubbish, isn't it?"

"What on earth does it mean? *This* is the, um, Ossianic Prophecy?"

She nodded. "But it's more important to understand it *recto* rather than *verso.*"

The phrase fell proctologically on Poole's ear. She prompted, "Please turn over."

Poole flipped the yellow sheets and saw a skein of words and numbers in faint purplish handwriting—a looping, graceless scribble unlike the copyist's hand of the pseudo-poem. It seemed a jumble of notes and jottings, unheaded and unsigned.

"*That's* our key," *Ann* said. "Aunt Mary, as you see, was fascinated by the prophecy and tried to incorporate it in her research. That was when she first got truly hooked on the project, and I suppose she was naive about Epaphimandas and his schemes. So she trumpeted word of the prophecy around, and many people were curious about it. But—"

Fred Toller blurted, "But what's *really* important is that the old fox kept his books on the back of that load of gabble."

Poole squinted at the chaos of figures and entries.

Toller continued, "When Ann sorted this rubbish, we found some of old Ep's account books and other sheets with his figuring on them."

"It wasn't exactly double books," Ann said, "but Epaphimandas kept one set of figures himself and another he evidently showed Ebenezer Cosgrove and the bank. Sometime he made a little journal of his transactions when he totaled his estate. He put in on the back of the Ossianic Prophecy, I guess, because he knew he'd hang onto it—a vital document for other reasons."

"What's it mean?" Poole asked. "It's all chicken-tracks to me. How can you be sure he wasn't just totaling his grocery bill?"

Buxtrider chimed in, "Fred here has done some accounting. Hell, it's no secret—he's a CPA. He had the accounting people at the mall run it through their whatsis machine."

"IRMA," Toller said. "I put Drew Whitman on it as a 'hypothetical' problem, to show me how IRMA could do her stuff. We had her sort and compare the figures here and those in Ep's ledgers."

Toller shuffled papers and located an accordion-heap of computer sheets. "She come up with interesting comparisons. Enough to show how Ep was fiddling his books."

"So," Poole said. "Noble Epaphimandas was just another con man and fraud."

Ann grinned. "Not exactly. That's the amazing part. When Fred broke out all the figures and showed me, we were both mystified. It seems to show that Epaphimandas Lee developed a complicated way to *cheat himself.*"

"You're sure the ledgers are Epaphimandas' handwriting?"

"We had these pages, the bound ledgers and the letters checked by graphologists," she said. "They're as positive as they get. He tended to use indelible pencil, not ink—that's the funny purple color."

Margo lit a cigarette and stared around at them. "I ask again," she said, "where this paperwork has gotten us. What's this ancient history do to help us cancel the mall disasters?"

Poole riffled through more sheets. Many were lined notebook

paper initialed M.L.L. and dated in the 1920s and '30s. They contained columns of brief notations or torrential paragraphs of prose. He scanned a few pages.

"Aunt Mary's working notes," Ann said. "She tried to interview survivors of Leeland's pioneer days when she could reach them. She also made copies of letters and other documents which people wouldn't give her. I shudder to think how much time she put in."

"Are these *all* her papers?"

"No. There's a big boxful in the library—early drafts of the book. I suppose a lot of these notes were lost or destroyed. An idea that makes librarians and local historians ill. She was—is—a cranky old woman, and I'm sure she deliberately threw out materials that revealed her beloved Leeland and the sainted Lees in less than an angelic light."

"Where did these come from?"

A silence. Margo extinguished her cigarette and toyed with the ebony-and-silver holder. Toller finally cleared his throat and said, "No point in being bashful now. I hijacked them from Don's office safe. When Mary Lee went to Sunnyside, she give away her stuff, and Don ended up with these papers. God knows why. He'd been interested enough as a kid to listen to her jabbering about the book and the family. He got, er, focused on the Ossianic Prophecy. It's weird, and Don seemed to believe that old Lee had a gift of divine foresight. He said it predicts the future. So, Mary give him a sackful of her papers."

"So you jimmied the safe and left the, er, poison-pen note on Don's desk?" Poole asked.

Toller tugged an earlobe. "Nope—must of been little Ziggy or Heinie. When I was there...taking the papers, I heard somebody coming into the office, prowling around. I slipped out in the dark, but I wasn't eager to get caught prying open my boss's safe. I couldn't see who it was, but when Don told me about the note, I guessed it was them."

"But you don't *know* that? You didn't see them?"

"Nah. But who the hell else would pull such a dumb-ass stunt?"

Margo tapped the long cigarette-holder on the table. "I still want to know how this will extricate us from this…catastrophe."

"Where *is* your, er, stepson?" Poole asked.

"Perfectly safe and sound in his old trundle bed," Margo replied. "The doctor was in and out, gave his ingenious diagnosis of exhaustion from emotional stress and overwork and zapped the poor boy with a sedative. I see…you think we're holding Don in captivity, along with you. Mr. Poole, you may walk out my door without let or hindrance. And I'm only trying to see that my son doesn't hurt himself or have a *real* crack-up."

The room was still, and Poole heard wind and snow brushing the house like fingers, a scrabbling ghost begging admission from the cold. Ann Wilcox gathered and stacked papers.

"Could I talk with your aunt?" Poole asked her. "Can she still see people?"

"We could visit. But as I said, Aunt Mary's well advanced into senility. She has good days when she can hold a simple conversation and times when she remembers selected things clearly. Bu tit's hard to sort out sense from her babble, and she's so frail I hate to tax her. Would it do any good? I've questioned her over the years about all this. All we have left of Mary Lee exists on paper."

"I'd like to talk with her. Maybe seeing a stranger would be good for her. She's the only one left from the old days…"

Ann tapped a finger on the stacked papers and sighed. "Very well. But we mustn't strain her. It might be brutal to unlock some old memories now."

"Could we go this afternoon? It's not too late."

She glanced at the others. "If it's all right, I'll go with Mr. Poole. We've led him thus far into our confidence."

Toller and Margo nodded. Buxtrider glowered at Poole, saying, "I'm not real happy to have this creep in on the process, but if you want to drag him around, okay by me. I still owe you a pounding, Poole."

"Look, I thought I was evening things up for that whacking I got at the motel. Wasn't that you and one of your boys?"

Buxtrider stood up and slapped the table. "Hell, no! If I'd of wanted you out of the way, I'd of put you in your car and run you right out of the county. I don't need to pussyfoot around motel rooms in ski-masks or whatever. Jesus God!"

Poole shrugged. "Sorry. I've put my foot into a lot of fresh cowpies—but then I'm *paid* for meddling."

Ann bundled the old papers into a large briefcase, while Margo answered the hall telephone. She returned and beckoned Poole.

The phone connection was another crackly radio patch-in, with Len Howells on the other end, his voice thin, as if attenuated by the chill.

"Poole? Jeez, I've been trying to run you down all afternoon. I had a chat with the town genius—Randy Loggins. He's out of his little nap and is about as coherent as he ever was. I Mirandized him and taped him. Good old Randy just talked himself into a vacation downstate."

"He confessed? To what?"

"Nah. That's the next step. But he's involved up to his jug ears in the killings. With all that he's babbled and the ballistics report, I can pin him down for the works—the little guys and our caped captain."

"You've got *motives* for it?"

"Motives, schmotives! Whatta you think, you're Ellery fucking Queen? Randy Loggins is too dumb to have motives. Motives is for rich folks. Nope, I think Randy got tangled with Nugent's slick schemes and ended wasting the bunch. Only God can make a Randy Loggins, and God ain't gonna slide down a sunbeam and whisper His secrets in your shell-like ear. Mine, either. Come down to the office and I'll play Loggins' opera for you."

"Tomorrow?" Poole said. "I'm on another track here."

"I'll bet you are, up at the big house with the hoi polloi."

"That's wrong," Poole said abstractedly.

"What?"

"Hoi polloi means common people. The mob. And it's not *the* hoi polloi. *Hoi* means *the*. Redundant. Just 'the polloi.' I think people get it confused with something like 'hoity toity.'"

"Poole?" Howells said in a tired voice. "Fuck you, huh?"

As Poole escorted Ann out the front door, Buxtrider appeared behind them, tugging up his sheepskin collar and clapping on his D.I. hat. "Talkin with that weasel Howells, weren't you?" he asked. "Watch your ass there, sonny. That shark would steal the nickels off a dead man's eyes."

He brushed by and descended the steps. Poole wouldn't have minded seeing the big sheriff execute a perfect pratfall down the twenty or so marble risers, but he strode manfully through the new snow like Randolph Scott in the last reel of *The Last Roundup*. Poole and Ann stepped timidly after him. Poole squeezed Ann's solid feminine shape through layers of down and kapok. She giggled, and Poole wondered if it was *with* him or *at* him.

* * *

Sunnyside Home for Senior Citizens smelled like decaying flesh, impending death, freshly mixed medicine and a chemical disinfectant powerful enough to sear the tissue from anyone's olfactory and bronchial systems. While Ann Wilcox reported to the nurse's desk, Poole gazed around the large common room. It was as big and barren as a blimp hanger, lighted by ranks of fluorescent fixtures which threw deathly green rays and made the spartan furnishings look even more bleak. The raw light also made the dozen or so Struldbruggs parked in the room appear as cadavers arranged in accidently comic poses, an exercise in black-humored Pop Art.

One ancient man sat in a chromed wheelchair, strapped and padded with pillows. He looked like a survivor of Dachau or a specimen excavated from Pompeii, impossibly desiccated, sticklike, his face collapsed into itself as he sucked at his lips, trying perhaps to turn himself inside-out. A stumpy woman slumped in an upholstered chair, one leg out-thrust and swelled to elephantine size by a cast and bandages. She pulled absently at stringy hair the color of jute and drooled extravagantly. A small man who reminded Poole of an even more dehydrated Don Knotts shuffled across the lengthy room with the aid of a steel walker. Poole calculated it as a twenty-minute journey.

Another woman, made up in flat white and garish red as for a silent film, crouched on a kitchen chair, a yard or so from a giant color TV set whose picture was on and sound off. The colossal face of an especially moronic soap-opera heroine filled the screen like an apocalyptic vision, leered, opened a huge maw and emitted a wordless cry of pantomime angst. The little old woman stared unblinking and uttered one sharp snort of laughter.

While Ann guided him through twisty corridors, Poole saw more specimens scattered in and out of cell-like rooms. A wizened man in floppy pajamas, his hair long and wild, approached them, one trembling hand extended, eyes glittering like the Ancient Mariner's.

"Bu-bu-bu," he sputtered. "Buy me c-c-candy, mister?"

A bulky nurse in a prison-gray uniform caught him and led him off, whispering, "There, there, Harold. Let's find our own room, shall we?"

Poole shuddered. In the background, a Muzak system howled, a few decibels louder than the one at the mall: "O Holy Night." In counterpoint to the slow lyricism a high voice screeched, "Forgive them, forgive them, forgive them" in an endless triplet rhythm. The aseptic halls reminded him of the mall, this place however a mart without merchandise, all sales final, no returns, no credit extended a perpetual last-chance sale.

As if prescient, Ann caught Poole's arm and muttered, "I *hate* these places. Holding tanks for old people. Warehouses. Dumping grounds. Ugh. I *wish* I could take Mary Lee out."

She pulled Poole into an open door at the end of the hall. Mary Lee Llewelyn lay in one of two massive hospital beds. The other was empty and neatly made. She was a tiny woman now, although Poole guessed she was once robust. She lay pale, flattened and insubstantial against white sheets and pillows, like a grotesque cut-out doll, a caricature of humanity compressed by the sheer weight of age and life.

Her eyes were open, black sharp eyes that tracked Ann and Poole precisely as they approached her bedside. Aside from the movement of the eyes, Mary Lee was inert. Her face was seamed into a network of folds and creases like ancient geological trauma. Her mouth was a straight slash of pink lipstick, applied by some thoughtful nurse but seeming a final parodic touch in an awkward child's impulsive crayon portrait.

Ann leaned over the bed and kissed the withered cheek and patted one hand. Mary Lee glared at her grand-niece and then at Poole.

"Aunt Mary? You're looking well," Ann said. "I brought a friend to see you. You don't know him—he's visiting Leeland. This is Richard Poole. Mary Lee Llewelyn, the author whose book you so admired."

Poole mustered a smile. The little black eyes fixed him, as if in final, cosmic summary, an assessment from which there was no appeal.

Ann continued, "We came out so quickly I didn't have time to bring flowers. It's so hard to find fresh ones this time of year. The florists are all holly and poinsettias, and I know you detest them, so—"

Mary Lee spoke, a small, remarkably clear voice, "Of course I don't expect you drag silly plants through a blizzard, Ann. Don't blither. And don't talk in that idiotic sing-song. It's intensely annoying. Be still and let me speak with Mr. Poole."

Poole gawped. The ventriloquistic effect was startling, the voice of a robust woman of tough intellectual fiber projected sybil-like through this ruined facade.

"Well?" Aunt Mary said. "I presume you accompanied my scatter-brained grand-niece for a good reason, Mr. Poole. I'm long past expecting strangers to call for social pleasure. Why don't you tell me why you want to see me. You seem a young man with a purpose."

"Why, yes," Poole managed, "you're right. Ann—Miss Wilcox—has helped me read up on Leeland's history, and I had questions about Epaphimandas Lee and his, er, work. Things not covered in your marvelous history."

"Cut the axle-grease and peach-butter," Mary Lee said, the slash of mouth almost a smile. "You needn't flatter me. I left out most of the *real* stuff in my book. It was hard enough finding a publisher for such a nice, sanitized tale. I knew I'd never find anyone witless enough to print the bald *truth*. Everyone thought I was a sentimental old busybody too soft and simple to put truth on a page. Horseshit!"

Poole glanced at Ann, who openly gaped at Mary Lee.

The old lady glanced at her and chuckled, "Oh, Annie here and a few *real* friends knew I wasn't just a harridan with a shopping bag full of trivia. But they…humored me. You know you did, sweetheart. I'm not blaming you. You were too young and soft to stand a sharp dose of reality. So, I played my part as a nice old gentlewoman. It was easier than teaching you to grow up, wasn't it?"

She paused, and her eyes fluttered shut. Ann leaned forward, frowning in concern. Mary Lee opened her eyes and essayed the ghost of a wide smile.

"Don't start worrying now. You're a quarter-century too late. You never were a whited sepulcher, anyway. You cared about me in exact proportion to your needs, which is perfectly…human."

"Aunt Mary!"

"Go on. You, Poole. I can see you have a batch of questions bubbling away. Best ask them now. I…drift, you know."

"We were reading the, er, Ossianic Prophecy, Mrs. Llewelyn. Interesting. But it has accounts written on the backside. Did you pay any attention to them?"

"Ossianic Prophecy," Mary Lee whispered. She paused to summon the spirit of ancient memory. "What a load of godawful tosh! Let me tell you, that old man Epaphimandas Lee was as crafty as a sackful of weasels. I believe he wrote that drivel as a cover for the accounting scheme. You know 'The Purloined Letter,' surely? An old trick, even in Mr. Poe's time. I think Epaphimandas had the accounts in hand and got some scrivener to copy that hideous effusion on the back. But I couldn't put that in my book, could I? Not if I was writing about saints and sinners, and Epaphimandas was counted amongst the angels."

"What was the, er, significance of the accounts?" Poole asked.

"Ah, that's where genius enters. He was concocting a will, you see, to put all his schemes into effect. Nail them down for all history and time to come. We Lees are nothing if not stubborn. I suppose the 'prophecy' part was a joke and a clue. If you read the *right* side of the paper, you see his plans for the future."

"How was his… juggling of the accounts a will?" Poole asked.

"No…" her voice faded slightly. "I was stuck with a role when I came to write the book. Saddest realization of my life. I had to abandon the light of truth just to…make the story come out right. It could have been a wonderful film, too. Do you love the cinema, Mr. Poole? I loved it with all my heart and soul. You know, I met the Gish sisters and Mr. Griffith in St. Louis. At a gala premier for…oh, I think it was *Way Down East*. Wonderful people, not like show-folk at all. Like great artists from the Renaissance, as Mr. Browning might have limned them. I felt a thrill like electricity when I entered a movie house, the way other young girls might have felt in church. I was never ashamed of it, either—not an iota!"

Her eyes fluttered again, and her face relaxed into something like youth returning unbidden. She sighed and continued, her eyes shut, her voice a mechanical recitation, as if reading yellowed notes.

"Epaphimandas decided to leave Leeland. His work was done, and I think he felt it. He had great optimism—confidence in the unquenchable light of generous liberality in our future. He had planted seeds enough, so he arranged to turn over his holdings and moneys to the bank, to Ebenezer Cosgrove. The industries, the properties, all. But it was a momentous decision and a back-breaking responsibility. Lee saw it, you know, as the future held in trust. Not just stacks of deeds and heaps of old greenback bills."

She paused, and one shriveled hand plucked at the nubbly thermal blanket, as if she were Penelope unraveling a life's weaving. The pointy little fingers fretted and fretted, and her voice faded further.

"I interviewed Clevis Ogden several times. An old man. We treated him as the town fool and tosspot. But he had a sharp eye and memory, when he wanted to use them. He was there, you know, when Epaphimandas and Ebenezer had their last… confrontation."

"He tried to break up the fight," Ann said softly.

Mary Lee's eyes popped open, an odd, doll-like effect. She glared fiercely at the younger woman.

"Don't prompt me like some drooling bumpkin you're

shepherding through that…book-heap where you work! There *was* no fight. That's my point. Poor Clevis got flustered when the old men exchanged such heated words. He started waving his popgun, and both Epaphimandas and Ebenezer were hurt in the fray. But I couldn't put *that* in my book. Low farce. Chaos. I strove for order, you see, in all my innocence of history. Epaphimandas tried to force Ebenezer to assume all his properties and finances, to guide the town in its destined course. Dull Clevis entered and found them in high dudgeon. He misunderstood the import, as everyone would do later. So those grand old patriarchs died ignominiously. And I couldn't force myself to write it down."

Poole glanced at Ann, who frowned and patted Mary Lee's hand.

"We've tired you. You must rest, Auntie."

Mary Lee shook her head fiercely. "Let me say it all. I've *got* it now. Some days it circles away, you know. Like a bird flapping big, black wings, going away from me. I *do* wish Mr. Griffith had read my script. The Gish sisters were darling—so diminutive, but tough as old boots, I could see. I…oh, yes, the accounts: Epaphimandas laid out the city boundaries and apportioned his holdings to his heirs and to the bank as permanent trustee. Ebenezer thought this madness, a gigantic folly bound to create legal and familial quarrels for generations. He wanted everything on a firm legal footing, while Epaphimandas was unshakable in his vision of a cooperative society, busy little bees, each with a duty and a cell in the hive, all crowned with sweetness and light from their endeavors. Or some such. I forget his exact words. A grand clash of ideologies, and in my idiot book I reduced it to a tawdry three-decker romance. *That's* the unforgivable sin…"

Her voice trailed to a whisper, a tremulous gargle. At that instant, the bulky, gray-garbed nurse bustled in from the corridor, stared at Mary Lee and then glared at Poole and Ann.

"You've gone and wore Miss Mary Lee out," she said. "She *does* relish a visitor, but she *is* a old lady who—"

Mary Lee's eyes popped open again, and she hissed, "Who never suffered fools gladly, Earnestine. You get out and..." She stared up at the ceiling, raising one hand tentatively. "It's that damn corby-crow! Catch him before he lights. Ugly great brute, fouling everything. Never could abide..."

Mary Lee Llewelyn seemed to sink, almost to melt like translucent wax, into the bedclothes. The nurse hurried around the large bed, touching and tucking.

"We'll go now," Ann whispered to her. "I'm sorry we upset her."

"That's all right, honey. Most folks just let 'em lay here and die. Don't visit or call nor care a tinker's curse. I think Miss Mary would druther wear out than rust. But she's so frail..."

They hurried through corridors where nurses and orderlies wheeled carts laden with chromed dishes and stacked plastic trays. The aroma of institutional food vied with the pervading stink of antiseptics and decay, a faint fecal scent of loss. Poole and Ann stopped outside on the doorstep in a squall of fresh snow and breathe deeply, in unison. The gray twilight was a relief to Poole, a promise of reprieve from an awful precognition of inevitable decline.

* * *

Poole drove Ann to the looming bulk of the Cosgrove house, again partially curtained by falling snow. They rode in sober silence, a backwash of Mary Lee Llewelyn's confession. Poole was too lost in reflection to make a pass at the librarian, although he mustered a Grade-A leer when she stepped from the Ferret and waved a mittened hand.

He followed wheel-ruts down the streets to the SleepyEye House Motel. As he walked toward his door, a stumpy figure beckoned from the office. It was Elbert Bastin, swathed in an oversized sweatshirt, clutching a folio. As Poole approached, Elbert scowled.

"Those cops said you didn't kill Captain Cosmo. Is that true?"

"Elbert," Poole sighed, "if I *had* killed him, do you suppose I'd electrify the world by confessing to you?"

The boy muttered, "Aw, shit—nobody'd ever tell me nothin." He stepped into the office and Poole followed on a squall of mite-sized snowflakes.

Elbert laid out his book, a dime store scrapbook, overfilled to bulging, on the desk. "I wanted to show you this stuff. It's all about...Cosmo. I been keeping it for years, and it's the most complete collection of anybody in the fan club. If you wanta look at it for clues..."

Poole flipped several manila-paper sheets, each heavily pasted with newspaper clippings, gaudy chromo pictures, pages from a newsletter headed *From The Corners Of Cosmo's Universe*, ticket stubs, all manner of useless memorabilia.

"I got every issue of *Cosmo Comix* at home. Course, they only published a dozen."

Poole looked at the boy, who slumped dejectedly in a sagging chair, picking his nose without enthusiasm. Portrait of a follower bereft of leader. Poole turned the lumpy pages.

He scanned columns of violently purple prose about the evil-busting adventures of the Captain in far-flung regions of The Known Universe. He examined offers for Cosmo Rings, Cosmo Space Kits, a polystyrene model of the traveler's galaxy-roaming starship, the XCC-R1A. Several eight-by-ten glossies of the Captain in full regalia, posed heroically. Signed in felt-tip ink, a fluid careless scrawl, "From the Captain to His #1 Fan, Albert."

"You said you never met the, er, Captain?" Poole asked.

"Nah. Not till...you know, your car. He sent that stuff. Ma would never let me go to St. Louis. She said I'd get in trouble. She never understood."

Poole's attention was caught by pages of blurry "live-action" shots from the TV series. The Captain engaged in hand-to-hand (or hand-to-tentacle) combat with a tall, lumpy creature that seemed to have been fabricated from cast-off shag rugs. A caption read

FANS VOTE ADVENTURE OF THE
MULTIPLYING NICKNOCKBEST FOR 1984.

Elbert leaned over Poole's shoulder, exuding a close-range blast of super-sweet mint scent from his bubblegum.

"Hey, that was really great," Elbert said. "They had people write in and guess what was going to happen and what the Nicknock was. It went on for a couple months."

The final shot of the sequence showed the phantasm reduced to two smaller shaggy lumps, equally tentacled, trying to surround the Captain, who pointed a pistol-like weapon of rococo elegance at one avatar.

"See, every time Cos'd get it cornered, the Nicknock'd *divide*. It was a, like, amoeba, see? He realized if he shot it with the particle disintegrator, it'd divide up into about a *billion* Nick-nocks and overrun the universe. So he had to *tame* it. He was always showing how you couldn't win all the time by force. You had to *think* your way out of bad spots. And be kind to all creatures, even if they are ugly aliens."

Poole studied the photos. There was something disturbing about them, more than the toothpaste-ad smirk Nugent wore under the domino mask which was Captain Cosmo's habitual face gear.

"The way it come out," Elbert jabbered, "was that the Captain got it to change permanently into Nick and Nock—that's the two little ones—and he got them to go off on errands to different ends of the galaxy. He swore them into Cosmo's Legions in the last episode, and they got pins and everything."

Elbert dug into a jeans pocket and produced a small bit of spuriously bejeweled plastic with a flourish of puce script reading COSMIC LEGIONNAIRE * GRADE I.

Poole stared at the scene where the creature loomed menacingly over the Captain, one tentacle wound around a tights-clad Cosmic leg. He studied the last scene, with Cosmo in heroic pose, one arm thrown out to point, as if he were the Archangel Raphael banishing two bitsy lumps of carpet from a TV Garden of Eden.

A peculiar idea shaped itself amoebically in Poole's brain. He leafed through more pages.

"Do you have a...cast list for the show? Who were the other actors?"

"Oh, yeh," Elbert leafed purposefully in the back pages. "Here —this stuff."

He pointed to booklets like theater programs. Poole scanned the sheets until he found

MORRIS WEINER...NICK

and

JACOB L. GREENE...NOCK.

"By God!" Poole said. "Sure—they were acrobats." He drummed his fingers on the desktop.

When asked, Elbert fetched a Leeland phone directory. Poole dragged the desk phone and dialed a number for the LeeLand Mall, muttering, "Don't be closed yet, don't be closed."

The phone rang twice. There was a stentorian mechanical *clack* on the line, followed by a blast of music played on a marimba or glockenspiel, introducing a nasal feminoid voice:

"We're sorry you called when we were closed. We have everything you need for home repairs and yard and garden work. Please call again."

Another explosion of frenetic tintinnabulation, followed by a ragged barbershop quartet singing, to a tune something like "La

Cucaracha":

> *We're here to help when you must fix it.*
>
> *If you need cement, we'll help you mix it.*
>
> *We have nails and pails and patio rails,*
>
> *Screws and glues and tools to do it,*
>
> *Hammers, saws and bamboo rakes,*
>
> *All the equipment that it takes*
>
> *To make your home and garden…*

Poole slammed the receiver down, and stared balefully at it, momentarily convinced it might leap up and wrap its tentacle of cord around his neck: *death, by jingle.*

Elbert grinned, showing a pink pseudo-tongue of bubblegum, and handed Poole a smudgy slip of paper with a note inscribed by a prentice hand.

"Pop left this. I was gonna put it on your door, then I saw you comin in." The slip read CALL FOR POOL FROM HARVY LEWIS. CALL BACK RITE AWAY.

"Jesus," Poole breathed. "When did Harvey call?"

Elbert shrugged. "Pop ain't too good at takin notes. He went off-shift at two. Could of been anytime this morning."

Groaning, Poole lifted the phone. Elbert said, "You wanta keep my stuff, or what? I want a receipt for it. Ma said that."

Poole flipped the scrawled note over and scribbled

Rec'd from Elbert Bastin

1 Notebook in evidence.

12/4/86. R. Poole.

Elbert inspected the screed for hidden meanings.

Poole dialed, got an operator with a broad Midwestern twang who asked suspiciously what number he was dialing, refused to accept a long-distance call from the office number, argued about Poole's telephone credit-card and its current efficacy, grudgingly fiddled with circuits and finally mumbled to someone on the other end. After flurries of static, faint voices that wobbled in and out of focus, like damned souls calling for succor from a fiber-optic purgatory, Harvey Lewis's voice emerged, gruff and strong: "Poole? Is that you? What the hell are you up to? I've been trying to get through for two goddamned days. What's going on out there?"

"Sorry, Harvey. There's been a hell of a storm here."

"What? *What?* Speak into the phone, damn you. You sound like you're at the bottom of a pickle barrel."

"Yeh. Okay. It's the storm. The phone lines. Don't forget, I'm in the sticks." Styx, Poole thought. *Hix Nix Styx Pix. This is hell, nor am I out of it.*

"I want a report," Lewis blared. "I'm getting weird calls from… some geek named Samsa. Another one from…Cosgrove. And a sheriff who sounds like Tom Mix. What in Christ's name have you stirred up now?"

"It's very…complicated."

"What? If we're going to move on AmeriMall, we've got to go before the end of the Christmas season. You know how many shopping days *that* means. Or do you?"

"There've been these…murders."

A brief hiatus, a bird's-eye rest, on the line. Somewhere in the ether, a small wraithlike voice said, "…won't be able to be home for Christmas again, and I said…"

Harvey Lewis said, "What the hell kind of connection *is* this? It sounds like a conference-call from the U.N. Listen, son—I wanta straight report on the Telex tomorrow. Got that? Give me a situation assessment with all the figures you've mustered. I see the

AmeriMall board Friday. I want to walk in with something in my hands besides my pecker."

The connection faded, overridden by a snatch of music, a bit of Christmas carol just over the perimeter of Poole's hearing and memory.

Poole's boss rushed back, "...to have a solid logistical projection to make the decision. If it looks like your mall is sliding right off the charts, all of AmeriMall will be under review. You..." A cackle of static like demonic laughter. "...get everything on the computer and send it pronto..." Dismal thumping like hoof beats from the Four Horsemen of the Apocalypse. "...believe we can salvage it, then you need to *say* so. Capeesh?"

"Yes. Gotcha, Harvey."

"I want this spelled out in ten-foot letters, Poole. Let's make it a merry Christmas for TransAtlas all around, hey? And take care of yourself out there in the boonies. You'll probably have a whole shit-load of snow and bad weather before you get away. 'Bye."

Poole stared blankly ahead, receiver to his ear, a lonesome howl on the line, the voice of the prairie redux. He sighed and hung up. Elbert had switched on a small black-and-white TV set, on which an ancient cowboy film unwound—legions of white-hatted cowboys hurtling after legions of light-eyed Indians in a fusillade of blank cartridges.

How the West Was Lost.

* * *

Poole limped to Unit Eleven, feeling the first chords of a symphonic headache. He had not eaten in a decade, and he ached all over, the ghosts of eldritch football injuries rattling chains in every cranny of his carcass. As he fitted key to lock, he saw a stooped figure lurching out of the dusk at him.

"Oh, no," he moaned, "go the hell away."

A stumpy man swathed in an old corduroy duck-hunter's coat

and topped by a billed cap with earflaps held out one hand as if in supplication, one bare fingertip winking through a hole in his ragged cloth glove.

"Ain't you Mr. Poole?" the phantom whined.

"I don't care if you're Jacob Marley or Bob Marley or Bob Cratchit or Tiny Tim or the Ghost of Christmas Not-About-to-Come-on-a-Bet. I'm tired." Poole matched the man's whine.

"I don't know about them guys," the man said. "I seen Heck Ogden at the County Jail. I'm Jinx Washburn, and he said I had oughta talk to you about all the doins at the mall."

The man bared a snaggled grin, exuding a mixed aroma of marinated body odor, cheap rye whiskey and White Owl cigars. *An irresistible invitation,* Poole thought. He opened his door and nodded Washburn in.

"I got a helluva story to tell you," Washburn blurted. "But I'd surely savor a little somethin lively to drink. I'm cold straight through." He grinned again.

Silver Bells

MIDNIGHT PASSED BEFORE Poole sent Jinx Washburn on his way, trailing clouds of replenished whiskey fumes, with a five-dollar bill in hand for a cab home. Poole fell on his bed and crashed into sleep like a stunt driver colliding with a brick wall.

Morning seized him soon enough, and he groaned awake. He tried to remember a dream that had visited: something about a burning building—towers of red flame and black smoke in the background—and a tall, muffled figure. A man (Poole thought it was Don Cosgrove but couldn't see his face) struggled with this hooded figure. The scene shifted with the frightening jump-cut rapidity of dream-imagery, and a young woman strolled on a broad, elm-shaded street on a summer night. A rotund, white-bearded man stalked across a lawn toward her, when another man intervened, brandishing a gleaming pistol. This man turned, and Poole recognized Gregory Samsa, who leered from the face of a silent-movie vampire, raised his gun and...and...and...

"Shit!" Poole muttered into the shaving mirror.

If that dream came through the gate of ivory, it would solve the whole daffy case. If he could remember its denouement. Or the beginning or middle. He tried to recall if Harry Nugent, aka Captain Cosmo, was in it. Or Wilma Breithope or Ann Wilcox. Why the hell didn't he ever have *nice* dreams—or even merely *neutral* dreams? His thoughts belched up from the lowest depths of his unconscious with enough revolting cryptic material to galvanize an army of analysts.

He thought vaguely of Margaret Hopkins, a woman he had almost married who had become an internationally respected Jungian analyst. Margaret could gut that dream like a starving gourmand cleaning out a Maine lobster. Her phone number was in his ratty notebook, and he considered calling her from Leeland, Illinois, to Berne, Switzerland, to hear the astonishment in Margaret's fluty Brahman voice.

He returned to the monumental task (given his condition) of shaving, deciding Margaret would doubtless bill TransAtlas for her opinion, even if she perceived the gag. And he didn't really want to *know* if the dream meant his *anima* was out of synch with his *animus*, or whatever the damned jargon was.

On his way to downtown Leeland, Poole found a diner which served homemade cinnamon rolls of magnificent size, sweetness, stickiness and general succulence. He engorged one roll as big as an infant's head, swilled bitter coffee and toyed with the idea of attacking another roll. A rill of nausea deep in his gut warned him off. He left a dollar tip, however, in the glow of appreciation for his discovery.

He found a parking spot directly before the Leeland City Building. Little things were working for him. The world, swathed in the gun-metal-gray light of a cloudy winter morning, brightened. Even if he couldn't decipher his dream, it marked a change in his muddled consciousness of this world into which he had blundered. He braced himself for the talk with Len Howells, armed to listen to Randy Loggins' taped effusions. Now, he thought, *things will fit as snugly as bits in a jigsaw puzzle, nothing left over to accuse me.*

* * *

Randy Loggins had babbled for two hours into the tape machine, with interjected questions by Howells and Co. Loggins' slow country voice ran the gamut of emotions from total bewilderment to mild resentment. He felt the world had oppressed him in every way from the second of his birth on a rocky farm on Elkhorn Creek. He was clearly correct.

In the middle of a diffuse narrative, Loggins seemed to reach the heart of the matter. Poole sat up and stared at the cassette player, as Loggins droned: "See, I wasn't on the job Monday night. Mr. Samsa, he told me to take time off, cause I was on straight through the day after the, uh, troubles. I went home and caught some zees. Then I went out for awhile…"

A muffled voice in an interrogative tone in the background.

"Yeh. Well, I don't know what I had oughta tell you fellas. I mean, you're making me to get into trouble. Yeh, I went to see that Poole guy. Me and Jinx. We waited and…shoot, we didn't want to hurt him or nothin. But we knew where the body was. I mean Nugent. See, we found that rental car in the lot. I thought it was a good place to get rid of it. The body, see? It had St. Louis plates. I mean the car. I pried open the trunk and we stuck Nugent inside. Then I threw away the trash bag we'd put him in. I thought maybe somebody would haul Nugent back there, and people would think he was kilt in St. Louis, see? Then I found out that Poole guy was drivin the car, and he was sure as shit going to hang around. We thought…shit, I don't know *what* we thought."

A pause on the tape. Howells smirked faintly at Poole.

"We're not dealing with criminal masterminds here, buddy," Howells said.

"…had to rough Poole up some, to make it work," Loggins' voice continued. "But we didn't have no idear of killin him or framin him. It just seemed like a good idear at the time."

Howells hit the STOP button. "You want to press charges, sport? Our man in the county prosecutor's office is working up a charge-sheet on Loggins that looks like the Magna Carta."

Poole declined. He suffered mostly from injured pride, and he had no concept of compensation for memories of being terrorized by a rum-dumb stoker and an untrained rent-a-cop.

Howells shrugged and ran the tape on FST FWD a moment. He hit ON, listened and nodded to Poole. "More little gems scattered by our Randy."

"…and then," the voice continued, "we was down in the steam tunnels. We dragged Nugent there and found a place back of the pipes, a sorta shelf. Jinx and me was scared shitless, let me tell you. But we got him there. And I swear to you, on my daddy's Bible, we never seen them little men. I didn't even know about that trash till Samsa come and Toller and all them cops. I didn't see no gun nor nothin. I just knew it was real bad. Old Jinx couldn't get hisself fired. He's too old to get another job. Then I went back to the office, and my gun was gone. I tell you, I near shit a brick!'"

Howells squeaked the tape ahead. "I'm skipping the part where he talks about Sunday School and his sainted mother."

"…wouldn't of thought of that kind of stuff," Loggins' voice muttered. "We was down in Jinx's shop. Like I said, he was runnin a tape… Do I gotta say what it was? Aw, shit. It was *Dolores Does Denver*, I think. You guys took all them tapes. You oughta know. Then I saw it was real late, and I come up to take a look around. Mr. Samsa, he was real nervous, and he said he heard there was gonna be a robbery. Well, I thought that was pure-dee chickenshit, but I went up to the balcony level to look around. That's when I found Nugent. God—it was awful. I never seen nobody shot to death before. Jinx come up, when he heard me hollerin. That's when we done it. Took Nugent's body. And I swear that's all we done!"

Howells clicked off the machine and lit a small cigar. He examined its coal and glanced at Poole.

"This filling in your education?" he asked. "There's a lot more, but it's mixed in with Loggins' endlessly boring autobiography."

Poole nodded and produced his notebook. "I have Washburn's version—in edited form. With some wrinkles Loggins may have preferred to omit."

Poole gave Howells a synopsis: Jinx Washburn had detected a problem in the heating system, with one side of the mall nearly shutdown. He called Loggins around midnight, and the two fiddled with the computerized tracking system until they located a main valve that had been closed. Washburn was baffled but blamed that "stuck-up, half-yeller dinge on the day shift," i.e., Pruitt Bastin. They decided to sample Washburn's modest archive of videotaped pornography, to celebrate their victory over error. When Loggins insisted on a break to make his rounds, Washburn stayed behind and took a call from Gregory Samsa. It was about twelve-thirty, to the best of Washburn's vagrant recollection. Then, after just coming off the phone and his earnest reassurances to Samsa that all was well, Washburn heard Loggins howling. He ascended from the sub-basement to find the security man on the balcony, hunkered next to Nugent's corpse. Loggins had vomited. Neither man had come through the central atrium but had taken the maintenance staircase. Neither had seen the elves at the fountain. The weird half-light of the security lamps made the halls spooky, and Washburn and Loggins were in shock and terror. For the next forty-five minutes, they were busy moving Nugent's body to the steam tunnels. By around two o'clock, they were back in the maintenance shop, swapping snorts from a fifth of plum brandy to quell their terrors.

Poole thought of the soldiers at the beginning of *Hamlet*, posted in the dead-of-winter night, way out of their depths in dealing with a fearsome (royal) specter. If Hamlet and old what's-his-name, his college buddy, hadn't come along, who knows how Bernardo and Marcellus might have buggered up the case?

"So," Howells interrupted this vague meditation, "Jinx says it was Loggins' notion, and Randy pins it firmly on Washburn's ass. But that's small potatoes. I think the two morons are essentially giving us the straight poop. It's an age of cover-ups, Poole, and I suppose these two aren't any dumber than Nixon's gang or those klutzes in Reagan's basement, when you think of it. *But*—there's a helluva lot happening offstage I want to tie up."

"What's Samsa's tale?" Poole asked. "He was prompting both Loggins and Washburn."

"Yessir. He's given only a minimal statement and has a tight-ass lawyer in. But we have him on record Monday morning as calling in that night. He said he was tipped that a robbery or vandalism was going down. That was his tale when he arrived at the mall."

Howells flipped through typed sheets in a folder. "Here's the sequence Monday morning, when the whole thing was called in: Two-twenty-seven a.m., our desk gets a call from Greg Samsa, saying he thinks there's a robbery in progress at the mall. Says he can't locate his security man. And…two-forty-four a.m., the sheriff's office gets a call from Fred Toller. Says Samsa has called him, queries what the hell's up. Says he can't raise Loggins either, asks for a patrol car to check around. We send a call to…Unit One-Oh-One. The officers have to cross town, it's black as Ned's hat and trying to sleet. The officers cruise the mall lots and see nothing unusual. They find the back main door—that's across from the security office—unlocked. They call in here at two-fifty-one. The night captain gives them the okay to enter and check it out. At…three-oh-nine, the deputies arrive and go through the same drill. It's a damn wonder we didn't have a Dodge City Shootout then, those clowns all creeping around the mall with their six-shooters. Damn. Anyhow, it must have been then the Leeland cops found the elves. It was strange, because Loggins and Washburn had taken Nugent away and cleaned up the blood and assorted puke on the balcony.

Just these two dead midgets at the fountain."

Howells stubbed his cigar out in an ashtray made from the base of a brass 105 mm howitzer shell casing. He flipped pages.

"After that, all hell broke loose. The assorted lawmen converge on each other and trip on their dicks. Buxtrider knew Doc Grimes was in East St. Louis and called him. The county coroner guys went into a snit. Our forensics guys were arm-rassling the sheriff's men. And Samsa and Toller show up in the middle of this circus. I have Toller there at three-thirty-nine a.m. Samsa there at three-forty-five. Both guesses, but somebody scribbled that down for the report."

Poole eyed Howells. Two minds without a single thought. *Why don't you do something to help me?*

"The place was supposedly sealed off, but everybody was running in circles trying to get the lights on, to check out the nooks and crannies for intruders with fell purposes, and so on. In the middle of this, Loggins and Washburn put a trash bag over Nugent and drag his carcass out to your car. That's gotta be a lot later, when we were trying to get out of Samsa's way, so he could have a nice shopping day. All I got from Loggins was it was daylight. So, what we know is that Loggins and Washburn didn't *do* anything significant here. Except fuck up the investigation. Give you a concussion. Commit perjury, mopery and general screw-uppery."

"So," Poole said. "You're looking hard at Samsa. And Toller?"

Samsa, yes. His part in this stinks, and we have him on a slew of charges now. Toller? Nah. I've known Freddy since fourth grade. He has odd ambitions, and sometimes he has the social grace of a mad warthog, but he's straight. He's also about two hundred percent smarter than he looks."

"I'm going to see Charles Cosgrove this afternoon," Poole said. "You want in on it? Could you bring Ziggy and Heinie? And Samsa?"

"Everybody's bailed out. I can't force them, and Samsa has this cornbelt Clarence Darrow in tow. But I can try."

"I think I have a handle on fifty percent of this mess," Poole said. "And the Cosgroves can lay out the rest, if we fit together who did what to whom at the right times. Samsa's dead-center, along with Heck Ogden. It's nastier than it looks. I mean, it's bad enough now, with all the shoot ups and mayhem floating around. But you've got a chance to wind it all up. Including the mess with the Gerties, the Ossianic Prophecy and every other rat's-nest of an idea fetched on."

Howells grinned at Poole: "Sic 'em, Tige!"

* * *

Poole supped a greasy lunch from a greasy spoon on Water Street. He passed the opportunity of ingesting yet another factory-fabricated meal at Burger Prince or Hot Dog Heaven or General Chicken. He ordered the Special of the Day, grilled pork chop, mashed potatoes, canned peas and a slice of *pie de jour*, which turned out to be desiccated apple, about a half-inch thick, more like a wedge of unidentifiable fritter. The whole meal tasted vaguely *yellow*, Poole decided, and he was pleased: small cities were as predictably tired and culturally pauperized as he recalled. He paid his dollar ninety-nine to a big, worn-looking woman of uniform henna color and complimented her on the meal. She seemed mildly astonished, as if he had arrived from a capital of civilization with news that the earth was round or gravity had been discovered, some idea that flew in the face of Leeland's smugly introverted crackpot realism.

As he left Junie's Civic Restaurant, Poole was accosted by a thin young man in a grimy trench coat. For a second, Poole thought he was being spare-changed. But the man only insisted on shaking his hand.

"Hi," he said in an urgent counter-tenor, "I'm Norm Bates—of the *Eagle*. I've been trying to catch you, but you're a hard man to pin down."

Helpless to resist, Poole shook the mittened mitt. Bates beamed. He wore a shapeless rag-wool sledding cap and unbuckled boots, and his whole demeanor was of a high-schooler sneaking off to join the little kids in belly-whopping or building snowmen.

"Mr. Poole, we're anxious to get your perspective on the trouble at the mall. We've interviewed nearly everybody else we could locate."

Poole backed a step, and Bates followed, like a tango instructor pursuing a beginner. "Sorry," Poole started, "but I don't give interviews on—"

"Look, I had a long talk with Annie Wilcox, and I know you've been digging in history. Here," he produced a newspaper from under his arm, "we've got dandy files. The *Eagle* has tracked these stories for years."

The paper unfolded in Poole's grasp, at its top a black-letter banner in high Victorian style, a glaring rampant eagle clutching a guidon etched with a script motto:

AND THE TRUTH SHALL MAKE YE FREE.

FOUNDED 1859.

Bates crowed, "I know this is small town stuff for you, but we do a good job. Come to the office and talk. Off the record. *Then* you can decide about an interview. We can help you."

Despite blinking mental warning lights, Poole was beguiled. Bates' periwinkle eyes twinkled urgently. *What the hell?* Poole thought. He also recalled Prime Directive No. 3 periodically reiterated From the Desk of Harvey S. Lewis: *Thou Shalt Not Talk to the Media on Pain of Banishment.*

"We're just around the corner," Bates said. "Give us ten minutes. You can stroll out any time, man."

Reluctantly, Poole fell into step with Bates, whose boots jingled with seasonal jollity, counterpointing the squelching of taupe slush beneath their feet. Poole scanned the paper, its tabloid-sized front page built around a center-column photo of Don Cosgrove looking earnestly upward and outward, as if caught by the Speed Graphic in a moment of evangelical prayer. The caption read LOCAL BUSINESS LEADER UNDER FIRE. Two columns to the right were slugged in 48-pt. Bodoni Extra-Bold Italic:

Cosgrove May Leave Mall. Business Future in Doubt.

"How the hell did you get this story?" Poole asked. "You know Don Cosgrove is having a…nervous breakdown."

"Yeh. That's the story," Bates said. He stopped and opened a plate-glass door set between two shop fronts. The *Eagle* banner was traced in chipped gold leaf on the glass. Poole followed him up a narrow, dim staircase to emerge into a large suite of small cubicles. The place smelled like every newspaper office Poole had entered—a vague whiff of burnt tobacco, sweat, benzene-based rubber cement and other elixirs he imagined as essence of typewriter ribbon, hot transistors and cold photo chemicals. It seemed as busy as a laboratory maze with obedient rodents running pre-assigned courses.

Bates waved negligently at a plump, harried-looking woman behind a CRT and led Poole down a corridor to a door of old oak and frosted glass, with the word EDITOR stenciled on the oak. Inside, Poole saw Ann Wilcox sitting by an ancient roll top desk. Astin Lee rose from a swivel chair.

"He came willingly," Bates said, unraveling an endless green-and-white coaching scarf and shucking the rest of his outer gear. He pointed to a kraken-armed oaken coat rack. Poole hung his coat gingerly on the heap there.

Lee shook Poole's hand and said, "We hoped to head you off from the downward path to wisdom, Poole. Good to see you again." Ann Wilcox shot a warm smile.

Poole sat in a big crushed-looking leather chair and declined Bates' offer of coffee, knowing that journalists' brew was always sludge boiled to a potency designed to murder brain cells.

Bates decanted a cupful of toxic brew and sat in another oaken swivel chair. The room looked to have been appointed by James Gordon Bennett about the time of the *Eagle's* founding and kept in museum order since. A concession to modernity was a big switchboard-style telephone on the desk, perched above an L.C. Smith typewriter as big as an eighteenth-century organ console.

"What is all this?" Poole asked.

"Recent history, Richard," Ann said.

"And a bit more," Lee amended. "After Ann and I talked with you, we decided Norman's supplications for news on this…crisis were justified."

"Meaning you decided I should talk to the press? Or that I should front for your, what, cartel?"

Lee chuckled. "It may seem a tad conspiratorial, but it's more in the line of an *ad hoc* citizen's committee."

Poole massaged his neck. "That could be a fancy title for a lynching party."

"Oh, Richard," Ann said, "don't stretch for melodrama. We came to convince Norm this isn't the scoop of the century but just red-hot gossip."

Poole waved the newspaper. "This hits the streets today, right? Is that the jargon, 'hits the streets'?"

Bates beamed. Out of his trench coat he looked even more the Junior Reporter, out of a weird amalgam of *Superman* meets *The Front Page* byway of *Brenda Starr.* Poole decided he wasn't about to be typeset as Clark Kent. He always hated people with reversible names.

Lee said, "Hits the mailboxes. Norm doesn't command a cadre

of snot-nosed newsboys hollering *Wuxtry wuxtry!* It's all done by a computer mailing service."

"Whatever," Poole sighed. "But this story isn't right. Don Cosgrove, when I saw him yesterday, was in no shape to resign. Or to decide anything else. You know damn well Margo must have—"

"Hold it," Ann said, with a tutting sound. "We know that, Richard. Read the story. It sets out everything you're about to dump on us."

"What's the point, then?"

Lee handed Poole two bulky folders, one labeled COSGROVE, C., the other SAMSA, G. "Here. I assume Norman said he wanted to *give* you information not receive it."

"Don't say Greeks bearing gifts," Ann warned. "Just fill yourself in on our recent history. There are other files. Heck Ogden's weighs about a ton."

"Hey, I'm in *business* here," Bates squeaked. "This ain't the Christian Science Reading Room."

"Good God, Norman!" Ann said. "Have you been working on your novel again? I heard Warner Baxter say that on the late movie last week. Or was it Warner Oland? One of the Warner Brothers, anyhow. About 1934."

Bates flushed and dribbled tar-like coffee onto his shirt. "I've gotta keep the old *Eagle* flying."

Poole scanned yellowed clippings, typescripts and notes. He eyed photos of Gregory Samsa, young, earnest and rigid. Charles Cosgrove's dossier was fatter and more worn, ravaged by time and the ceaseless accretions of fame.

Poole read after Cosgrove in *Eagle* notices from the late 1920s, when he appeared in stories about the Cosgrove family or about Charles' father Maurice. The 1930s yielded a harvest of depressed and depressing items on the collapse of Leeland's commerce and industry. As he paused in reading, Poole noticed the ubiquitous Muzak even here, pip-squeaking a dirge-tempo rendition of "In dulce jubilo." Poole plunged on into the wartime editions of the *Eagle* and the swelling progress of Charles Cosgrove as his own man, a story of evidently blameless success in pure capitalist enterprise.

Poole found the notice of Charles' first wedding, a full page in the old, wider *Eagle* laid out in pictures and breathless tittle-tattle, the zenith of 1940 Leeland. In the largest picture, a young, rubicund Charles Cosgrove plunged down the steps of a Victorian church, leading a grinning girl in a swirl of wedding dress and a fusillade of pelleted rice.

The caption: MISS AMELIA SWAYNE BASTIN WEDS CHARLES OGDEN COSGROVE. A paragraph retailed details of the ceremony and the variegated couture of all present. The two very young people in the picture seemed to plunge directly at Poole in the late twentieth century. A small cameo of Charles' first wife, Don's mother he never knew, occupied a lower corner, a frozen figure as blank and expressionless as a Dutch doll in the studio portrait.

Cosgrove's second marriage was covered by a brief note, un-excited prose describing his return from a tour of the Eastern states and Europe in autumn 1954 and his new wife, expatriate Leelander Miss Margo Thwaite Ogden (20), who had studied painting in Paris. Poole willed the column to yield more. It was only sere paper.

Poole scribbled names and dates in his notebook. He stared out the window at a fresh swirl of snowflakes. Then he turned to Greg Samsa's modest file. The Muzak segued into a Tex-Mex version of "I Saw Three Ships A-Sailing." *Mariachi Xmas!*

Gregory Hunt Samsa rose in Alger fashion from a graduate of a Davenport business school to sub-manager in the rejuvenated underwear factory to vice-president of the Leeland Chamber of Commerce to assistant manager of the new LeeLand Mall. A photo commemorating that project showed Charles Cosgrove, Don

Cosgrove and Samsa on a barren field, muffled in topcoats and fedoras, with stainless steel spades at port arms. A second shot showed them trying to dig on frozen turf while looking at the camera. They looked mildly angst-ridden, like a Soviet-sponsored comedy team in a broad satire on imperialistic decadence—The Three Stoogeskis. He expected a third photo of them battering one another with the chromed shovels. But it was merely a relaxed instant, the three men *sans* implements, shaking gloved hands, grinning with ersatz self-satisfaction.

Poole noted dates and looked up when Ann said, "Let's find a quick lunch before we go to the Cosgroves."

* * *

Charles Cosgrove's sickroom was a drafty box, a warehouse of Victorian memorabilia—wardrobes, highboys, scrolly mock-Chippendale everything, a bed the size and configuration of Noah's ark. Charles lay in it like a shriveled pharaoh laid out for his voyage to the next kingdom. He was hosed to an intravenous feeding station, a vital-signs monitor and tanked oxygen. He could be shot into outer space and exist for a week.

A massive nurse in a starched white uniform sat at the head of the bed below the monitor, alternating glances at the oscilloscope, her patient and the people pressed around. She looked displeased.

"You mustn't tire Mr. Cosgrove," she said gruffly. "He's doing well today, but he must preserve his strength."

With a palsied swipe, Charles jerked the respirator cup from his face. "For sweet Jesus' sake," he rasped, "please butt out of this, Nurse Howarth."

With his face unshrouded, Cosgrove still looked vital. He was nearly bald, a wisp of cottony tonsure around his ears, and his features were collapsed, as if gravity undid him. But he was unlined, an ancient infant glistening with foreknowledge of death. His eyes were light blue and bright as they scanned the crowd. Margo held one arm around Don, the other gripping Lainey's elbow. Len Howells stood between Ziggy and Heinie, while Toller and Buxtrider hovered behind them. Wilma and Poole were furthest back, incidentals. The room was lit by discreet floor lamps flanking the bed and a flow of uncertain gray daylight from the tall windows. It was an oddly ceremonial vignette from an old novel: *The Passing of the Master*.

"No time for shenanigans and temporizing," Charles said. "I must settle my mind about this disgraceful rumpus before I...exit."

"Charles—" Margo said, clasping his hand. He pulled away and turned for a pull on the oxygen cup. He glared at her and continued.

"I want to know what my grandson and daughter are mixed up in. But let's start with you, Donald. You're on your own, sonny. That's what you always wanted. Now measure up to it."

Don wore a man-sized robe now, baggy pajama legs showing below, but he still looked in search of a lost teddy bear. His face was blanched and haggard, his mouth working.

"Papa," he said. "Oh, Papa, don't die!"

"Nonsense," Charles said. "No time for that now. I demand an explanation of the...folly occurring under your nose. I didn't put you into that mall so you'd have time to putter with your damn-fool toy trains."

"It'll be all right, Papa. The police, the sheriff, Mr. Poole. They've got it...fixed up."

"Damn it, boy! It's *your* job, not theirs. I told you a thousand times the Cosgroves take care of their own business. Always have and always will."

Don hung his head, whispering. Margo caught the loose sleeve of his robe.

"What?" Charles said. "You were ever a mumbler and mutterer. Never could stop you swallowing your tongue. You keep hands off, Margo. He's got to speak up for himself now. What in hell did you say?"

"I said…" Don looked waveringly around. "I said I'm *not* a Cosgrove. I'm just a…foundling." He giggled and then stifled the sound. "A lost-and-foundling."

Charles stared at him. He uttered a snort then clasped the respirator to his face. Margo caught at Don's arm, but he fended her off. She started to speak, but Charles' voice intersected hoarsely.

"Wrong again, sonny! Even when you think you got hold of a damn smart grievance, you get it bass-akward. You're one hundred percent Cosgrove. Couldn't get more so. Tell him, Margo. No—now's the time. Damn this clutch of jackals to hell. Let 'em listen. Soak it all up. It'd be all over the *Eagle* tomorrow anyhow. Somebody would blab if we were all in the middle of the Gobi Desert."

"Donald…" Margo glanced at Charles. "Oh, very well. You *are* my son, Donald. You were adopted, yes, but it was a ruse, a charade. I knew it was wrong but…there were considerations. People we couldn't hurt. So we deceived them. And you. As if that were better."

Lainey stepped from the shadows. She grimaced and caught at Marge's shoulder.

"Damn it, what are you saying?" she bawled.

Margo detached herself and pushed Lainey away. She said, "Keep your hands off and your ears open and learn something. Not that you'll like it."

She turned to Don and caught his hand. He was frozen, unfocused. She rubbed his hand, as you comfort a tired, chilled child before you administer medicine.

"Your father and I had…an affair. Before *she* died, Donald. You're…our child. I was tangled. I was too young to know if I was doing the right thing. Your…Charles' wife was so ill, so weak. He was desperate with grief, and I was crazy in love with him. That's all —crazy, all of it. Lainey was tiny, your father didn't know what to do. We didn't know how long she…Amelia might live. So…"

"You witch!" Lainey hissed. She lunged for Margo, but Wilma

Breithope interposed. She caught Lainey in a wristlock.

"You...you dreamed this up! You and that worn-out coot are trying to cheat me, to rob my boy." She glared at her father, and whined, "Please don't, Daddy. Daddy?"

"Stop it!" Charles' voice was like a breaking wire.

Lainey ceased struggling and stared at him.

"It's all true, sweetheart. This is no time for lies. Or evasion. Just listen to your...to Margo."

"Think about it," Margo said. "You two have always been alike yet different. You look like brother and sister, but you're not. What's the phrase? A little more than kin and less than kind?"

Lainey whipped her head, her face fiery, under pent pressure. "Not, not!" she sputtered.

Don stared at Margo with round, blank eyes, like a character from *Little Orphan Annie* who waits for a balloon of words to form over his head.

Margo continued flatly, "I never considered giving you up, Donald. I was going to California to live with my cousins. I should have done it. God, I was *eighteen* when you were born! I had life in front of me. I had no way to imagine what it would be. People were making new lives after the war. A brave new world. I was so young and so damned dumb! And your father knew what he wanted. Yes, indeed, he always knew what he wanted."

Charles lay with his eyes closed, sunken on the pillow. He nodded slightly.

"He wanted me! Yes, little missy, he would have dropped you and followed me anywhere. But I gave him the right thing—a son and a home!"

"You conniving bitch!" Lainey whispered.

Don made an odd sound. He smiled oddly, a half-swallowed Cheshire Cat grin. "I'm a...bastard," he said to Margo. "I'm only a bastard!"

Heinie snorted, "You got that right, you fucking moron," ending with a hyena cackle.

"Chance!" Lainey wailed. "You get out of here."

Heinie held up cuffed wrists and smirked. "Fat fucking chance, Ma —so to speak. The only *chance* you gave me was my useless fucking name!"

"No, no, you don't see it," Don said. "Don't you see? That's *all* that was wrong with me. I thought I was crazy, I thought it was... I don't know, a curse, voodoo. Those fires, Rita, that terrible analyst. Why? Why, Mother? Why did you want me to believe it all? To think I was crazy?"

"Oh nooo," Margo moaned, "it wasn't like that..."

"Please, please!" Nurse Howarth said. "This is far to much stress for Mr. Cosgrove. Stop it, please!"

"Get away," Charles said, batting feebly as if to swat a small insect. "Shoo!"

"Hey, Gramps, it's gettin juicy now, ain't it? C'mon—sic em, Chance. Ma! Get her, Margo!"

He cackled, and Toller yanked on his cuffs.

"I'll call the doctor," the nurse said in a steely voice. "I wash my hands of it..."

"Like jesting Pilate," Charles called at her as she bustled into the hall, "who would not stay for an answer."

"A bastard," Don said in fatuous wonder, "that's all. That's no problem. No big deal. I can handle that!"

"You're not," Margo said. "Don't say that! Don't use that word. You're my son. Charles' son. That's what matters. We've always loved you, given you everything."

"Oh, love," Don said offhandedly. "I *know* that. Never the problem. Too much love, Mother. Mother-smother love, Mother. I just wanted...respect."

Charles shifted feebly. "You've got to *earn* that. It's all I wanted you to do. That's why we decided about the mall. Now you've balled that up."

Don stepped forward and stared at Charles. He seemed to make a cold, cruelly scientific assessment. He touched the back of Charles' blue-white hand.

"Cold," he said. "That's what I remember. Margo…Mother used to say 'cold hands, warm heart' but I didn't believe it. You said I had cold feet when I wouldn't do what you wanted. When you took me to the river with Og to teach me to swim. I stood on the bank, *so* scared. 'Cold feet,' you said. With such…disgust. I was seven years old, and you wanted me to be *brave*. You said Og was a war hero. He wasn't afraid to jump in a muddy river and swim, when he was chased by a million Chinese. Then poor old Og had to jump in, shoes and all. To keep you from being a liar!"

Charles lifted his hand and clasped his son's. His eyes glittered. He whispered, "'What is Truth? said jesting Pilate…'"

His blue eyelids fluttered. The cardiac monitor beeped, uttered a syncopated rhythm. Nurse Howarth loped from the doorway, bustled Don aside and leaned over Charles.

Margo stepped to the bed. Then there was a swirl of motion, a shout of "Hold it!" and sounds of rending materials, a carillon of shattering glass. Poole whirled to see Fred Toller half-swathed in billowing velvet curtains, Len Howells drawing his stubby revolver. An arctic wind tossed the heavy drapery, and Toller went down like a yachtsman trying to reef in a spinnaker in a gale. Snow and glass fragments spun in the air.

Howells bawled "Lights!" like an attendant in *Hamlet* then "Lightman!" Poole imagined a torchbearer in medieval dress rushing forward. But it was Wilma who dove forward, service revolver drawn.

At that instant Chance Cosgrove threw a Pop Warner cross-body block into Poole. *'I've been clipped!* Poole thought erratically as he folded up and overturned Wilma.

From hands and knees, Poole watched Chance dart out the bedroom door, running apelike, shackled hands held out and down.

"Jesus, out of the way!" someone howled. Poole tried to lever Wilma from the twisted carpet. Len Howells sprinted past. Fred Toller leaned out the splintered window frame, his big bottom canted dangerously. He shouted, "God damn it, there he goes. *Grab* his ass!"

A dapper man in an expensive suit stood in the doorway. "You…you can't *do* this," he sputtered, "in a sickroom!"

Wilma scrambled after Howells, while Poole stared at Margo and Nurse Howarth bent over Charles Cosgrove's form. Then he brushed past the doctor, who clawed at his arm, hissing, "You, sir!"

Poole pounded down the sweeping staircase to see Sheriff Buxtrider, dappled with tan slush, burst into the house, waving a huge pistol. Wilma skidded on the parquet flooring, and Buxtrider caught her.

"Ziggy's gone around the house," Buxtrider wheezed. "I think I busted some ribs jumping out that window," he added.

Poole hit the Turkey carpet at the foot of the stairs in full flight, felt the rug bunch, did a fandango side-step, turned sharply and reeled down the corridor toward the back of the house. He managed not to fall.

He heard Don Cosgrove's voice from above, wailing, "Oh, Papa —don't you dare die!"

***

"Your half-assed Deputy Lightman was in the kitchen drinking hot fucking chocolate," Howells said. "And the dim bulb I posted at the front door went to his unit to put in a call."

Howells had run Chance down, found him at the top of the stairs in the garage, battering with his cuffs at a locked door. Chance was bundled into a police cruiser and returned to jail. Wilson James, aka Ziggy, was still loose in the snow.

They were gathered in the big kitchen, Buxtrider at an end of a chopping block, his shirt stripped off. Wilma assisted Dr. Morganthaler in winding a strip bandage around Buck's torso. Margo and Don sat, stupefied and bereft, in kitchen chairs. Howells pushed his new homburg back on his skull and sucked coffee.

"Whose lousy idea was this town meeting?" he growled. "Poole, I seem to remember your eloquence." He sighed. "Ah, well—they'll track Ziggy down. Or he'll freeze his ass to the ground. I hope somebody at the shop is twisting the Brewster kids'…" He glanced at Margo and muttered, "Sorry."

Poole looked at the interlocking rings of mug-stains on the table before him. Everything connects. But how?

Lainey had accompanied her son, screeching imprecations at the police. "I'll sue this chickenshit city off the map!" she bawled. "Hurt one hair of his head, and you'll die! My father's an important man. He'll fix you!"

The doctor finished with Buxtrider and went to Margo. He patted her shoulder, saying, "I'll call from the hospital, Mrs. Cosgrove. I warned you it would come quickly. He's not in great pain, you know."

An ambulance had carried Charles Cosgrove's frail body away in convoy with the police cruiser toting his daughter and grandson. The red and blue lights of the vehicles splashed happy Christmas hues across the drifted snow. The ambulance siren hooted musically, like remote carolers approaching the Cosgrove crèche in song. "Angels I have heard on high," Poole thought.

Howells sat next to Poole, dropped his hat into his lap and toyed with its razor creases. He glanced at Poole and said, "Any big ideas on where we go next?"

"Heck and Samsa. That's all we have left."

Howells blew a muted raspberry. "Yeh. You're goddam welcome to chat with Heck. He tells anybody with an ear his life history. Samsa —he won't say *boo* till his lawyer gets the case worked up."

Buxtrider walked gingerly, wincing, while Wilma watched attentively.

"Heck knows it all," Poole said. "He can put it together, if he'll talk without running off the map."

"Yes, and good luck to yez there," Howells said.

A housemaid in a blue uniform leaned into the kitchen from the hallway. "Excuse me, Ma'am. It's all so confusing. There's a phone call. Is there anybody here named Pole?"

"Poole?" Poole said. Echolalia.

The maid gnawed her lip. "Maybe," she said.

Poole struggled to use the kitchen phone, punched several buttons and finally heard a thin voice.

"Mr. Pole, that you? Earline here. You recollect? Missus Handyman Harve?" Her voice was light but clear. "You ast me to call. They give me this number at the motel."

"Yes, yes: I wanted to know if you remembered anything else about the person who bought that rope."

"That's real odd, Mr. Pole. Lewis and me was talkin about it last night, late. Kind of pillow-talk, you know?" She giggled, a sound of light chains jingling. "I *did* recall something. But it's so *strange*."

In the dull silence, Poole ground the receiver into his ear. "Earline? You there?"

"Oh. Yes."

"Well, what do you mean? How strange?"

She giggled again. It was like a beginner's obscene phone call.

"It's...nutty," she breathed.

"Mrs...Halberstam," Poole prompted.

"You said to think about them hands. You remember? A big guy in a parka, and hairy hands. How I told you?"

"Please, Mrs. Halberstam," Poole said. Her voice evoked in his frontal lobe the Ghost of Headaches Past.

"Well, Mr. Pole, I'll tell you. I *revisualized* it. That's what they teach us in my relaxation-therapy group. You have to make up a new body for yourself. You close your eyes and revisualize what you want to look like, see?"

Poole massaged the back of his neck. He thought, randomly, of an old vaudeville tune called "I Wished I Was in Peoria." He fondly wished Earline Halberstam up to her fat lips in boiling acid.

How far away *was* Peoria? Tiny red-and-blue spots danced before his eyes like Christmas ornaments from Cloud Cuckooland.

"...you assemble all the parts and come up with a whole new self-image. I'm here to tell you, it works, Mr. Pole."

"Mrs. Halberstam. I...my name is *Poole*. Forget that. I just need to know what you remembered."

"I'm sure sorry," she said stiffly. "You *said* it might be important, and I tried to call you all day. Them people at the sheriff's office are a sorry bunch."

Poole banged his head softly on the wall. *Will no one,* he moaned to himself, *rid me of this prolix succubus?*

"...saw them hands again. And Mr., er, they was tiny. That's what's nutty. I could see a great big guy all muffled in a parka. Big, heavy coat, see, hood an all. But the sleeves was pushed up, and them hands was real...small. That don't make sense!"

Poole sighed. Earline laughed again, the girlish titter amplified by the phone into booming silver bells.

"Listen carefully, Earline: was there anything odd about the *shape*—I mean the way this man's...body looked?"

She blurted, "Why that's it, Pole! That's what Lewis and me talked about! He was all...lumpy. I mean, like somebody in a Santa Claus suit, with pillows inside. It was...nutty."

"Could it be..." Poole hemmed. "Listen, could it be something like one small man on another small man's shoulders, inside that coat?"

The line was as void as interstellar space. It whistled, and Earline said, "Mr. Pole, I think *you're* the nutty one! It's some kinda joke!"

"No, no, I assure you. It's dead serious, Earline. Think. Er, revisualize, Earline. Could it be?"

Her voice warped uncertainly. "Well...I guess that might explain it. But I never heard of any such of a thing!"

"A small hand," Poole prompted. "A tiny, hairy hand?"

"Well...Yes," she whispered. "But what does it mean?"

"Earline, you've done very well. God bless your relaxation-therapy classes!"

"It's for the weight," she said hoarsely. "I don't tell Lewis, because it's going to be a surprise. But that's what I do it for."

"Thank you, thank you," Poole babbled. "And Merry Christmas to you and Lewis and Handyman Harve and everyone!"

* * *

Outside, Poole surveyed the sky, a genuine midnight clear. Wilma was by him, waiting for the Bronco's motor to warm.

"You're, er, stuck on Bucky, aren't you?" Poole said.

Wilma shrugged deeper into her bulky coat. She wore a kind of astrakhan cap with a sheriff's star on the front. She looked like the most attractive sergeant-major in Mao Tse-tung's army.

Her breath burst in a long plume. "I guess you could say that."

"You don't think this is a rerun of your marriage?"

"No, Richard. I mean, maybe...but I guess I'm willing to take the chance."

Poole felt his left foot giving up its life. He stamped it and winced, as capillaries reported in to his central nervous system.

"Jesus, when will I stop being cold?" he mumbled.

"Wish me luck?" Wilma asked quietly.

"Sure. All the best. But I was just a, er, decoy?"

She stepped to him, pressed him back against the Bronco's steel flank and gave him a warm, whacking kiss. "No, indeed," she said, nuzzling. "But..."

"Yeh. I'm a footloose stranger on the scene." Wilma held him, and he absorbed some sweet warmth, a faint elixir of home-and-hearth.

She turned to the Bronco. "I don't cry anymore," she said. "Not over men."

"Good resolve," Poole said. She climbed into the cab, the interior light giving him a flash of the sadness in her face. Poole waved as the Bronco snorted and backed away, its headlights flashing in his eyes and putting out the myriad of stars in the deep sky.

Santa Claus Blues

GREGORY SAMSA SAT at a long table in the police interrogation room, next to a stubby, bald man in a rumpled tweed suit. This man wore thick bifocals and toyed with a portfolio of legal papers. He might as well have worn a badge declaiming *I Am a Big-Time Attorney, So Look Out, or I Will Sue Your Miserable Ass into the Pavement, Scum!* He had a mild, professorish face, betrayed by wire-like tension lines at the corners of his mouth. Obviously a jackal in wolf's clothing.

"Counselor," Len Howells said patiently, as if explaining the mere rudiments of sex education to a retarded delinquent minor, "we don't want to compromise any, uh, facet of this case, but—"

"Cut the crapola, Lenny," the bald man snapped, snatching off his horn-rimmed specs as if they were ablaze. "You have no case on my client, and I won't watch you build one on loose lips and slight slips, kiddo. So let's cancel the next waltz, huh?"

Poole sat at the end of the long table. He tried to maintain eye contact with Samsa, possibly to shame or intimidate a dramatic, wholesale confession from the executive. Thus far, the tactic had failed. Samsa looked bored and restive, a man with more important things to meditate than a potential multiple-murder-mayhem-conspiracy charge, spangled with subheadings and addenda.

Samsa scrubbed at his thin, sandy hair and sighed. He glanced from Poole to Howells.

"Gentlemen," he said, "I want to get this miserable business—"

192

"Can it, Greg," the lawyer said. "You promised to abide by my instructions, and my instructions are to button up till the DA comes up with a real-life statement for us, huh?"

Howells sighed and stubbed out his cigarette. He eyed the owlish lawyer sourly. "You always were a smalltime prick, Jess. Everybody on the playground at dear old Warren G. Harding High used you for a lunchtime punching bag, and you're going to get your revenge by being a massive pain in the ass for the entire population of PawPaw County. Congratulations on your wisdom."

Jesse P. Meister replaced his glasses and glared. He turned to Samsa and said, "This is not a productive meeting. Back to my office, Greg. Let these cops and the DA play jacks till they come up with something we need to hear."

Samsa shook his head. "I wish to cooperate with the, um, authorities," he said. "I want my name and reputation cleared."

"Good," Howells pounced, "let's have a statement on your whereabouts on the nights in question, Mr. Samsa. All I have is notes from investigating officers at the crime scenes."

"I can only repeat what I told the officers."

Howells flipped through a sheaf of typed notes. "That's a start," he said.

"Not a chance," Meister said. "You button up, Greg, or call a hotshit lawyer from Chicago with a lot of practice plea-bargaining amateurs off death row."

"Ah," Howells said. "I take that to mean your client has done something truly naughty, Jess? Can I make a note of that?"

Meister stood, scooped his papers into a worn briefcase and hooked his arm around Samsa, levering him upright. "March now, or I'm off this case," he growled at Samsa.

Samsa glanced at Poole and Howells and smiled feebly. "You see?" he murmured. "It's out of my hands..."

* * *

Heck Ogden sat in the battered captain's chair Samsa had occupied. The curved back kept him from slumping. Otherwise, he looked like a poor model of a man, a manikin stuffed with inferior excelsior, about to collapse in a heap like Dorothy's Scarecrow before he discovered his spine.

When Heck tried to create a cigarette from a bag of Bugler and a ZigZag paper, the product disintegrated into refuse under his quivering digits. His eyes were red-rimmed and flecked with mucus at the corners. He could have modeled for a modern Hogarth about to engrave the final panels in a *Drunk's Progress*. He flinched when Howells spoke,

"Come on, Og," Howells cajoled. "We want to help you out of this heap of shit you fell in."

A young policewoman sat at the far end of the table with a tape recorder and a steno pad. She was a perky brunette with an enticing ear, Poole had noted. But she was a shade walleyed, he decided. What the hell? He tried not to look her in the eye. Or eyes. Or *was* he?

"Mr., er," Ogden said abruptly, "what you think?"

"I think you must tell us what you know," Poole said.

Ogden sighed, scrubbed a hand across his lips, slumped lower in the chair and mumbled, "Okay."

After minutes of rambling, punctuated by sharp questions from Howells, Heck Ogden began to unravel his tale:

"I run into Nugent a couple times in the last few months. He was into some really bad shit. When Jake and Mo come this year, I tried to tell 'em what he was doin. I went with 'em that Sunday. We was…we knew he had the shipment of Gerties, see? He had them stored out at Don Cosgrove's place, that goddam cute little barn. Shit. Jake and Mo and me, we decided…I talked them into it. That's what really hurts—I got them to do it. I said we wouldn't get caught, and we'd fix Nugent's wagon. And Samsa. He was in it all the way.

"They got the rope at the mall. I don't know how. I was out in the truck. I had a bottle. You know. We had some drinks, and it got dark. I took the old River Road out, back of Cosgrove's place, and we waited around. Jesus, was it cold! Jake and Mo had a couple drinks with me. We set in the truck an watched the place. I thought it was clear, so we snuck up an fiddled around. The barn was padlocked, like I told them, but they had the rope. They threw it up on that beam on the barn, the hoist, see? It was amazing what those two guys could do. Jake swung up an jimmied the loft doors. He got in, he opened a window for Mo, but I couldn't get through it. Too fucking small. Oh, Jesus—excuse my mouth, Ma'am! Anyhow...shit, I wisht I had a drink..."

Howells sighed and said, "Later, Og. Let's get through this, huh?"

"Yeh. Hell, yes. I...waited outside. Mo and Jake got a light on, an I could see inside. A big shitload of boxes and stuff in the back room, a kind of storage place, see? Mo opened a box, an it was full of Gerties. He showed me one an laughed to beat hell. I had a can of white gas in the truck, an I gave him that—handed it through the window."

"White gas?" Poole said.

"Kerosene," Ogden said. "See, we decided we was gonna screw up the whole operation. I thought if we poured that on the Gerties, it'd ruin 'em. Hell of a stink, anyhow. So Jake and Mo opened the boxes an splashed the kerosene around, laughin and screwin around. We was all pretty tanked up. It was cold as a bastard, an I keep hollerin at 'em to move their asses. Then I saw a car comin up the drive I nearly shit...I mean, I was real scared.

"I yelled at 'em to get out, but they was rippin an tearin, an Mo just give me the finger. So I run around the barn an hunkered down in a cut. The car come up, an I seen the lights go off in the barn. They must of heard or seen it—Jake an Mo, I mean.

"I was scared, an I started gettin puke-sick. But I kept watchin. It was Nugent. He unlocked the barn—he had a goddam key, see? Then the lights was all on, an I snuck up to the window, when I saw nobody was with him. I couldn't see a lot inside. Nugent stomped around, an he must of smelled the white gas right off. He finds boxes scattered around, an he opened the cabinets an starts throwin the goddam dolls out. Then I see him drag Mo out of the cabinet… Jesus, it was like another doll! He…"

Ogden shuddered and buried his face in his hands. He sobbed, a racking cough of tissue rending. Howells glanced impassively at Poole, a look of compassion—or perhaps only professional boredom.

"We was just gonna screw up the Gertie job, see? I didn't mean to put Jake and Mo in the shit. I…run away. I started for the truck, but it was a quarter-mile off, an I floundered around in the snow, up to my ass. I thought I'd get a tire iron—something. I knew Nugent would have a gun. The kind of bird who does. I…Jesus, I don't know what I thought. It was like Korea. All that goddam dirty snow. I got a hundred yards, maybe. Then I stopped to look. He comes out—Nugent—carryin…things. I think it's Gerties, boxes, whatever. But it was Mo and Jake. One under each arm, like you'd carry rag dolls or…dead meat."

"How long did this take?" Howells asked quietly.

"I…don't know. Jesus, can't I have that drink?" Ogden shivered again. "Okay, okay. I know." He stared at the scarred tabletop and drew a long breath.

"That bastard. He threw them in his van, in the back door. I thought they was dead. By the way he did it. Like some guy takin out the trash. I was freezin. It must of been a long time, see? Nugent gets in the van, an I cut across the field. I thought I'd lose him, but I saw his taillights, an when I come down the River Road, he was goin along, just drivin like nothin had happened. I followed, an I saw him go toward the mall. No place else out there he could go. I couldn't figure why he'd go there. But I went along with my lights off. The bastard parks right by the back entrance, an he has *keys* again, for Christ sake, an lets hisself in. That's when I knew Samsa musta been in it. I waited, then I went in after him. That prick just left the key in the damn door! It was dark inside, but them yellow lights in the halls was enough to see by."

Ogden sighed and rubbed a gnarled hand on his forehead. He seemed to Poole an eye-witness to the harrowing of hell.

"I come after him, real careful, but he was walkin along like nobody could care less. I cut back to the security office, all lit up like it was supposed to be. Nobody there, but Randy Loggins' gun was on the desk bigger than shit. I didn't think twice. I grabbed it, broke it an checked the load. Then I went back after Nugent. I seen him comin from the phones at the front. I figure he called Samsa— or somebody. Not then, I didn't figure, but now, see? I thought he seen me, but I jumped back into a side hall, that one goes to the maintenance room. I could see out. Nugent come and picked up Mo and Jake. They was stacked on the floor. He picks them up an starts up the main stairs to the balcony. I don't know why he's carryin em up, but I cut around up the fire stairs. I can head him off on the second level, see? I get there, an Nugent's staggerin along, wheezin an panting. He's a big guy, but he's luggin Mo an Jake, an his face is all red...

"I come out of the fire stairs just as he gets to the top of the main stairs on the...what, mezzanine, balcony, whatever. I step out, an he sees me. I got Loggins' pistol in his face, an Nugent looks like he'll shit a red-hot brick! He stands there wheezin, an says, 'Good Christ, Heck Ogden!' like we was at a class reunion.

"I don't think I said anything. Maybe I said 'Why?' Or maybe *he* said it. He stepped back against that skinny railing, and I said,

'Put your hands up' or somethin. He had Jake and Mo on his shoulders like goddam feed sacks. An they slid off backward. Ah, Jesus, it was so horrible, they was fallin down, an I thought *Maybe they're alive—stop!* But I didn't say it. Maybe I thought I was sayin it. What I was doin was pullin the trigger. Like firin a friggin cannon in there. I thought I was deaf. I saw Jake and Mo fallin through the air, an it was like I could *catch* 'em if I pulled the trigger. See? Then Nugent takes the wallop. I thought he was doin a backflip off the railin, but he just slid down to the floor. He jerked an folded in half, an I heard these echoes, an...I heard them little guys hittin down below. I run an looked down an knew they was dead. I was so scared an sick I shot my lunch. I wished to God I'd of puked in Nugent's face.

"I crawled around on the floor, then I got up an run down them back stairs. I thought I heard 'em behind me, blowin those crazy bugles. A million gooks in rubber-soled shoes, trampin through the snow. I got to the truck, finished that bottle of rye an drove home. I don't remember nothin about that. Then the sheriff's men was draggin me around, said I was guilty as shit, an I knew I *was*—but not of hurtin Mo an Jake. I wouldn't of hurt them. But...see, I did. It was my fault, ever goddamn bit of my fault. If I could of... thought. But there wasn't no time to think. It all happened like I was caught in some movie, an I *had* to do what I was supposed to—go here, go there, watch Nugent kill Mo and Jake, pull the trigger on Loggins' gun. All my life I been doin what somebody else said. 'Heck, get your ass over to Korea an kill a buncha slopes for me'...'Heck, weed the fuckin garden till your back goes out.'...'Heck, teach my wimpy kid to drown worms, make him a man.'"

Ogden sagged further in his chair. He looked gray and deflated, as if he had exuded a mass of guilt and turmoil that kept him intact. Howells asked, "How did you *know* about the...Gerties?"

"Mo an Jake was in it. I mean, Nugent told 'em some. They wasn't really doin nothin, but they picked up on the game, an they thought Nugent was scum. He told 'em he knew they'd done some little jobs, break-ins.

Mo an Jake weren't no angels. They did bad stuff, but they weren't really bad guys. They didn't want to get twisted in a heavy-duty dope operation. They got scared. We thought we'd spook Nugent, get him to stop it. I don't know what it was about, except they said the dolls was used to bring in that brown Mexican dope, the real nasty kind. Up from New Orleans."

Poole asked, "What happened to the gun? Where did you leave it?"

Ogden stared. He shrugged, "Shit if I know. I must of dropped it somewhere. I didn't care about that. I didn't care if the whole goddam sheriff's office found it."

Howells signed to the policewoman, who shut off the recorder. "You wanted a short drink, Heck. Come down to my office," Howells said. "You earned it."

* * *

In late afternoon, Poole arrived at the mall. The lots were nearly scraped clean, dotted with cars, and new banners and guidons flapped in the stiff river breeze. They announced sales, pre-Christmas *Buying Incentive Plans*, layaway no-down-payment schemes, free credit on long-term big-ticket items, deals on new merchandise, deals on old merchandise, last week's models *Half-Price Today Only! Buy, Buy—Bye-Bye.*

Poole jostled in thickening crowds. In the atrium, a new, improvised SantaLand seemed more a dumping ground for tots, a holding pen where toddlers were corralled. Poole rode the escalator to the office tower.

He entered the wicket gate leading to LeeLand Mall's micro-circuit brain. He found Drew Whitman and Alicine Mungo holding vesper services before the altar of IRMA. They handled reverently the stacked scriptures of accordion print-out sheets and toted crystal chalices holding hard discs. The sybil meditated in deep silence.

"Mr. Poole," Whitman said, rubbing his stubby red hair and grinning. "Lissy's helping me assemble your data." Alicine was chic in the white duster, an extra in reel #3 of *Bride of Frankenstein*, attending the techno-wizard in his den.

"Here are printouts on the new franchises," Whitman said. "And the projection data we programmed. The legal documents aren't on file. I want the whole paper system digitalized, but this is still the late nineteenth century here, you see."

At a spotless, chrome-topped table, Poole spread the thick packets of computer pages. He began to interpret the filing and breakout system IRMA used. Then he could see a picture of the mall's projected new ventures.

Whitman and Lissy continued their votive labors. The room was silent except for a sighing from the climate-control system and tiny rustlings in IRMA's labyrinthine innards. The reading-room of the future, Poole realized. No reading aloud except for IRMA, when she regurgitated a python of ruled paper.

Finally, Poole called Whitman in a hushed voice. He tapped one large sheet.

"What's all this?" Poole asked.

Whitman adjusted steel-rimmed bifocals and said, "A glitch? Looks copasetic to me."

Copasetic? Poole thought. He flashed on Cab Galloway in floor-length lab coat over florid zootsuit, leading a hidden orchestra while he scatted out IRMA's charms in alliterative vocalese.

"It's not a...mistake," Poole managed. "It's added and organized okay. It's the...kind of data here. These are all estimated figures, rounded off. It isn't real accounting—it's all hypothetical."

"Ah, sure. These are projections. Models. Mr. Samsa had us work this up in August, to model trends. See: here's a one-year model, a five-year model, a projected lifetime model of fifteen years."

"You mean none of these places is actually operating?"

Poole showed Whitman his notebook listing of Sol's Tannery, Hickory Daiquiri Dock, Shoe Soul, The Harem, Tinker's Tottery, Lafayette Espadrille…and Little Fishes, The Wish Factory, Nightwear Alley and Interfaith Books. Whitman traced the entries on another ledger-sized computer sheet.

"Yep," he finally said. "This was a package proposal, a ten-year plan for expansion and development. See—" He pointed to a cluster of numbers and code abbreviations. "Here. This indexes the other sheets. We made projections on size, kinds and quality of merchandise, estimated turnover on items, and we ran a profile model of the whole mall, so you can see the share of total business we're talking. Then breakdowns on overhead, depreciation, estimates of inflationary trends, that stuff."

"But none of these businesses is open?"

Whitman shuffled another scroll. He scratched his nose and blinked. "Nope. Nothing on-line yet. Nothing shows new data since…September. I guess the big guys put the proposal on a back burner."

"Or in a closet," Poole muttered. "Could any of these be in operation but not, er, plugged into IRMA?"

Whitman winced. "Not a chance. Oh, I suppose somebody could do something by hand, or set up a mini-computer on their own. But that's absolutely against the book. AmeriMall would have giant kittens if *that* came out! Nah. No one could get away with it for long."

Poole tapped a finger on the top rank of figures. "Maybe they wouldn't have to do for long. A couple of months—say, October to December."

After a half-hour of thrashing through the accordion sheets, Poole beckoned Whitman again.

"Look here," he said, tracing a set of columns. "These franchises are marked with this code: N/F. What's that mean?"

Whitman frowned and shuffled back through sheets. "Um," he said. "Here...not funded."

Poole scratched his ear. "What's that mean?"

"These are all *models*, Mr, er," Whitman said. "Projections. Hypothetical records, see? We do it routinely for proposals. See: it's marked January through June of *next* year. Two quarters, projected during the slowest season, to show profitability, overhead, and so on."

It was a puzzle. Poole shuffled sheets. "Could...what's to prevent someone from entering these into the regular mall accounts? How do they get switched from models to operative accounts?"

"They must be okayed by the manager's office. Then we transfer them into current operating programs. It's an easy transition."

"What about purchasing, credit and so on?"

"Same deal. Once they're authorized, we reroute individual programs, put them on the master supply program."

"Look," Poole said carefully. "I'm wondering if anyone could have used any of these operations as a kind of...front. A dummy account."

Whitman grimaced as if Poole had just farted loudly in his sanctum. "I don't see how. We have a series of internal audit programs running. It's a daily audit, for all practical purposes."

"Who checks the audits?" Poole asked. *Who keeps an eye on the keepers?*

"I spot-check for errors, glitches, problems in the run," Whitman said. "Then abstracted reports are sent to the manager's office. The complete records are opened for external auditors whenever they come. The AmeriMall people get quarterly reports, and we're patched into their computers."

"But if somebody wanted to run a dummy franchise for a few months, they could get away with it? If nobody in the manager's office blew the whistle?"

Whitman scowled. "I guess. But it wouldn't last long enough to skim much cash. The disbursement program has a blue million security checkpoints built in. Nobody cuts a check without a lot of clearance."

"I'm not thinking about a penny-ante skimming operation. I'm thinking about lines of credit, enough to back orders, to make shipments coming in here look bound for a legitimate franchise."

Whitman leafed rapidly through sheets, stopped and traced a line of numbers with one finger. He sucked at his teeth and whistled tunelessly.

"Just between us, captain, I've noticed one anomaly. But I had no reason to ask obtrusive questions. It's this—" He tapped a column of crowded digits and acronymical abbreviations. The column was headed TNK TT.

"Tinker's Tottery?" Whitman nodded.

Poole watched while Whitman pecked out cabalistic phrases on a keyboard, lighted up orange on a screen before him. He paused, nodded and tapped a few more keys. A large, high-speed printer next to him clacked alive and rattled off lines of type. In seconds, a paper tongue lolled. Whitman picked it up and scanned it as the printer rattled on.

"I'll be double-damned!" Whitman whispered. "I think you're onto something. This place has been sending orders and establishing credit since late October. No manager's okay, no order to switch into the accounting program, no connection with the internal auditor. And nobody's reviewed it." He stared at Poole with something like fear on his face.

"You never handled any of it?"

"Hell, no! It's been funneled in from another office. After we set up the model programs for that batch of proposals, I never looked at this stuff. We make runs like this a couple times a year, and I just wait for go-ahead orders when anything is supposed to go on-line."

"Yours not to reason why," Poole said. "Interfaces to the right of you, interfaces to the left of you, into the valley of confusion ride the five megabytes, eh?"

Whitman shook his head and rattled the scroll. "What the hell is the deal on this Tinker's Tottery?" he asked. "Jesus Kay-rist! Greg Samsa'll have somebody's ass on a platter for this."

Poole took the sheets and added them to his heap. "Oh, I don't think so," he said. "That's not the scenario this time."

* * *

Harvey Lewis's voice was the sound made by a table saw with a dull blade, a rising howl of indignation mixed with vengeful snarls and a constant overtone of cosmic self-pity. He had made clear to Poole that speedy resolution of the muddled LeeLand Mall affair was not only desirable but imperative. He had stalled at the AmeriMall meeting, and Poole could imagine the mixture of genteel equivocation and high-level bafflegab Lewis had employed. But in the late night, in his empty, soundproofed office, Lewis had the voice of a *heldentenor* turned loose in the last second of the last act of *Gotterdamerung*. Hellfire, Armaggedon and universal apocalypse crackled over the phone line and sizzled in Poole's inner ear.

"You get back to me *tomorrow*, Poole!" he bawled. "I'll have a management team on the first morning flight, you get them with Don Cosgrove, and they'll contain this brushfire. But god *damn* it, I'm counting on *you* to keep this out of the media and under control! You copy?"

Poole sighed and went into his patented number-three soothing sustaining routine for Harvey.

He cooed assurances he was unsure he could guarantee and promised results no human could deliver. Slowly, Lewis's shriek subsided, modulated to a sullen grumble. "...and your report better be detailed and documented, unless you want a little trip to Patagonia to be your next...and last."

Poole stared at the receiver, hearing the hiss of the dead line…"And a good night to you, old sock," he said, cradling the phone. Harvey Lewis had discovered a mining operation in the hinterlands of Argentina, which he held as a stick before Poole on desperate occasions. Poole wondered idly if Patagonia were all that bad. He looked out at errant snowflakes dancing in the parking lot lights and decided it could be no more dismal than this Mississippi beachhead. It was *summer* in Patagonia.

Fred Toller bustled into the office, shucking his parka, showering droplets of ice water. "Cold enough out there to freeze the pecker off Prometheus," he said.

"Just got word Buck's run down little Ziggy. Got a call from the state cops down near Carbondale. Ziggy'd picked up a ride with a trucker, who dropped him at an all-night gas station. The guy saw the cuffs, and after a battle with his conscience gave in to a moral impulse. The smokies got Ziggy as he was going to climb into another eighteen-wheeler. Makes you wonder, don't it? The goddam highways of America are littered with hitchhikers wearing Smith and Wesson ID bracelets, maybe. Jesus, what does it take to make people give a shit these days?"

"Where was he headed?" Poole asked.

Toller sucked at his front teeth and sighed, "Just out, I'd guess. Heading south, anyhow, so he can't be as stone stupid as I thought. Buck's gone to haul him back. Meantime, Buck's been persuading Heinie to sing us a song. The kid's had a teensy change of heart, and he'll babble as long as you want about Greg Samsa and his evil empire."

"You buy the idea it was Samsa and Nugent. And Ziggy and Heinie were just, er, pawns?"

"A tad hi-falutin, but it'll do. Samsa had Ziggy and Heinie running a little terrorism and random vandalism, to keep Don Cosgrove on the hot seat and out of the way. Say, you have a line on that operation Greg was running, right?"

Toller waited, a groundhog alert outside a winter burrow. Poole grinned and said, "That's what we call a high-security matter."

"Shit." Toller picked up a coffee mug and inspected the green substance sprouting in its depth. "I thought we was just a couple old boys in this shit together."

"It will be unfolded in the fullness of time."

"Yeh, like Nixon's memoirs. Only the boring-ass parts ever get to me. Anyhow, I got it figured. Nugent was down here, and Heinie and Ziggy were lurking, when the elves was snuffed. I figure Samsa had them set up to do some vandalism or bust into a store, make a mess to scare Don. Nugent got it into his head to bring the elves here after he did them, maybe add to the scheme with some mayhem. Say, you think he had *them* involved? Heck Ogden said they were into smalltime B and E. Maybe they was all going to do some dirty tricks here, but Heck diverted the elves. How's that for a theory?"

Poole shrugged. "Sounds, um, copasetic to me. We'll never know all that went wrong."

"Loggins and Washburn was down in the maintenance tunnels, and all them creeps was in the mall. Helluva blotch on my record, huh? Some security chief. Even poor old Doreen was doing the double-shuffle up here. Shit."

"What?" Poole stared. "Doreen was here that night?"

"Sure. Didn't your buddy Howells fill you in? She's the A-One eyewitness corroborating Heck's story. Turns out she was in for the night, schlepping around to find a warm corner to bunk in. She saw Heinie and Ziggy, saw Nugent come in with the elves, saw old Heck drill him, the works. Course, she ain't the best-looking witness to set in front of a jury, even if you bathe her in Lysol."

"Oh, God," Poole muttered, "I've got to read the whole transcript."

"That'll be a bundle of yuks. It's weird—Doreen's hanging around to see her ex-husband wasted by Heck Ogden, which makes her happy as a lark. I think that's what made her talk to Howells. She couldn't wait to tell somebody she saw the old fool get his. Howells was ready to pin it on her, but even he couldn't buy the idea that Doreen could hold a gun steady enough to plug him."

"You don't think Heck's covering for her? *Could* she have shot him? Could she have swiped Loggins' gun?"

Toller scratched his scalp and snickered, "Jesus, you want to get everybody in on the job, huh? Sure—it's possible. Heck still wants to be somebody's hero. I guess he'd get off on a little self-sacrifice to save the life of Leeland's leading bag lady. Who knows? But she swears she just watched it all. Not that she was a bit unhappy to see Nugent's brains scrambled."

Poole struggled into his coat. He glared at squibs of snow blowing across the prairie-sized lots.

"Tell you what," Toller called after Poole. "Give me a *Reader's Digest* version when you get them records sorted out, huh? I want to know, but not so bad as to have to hear it all…"

* * *

Poole was astonished to find in Howells' office Margo and Don Cosgrove, Astin Lee, Ann Wilcox and Wilma Breithope. Their various degrees of dishevelment suggested an impromptu council. Howells sighed when Poole poked his head into the chamber.

"Jeez," he said, "come on in. Drag in a chair. Hell, we might as well of advertised this as a town meeting. I could of sold tickets."

Poole didn't place the short man in a scruffy warm up jacket sitting next to Howells. Then it registered: Marty Grimes, the elusive state medico. Grimes leafed through typed sheets in a folder, a small grimace on his owl's countenance.

"I said I'd fill in interested parties when the case was tied up," Howells said. "We're about ninety-nine percent done, and the DA will have his case worked up by the end of the week. So this is all the Q-and-A time I can give you."

Grimes shut the folder and said, "I'm out of here in thirty minutes, Len. You want me to lead off?" Howells nodded and lit a twisty stogy.

"The results of my workups and the local boys' reports converge," Grimes said, removing his thick glasses, which made him appear more than ever a small owl harassed by angry crows in daylight. "The, um, elves were killed a few hours before discovery, moved to the mall. Fiber packing materials on their clothing correspond to the materials used in the, er, doll shipments. Traces of low-grade kerosene fuel also present on clothing and skin. Ditto for your Mr. Nugent, on re-examination by the county coroner. Nugent's death: instantaneous by gunshot to the head, slug matching the weapon issued to your Mr. Loggins. Nugent moved sometime shortly after death and deposited in the car trunk where he was found, frozen, unmoved thereafter."

"Where was the gun found?" Poole asked. "How did it get there?"

"In a dumpster at the edge of, er, Kinglet Lot," Howells said. "Our resident geniuses, Loggins and Washburn, tossed it there when hey transferred Nugent to your car. It was right in the middle of the goddam investigation, when they sacked Nugent and carried him up from the steam tunnels."

"That screwed things up for me," Grimes said. "The body was kept at relatively high temperatures for several hours, then taken into the cold. About fifteen Fahrenheit, the local report says. Where it promptly froze. Left tissues in a hell of an odd state, not to mention blood settling in weird patterns after they slung him around. The one, er, elf in the pool was the same way—the water temperature and being inside and outside skewed everything for us."

"But modern science triumphs over all, eh?" Astin Lee said.

Grimes polished his glasses with a rumpled red bandana and blinked. "We ran samples through Northwestern's labs to double-check. It all comes out square now."

Don Cosgrove cleared his throat and glanced nervously around. He looked shrunken but in control. "You're *sure* Heck's story is true?" he asked.

Grimes said, "His description of the way the elves died makes forensic sense. Ditto his account of Nugent's shooting. He couldn't know about Loggins and what's-his-name dragging off Nugent's body. But it tallies as closely as anybody can make it."

"What about Doreen?" Poole asked. "How the hell was she involved, and how do we know she isn't tied into all the deaths?"

Howells sighed and set his cigar in the shell-casing ashtray. "We've grilled her and Heck separately, and unless you credit a conspiracy of some really high level of competency between the town drunk and the resident bag lady, we have it right. Turns out Doreen had a regular routine, staying in the mall on bad nights. Hadn't been caught by Loggins. Or maybe that dumb ass let her stay on, for whatever reasons. Her story is that she slipped out of a maintenance cubbyhole by the emergency stairs after Heck went up, watched from the doorway and saw him whack Nugent. She's not a hundred percent clear on how the elves fell. But her eyesight's probably worse than Marty's."

"What's...what do you do next?" Don said. He was pallid again.

Howells tipped back in his swivel chair. "Either we get a break and Greg Samsa decides to make a wholesale and cleansing confession, or the DA goes to trial with a tissue paper case, and we hope to hell the court sorts it out. I'd guess the latter, since Samsa has sealed himself up with Jesse Meister."

"We *must* have order restored to the mall," Margo said, leaning toward Howells. "And this must be kept as quiet and contained as possible. The damage to the business—to our whole local economy—could be tremendous. There are even...political ramifications."

Howells nodded glumly. Marty Grimes gathered a battered aluminum case and tugged on a wool stocking cap. He looked like a school kid about to embark on serious cross-country hitchhiking. He grinned around the room and said, "I can't say it's been a great pleasure being involved with this Leeland madness. And I sure as hell don't need to hear about your corn belt *realpolitik*. So, excuse my hasty departure. I'm due in Rock Island. They have a juicy poisoning case on. A disgruntled family-farmer did in a banker and his whole family with a herbicide-laced pullet. Now *there's* political murder for you. Merry Christmas, friends!"

Margo started to speak as Grimes shut the office door, but Don put his hand on her arm. "Mother?" he said. "Leave it. I'll handle it. Wilma: when will your boss be free to sit down with us?"

"He's back in town, and when the DA sorts out jurisdiction on Heinie and Ziggy and Heck, Buck, ah, the sheriff will meet you all." She smiled at Don. "He has a lively interest in the political and economic implications."

Ann turned to Poole. "What about your corporation? Are you still representing their interests?"

"I had instructions this afternoon. A management-consultant team is due tomorrow. They'll help Don sort out the mall operation over Christmas. Yeh, *I'm* still on the job."

"They're willing to be involved in the legal disputes over the mall location? Over local responsibility?"

Poole nodded. "AmeriMall will hang in with LeeLand Mall if there are negotiations in good faith. My boss says TransAtlas is an organization with a large soul. He makes it sound like a Walt Whitman prairie ramble."

"It will be a…confusing time," Margo said soberly. "We must put many houses in order. We have to know if your masters have the patience to deal with us on it."

"*I* think so," Poole said. "No long-term promises. That's Harvey Lewis's First Commandment for field reps. But I don't see why TransAtlas could object to a...clarification of your situation. Provided we don't catch a batch of lousy publicity out of the... murders."

Ann cleared her throat and smiled at Poole. "We have Norman Bates' attention and cooperation now. Thus far, Fred Toller has been ingenious in keeping the St. Louis radio and TV people on a leash."

The group seemed satisfied, like a family that has weathered a little domestic crisis and is ready for mundane plans—the reunion, a Sunday School picnic. They donned galoshes and scarves, breaking up and chattering as they milled from Howells' office.

"Got a minute, sport?" Howells caught Poole. "Hang on while I check with the duty officer. You and I need to tie a couple of loose ends."

Poole opened his notebook and scanned the last pages. Howells returned with a pair of steaming styrofoam cups.

Howells sipped the coffee, wrinkled his nose then settled back in his chair. "It all looks tidy. Do *you* buy the stories?"

Poole laced his fingers back of his head. Leeland Headache No. 6 was reasserting itself. "Up to a point," he said. "Heck has found another hero-martyr role, and if he insists on his confession, you're locked to him. Unless anyone else recants."

"Yeh. It's real convenient for the high and mighty that a dying lush will take the fall for everything in sight."

"Dying?"

"Yep. I got it out of Heck after I saw the county medical officer's admission report from the jail. Heck's got two–three months at most. Lymphoma. He's known since September. He's been under treatment, but he prefers doses from the bottomless red-eye bottle."

"Then he has nothing to lose if he sticks to his story."

"Not a thing. Not even time. He'll be…out of it before the case gets to trial, however the DA jumps. It might be Heck's last act of… contrition, repentance, whatever. Or maybe it's exactly what he says it is."

"Kind of the opposite of the usual deathbed confession angle."

"We're re-questioning them all," Howells said, "but the stories jibe, roughly, at least. Inconsistencies are what you'd expect from a bag lady, two strung-out juvies, a dim security guard and a pickled furnace-jockey. What evidence we sifted from the fire site at Don's is sketchy."

"You have enough to implicate Samsa?"

"Sure. He's the chief goat. Heck will shuffle off this mortal coil, Heinie and Ziggy are minors and probably will only get hung with malicious mischief or B and E. Doreen is at her same old stand, Loggins will get demoted and who gives a shit about Jinx Washburn as long as the steam pipes don't blow up?"

"But Samsa *will* be charged?"

"With anything we can nail down. There's another angle: We think we can take down a shipment coming in. When Ziggy and Heinie can put together two words, they say a big shipment of dolls and dope is due. They don't know the whole drill, but we have the DBA and FBI boys in setting up a trap. If the seller hasn't been spooked. That's why we're sweating to keep this out of the press."

Howells' phone buzzed and winked. He scowled and picked it up. "Look, I said no calls…" He blinked and said, "Okay." He covered the receiver and waggled his eyebrows. "A big time drug guy from the FBI. Maybe a hot flash, eh?"

Poole rose and waved, while Howells said, "Karl? Yeh, been waiting…" Poole shut the door as he exited.

At the front doors, he found Ann, Wilma, Margo and Sheriff Buxtrider in confab. They edged toward the doors as they spoke. Buck glanced at Poole and gave him a girls-will-be-girls wink.

Poole fell in behind as they passed out the glass vestibule into a gale of fine sleet. Astin Lee walked toward them up the wide travertine steps, saying, "Damn car won't start!"

As Poole looked toward him, he saw an apparition—a woman in a long red coat trimmed in pseudo-ermine, topped by a red stocking cap, with red suede boots and red mittens. She looked like Mrs. S. Claus or the Clauses' eldest daughter as she stepped from a long dark-blue Mercedes at the curb. Poole recognized her as Lainey Cosgrove the instant she raised her left hand, pointing a small nickel-plated pistol.

Lainey's mouth opened, expelling a puff of vapor like a comic-strip balloon, and from it a stream of words: "You bastards think you can cheat my Chance out of his inheritance, you…"

The little silvered gun, like a gag cigarette-lighter, then expelled a tiny 0 of smoke and a bright cartridge casing, which popped up like part of a conjuring trick.

Lainey seemed to say *Bang! Bang!* but Poole heard her soprano howl, "…then keep it all for herself, the interfering bitch!"

The tiny gun continued to puff and flip casings over the ermine collar of Lainey's coat. Idiotically, Poole noted that the gun tracked higher with each shot, as automatic pistols fired by inexperienced one-hand shooters do. He reasoned that the air around him must be full of lethal hunks of lead. He lunged into Wilma and Ann, and as his face buried in Ann's fur coat, he saw that Lainey's pistol had tracked up to a forty-five degree angle, still puffing away, as was Lainey's agitated mouth.

Poole bawled, mouth clogged with fur, "Don't shoot! For Christ's sake, *nobody* shoot!"

He rolled over soft bodies, took a hard elbow in one cheek and skidded on the other cheek across coarse, slimy stone. He wrenched loose of a body that had fallen across his knees and looked up. Lainey stood motionless, the pistol in her hand pointed downward.

Her mouth was open but nothing emerged. Poole turned to see Buck rising on hands and knees, fumbling an immense long-barreled revolver from under his coat. His eyes were red and his D.I. hat was crushed under one knee. Poole lunged at Buxtrider.

"Jesus, don't shoot!" Poole yelled. "She's nuts!"

Buxtrider shoved Poole, who grabbed the sheriff's wrist and twisted at the huge gun. For a second he peered down its maw, then he pulled it to his side. Behind Buxtrider, a uniformed policeman erupted from the glass door—now starred over with bullet holes—skidded on one heel and grabbed for his service revolver.

"Don't shoot her!" Poole howled past Buxtrider's ear. The policeman's cap shot off as he slithered, and he glanced at Poole in terror. "Drop it!" he said, swinging around, flourishing his revolver and aiming it toward Poole and the sheriff. They held the magnum revolver between them like a trophy in a hand wrestling contest.

Buxtrider shouted, "Let the fuck go!" With a wrench, he leaned onto Poole and twisted the ventilated barrel down between Poole's eyes.

Which was the last thing Poole saw for fifteen or twenty seconds.

He came to as someone lifted him to a sitting position. It was Wilma, who dabbed at his face with a handkerchief spotted with his own blood, Poole registered. He staggered upright. Wilma braced him, then Ann arrived to hold him from the other side. Poole shook his head, which throbbed.

He saw Lainey being handled up the steps past him by two uniformed officers. Howells stood at the top of the steps, taking the little shiny pistol from another cop. Buxtrider was stooped over his D.I. hat, dabbing at it and trying to reshape its pyramidal crease. Astin Lee stood about halfway up the steps, staring incredulously down at the front of his camel's-hair coat, on which erupted a fuzzy roseate stain, like a military decoration, near one shoulder.

"I believe I've been shot!" he said clearly. Then he buckled at the knees and sat heavily. Ann released Poole and skipped down to him, arriving in tandem with a policewoman.

Howells bellowed, "Is anybody else hurt? What the fuck is—" Lainey bucked against two policemen restraining her, half-wedged in the swinging glass door. "You killed him, you horrible witch! You killed my daddy—and you'll *die* for it!"

The policemen bore down and forced her back into the building. Margo stood in the middle of the steps, staring toward the closed door and then back at Astin Lee, who was laid back on the stone.

Two more officers converged on him, and an ambulance swung around the corner of the building, gumball light pulsing red.

Poole held the handkerchief to his forehead, while Wilma turned to Buck, asking, "Are *you* hurt, dear?"

Poole took the mottled cloth from his cut and looked at the gaudy blood. "Is this the unkindest cut of all?" he muttered.

In Dulci Jubilo

"YOU SAY WE'VE got a lot of things wrong," Poole said reflectively. "That's not big news."

He sat in Junie's Civic Restaurant at an obscenely early hour, facing Len Howells, Sheriff Buxtrider and Wilma Breithope, their bulky law-keeping bodies crammed into a semi-circular banquette, their table littered with the debris of a massive breakfast. Buxtrider debated with himself, half-aloud, about another order of buckwheat flapjacks.

"It's like Lainey's shooting spree yesterday," Howells said. "She fired seven .32-caliber rounds at pretty much point-blank range into a gaggle of immobilized people. And didn't hit a blessed soul."

"Oh?" Poole said. "How did Astin Lee get that hole in his shoulder?"

"The handiwork of a rookie cop, the guy drawing down on you and Buck. New kid on the force, hasn't been on duty six months. One Rhett B. Bastin, in point of fact—twenty-three years old. He managed to fire off his piece in its holster while he tried to decide who and what the malefactors might be, and his .38 slug ricocheted off those fancy marble steps and hit Lee. The good news is that the ricochet was pretty well spent, so it just broke the skin and Mr. Lee's clavicle. The bad news is that the impact deformed the slug, so it made a nasty wound. Lee probably doesn't look or feel much better than you, today, Poole."

Poole had inspected the salvage job the Mercy Hospital

Emergency Room gave his face, which wasn't highly cosmetic. He had two black eyes, now richly iridescent in hue—not at all black, strictly speaking—a big butterfly bandage on his forehead (covering stitches) and a smaller bandage on his left cheek over a contusion. His brief encounter with Sheriff Buxtrider's stout right arm had been destructive to his physiognomy. Poole felt his spirit was intact, anyhow.

"What else is new?" Poole asked. Buxtrider bellowed at Junie for his flapjacks, having decided in the affirmative.

"Odds and ends," Howells smirked. "Ann told me, for example, that your hero's name—old Epi-whatsis—is *wrong*." He produced a slip of paper. "Yeh. She says it was right, I mean it was *his* name, no problem there. But it's not a kosher name, see? It ought to be... *Epanimondas*. Something like that. However he got christened, it was the wrong batch of syllables. His name is...wrong."

Poole shook his head. "A little late to quibble over Victorian nomenclature," he said. "But, speaking of names: you say the cop who shot Astin Lee was named Bastin?"

"How's that for history repeating itself?"

"And what's Lainey's, er, condition?" Poole asked.

"The family lawyer is working to get her transferred to the state psychiatric hospital. She was the only one home when Charles died, took the call from the hospital and just *snapped*, is the story. She found that old Starr pistol in a dresser and went to the station. She claims she thought we were holding her bouncing baby boy illegally, and she was doing a thoughtful mom's duty in rescuing him."

"Hell hath no fury like a mother's love," Poole said.

"I can sympathize," Wilma said, drawing an odd glance from Buxtrider. "I mean, from her point of view, she's the only Cosgrove who's cut out of the family fortune. Chance isn't much of a kid, but he's hers. She just found out her brother's really her brother, and..." She gave up trying to make her point.

"About the basic case—Ogden, Samsa and the elves?" Poole said.

"Ah, tight enough," Howells said. "By this afternoon, we'll have the dope connection sewed up."

Wilma glared at Howells, and Buck nearly missed a stroke at his new heap of flapjacks. Howells shrugged and said, "It's cool—Poole isn't going to screw up the works. I filled him in on it."

"So your trap will be today?"

"Yep. You can come along, if you'll keep your head down. I told Karl Weiss, the FBI coordinator, about you."

Wilma started to speak when there was a rap at the fogged window next to them. Outside, face pressed to pane in a Dickensian grimace, was Norman Bates. His lips moved, and then he started down the street. In a moment, he clumped into the diner, stamping snow from his boots.

"Just the gang I sought," he shouted. "I want the straight poop on the case—now. I could sit on it when it was a little ancient and out at the mall, but everybody in town heard the shootout at your corral yesterday. I need copy, folks!"

In a concerted pincer-movement, Len, Wilma and Buck rose to meet Bates, Buxtrider in the act of shoveling another slab of flapjack under his bravo's mustache.

"Norm, buddy—we were just *talking* about getting together with you!" Howells exclaimed.

The editor squinted uncertainly through misted specs. "Really?" he said. "You've been giving me the royal run-around."

"No way," Howells said, arm over Bates's shoulder. "Let's stroll over to my office, and we'll fill you in…"

Poole watched them go and stared morosely at his cold coffee. He realized he had been stiffed with the breakfast tab. *Ah, well,* he thought, *another mysterious item to confound the Argus of Trans-Atlas accounting.* He preferred this moment to himself to the hour of bafflegab the law officers would feed Norm Bates. Poole paid Junie, who sucked a toothpick and expressed outrage at the condition of her bunions. He buttoned his coat and headed into the windblown snow, across deserted streets to the library. A wizened janitor admitted him to the lobby after Poole proclaimed his friendship with Ann Wilcox, his status with TransAtlas and his low body temperature. He sat on a marble bench under a blackened bronze bust of Henry Wadsworth Longfellow. There was no wind inside the building, but the Victorian stonework oozed a wintry chill. Longfellow, he assumed, had turned black after freezing to death.

He shuffled papers in his notebook and read scraps of data. He found pages on which he had tried to outline the status of the Cosgrove family: Margo Cosgrove (nee Ogden) had married Charles Cosgrove in 19(?), after the death by uterine cancer of Amelia Cosgrove (nee Bastin). This (it was now clear) after Margo had borne Donald Cosgrove by Charles. Elaine Cosgrove (Brewster) was born in 19(?), Donald in 19(?). Donald was brought back from Wyoming, where Margo had given birth, and raised as if he were Amelia's last child. Poole scratched at his sore cheek, whose bandage pulled and itched, and scribbled emendations. Donald and Elaine had grown up assuming they were sister and brother. Hector Ogden, one of Margo's shirt-tail cousins, had been the family's Admirable Crichton and a wolfish father-surrogate for Charles. At some point, Ogden had intimated clumsily to Donald the relationship between his father and stepmother before his mother's death. Young Donald had fallen into a family-romance neurosis, which eventually bloomed into obsessive-compulsive behaviors. Pole sighed and sat back: How the hell could he pass this psychobabble through a TransAtlas WB-220 Field Report?

He scribbled. An accidental fire at the Cosgrove stable, possibly started by Heck Ogden in a drunken fit, left Donald further traumatized. His affair with another Bastin—cousin Rita, was quashed by the family. Rita had been shipped West, when Donald assumed she was pregnant. She was not. The Cosgroves paid for Rita's fancy education and made a cousinly settlement on her when she married in 1970. Don was left to his fantasies. In 1967, Elaine married Alvin Brewster, a monied lout and layabout she met when she was at Radcliffe and he at Harvard. The marriage disintegrated after three years of Lainey's tantrums and Alvin's stoical indifference. Lainey returned to Leeland with son Chance *in ovum,* to raise him on an obscenely large allowance from her father. Lainey later claimed Brewster had married her only to acquire married draft-status at the peak of the Vietnam War, that he was rampantly homosexual and dull to the point of insensibility. She had no rationale for her motives in their union.

Chance Cosgrove Brewster (aka Heinie) was an annoying fly in the tainted Cosgrove ointment. Was he a legitimate male heir to whatever fortune the bank, manufacturing complex and mall would yield? Was Don a contender for anything, as a jury-rigged half-uncle? It sounded like the muddled middle of *Hamlet,* and Poole imagined Chance running around Leeland in doublet and hose, waving a bent rapier and shouting epithets about "uncle-brothers and sister-mothers." He could not envision Don as Claudius.

"You got up early and ate the canary," a low voice said, causing Poole to scatter his papers. It was Ann Wilcox, ruddy-cheeked and cheery from the cold, bending toward him as she tucked away a giant key ring. She smelled like fresh snow.

"Hello. No canary on Junie's menu today. Probably out of season. Penguin, maybe…"

"Well, you were wearing a truly *fatuous* smile, Richard." He gathered notebook and papers. He found one in Ann's schoolmarm copperplate, a bit she had copied from Wordsworth's *Prelude* when he was ransacking Leeland history. It read: *Not in Utopia— subterranean fields, —Or some secreted island, Heaven knows where!*

But in the very world, which is the world Of all of us,—the place where, in the end We find our happiness, or not at all! He showed her the scrap.

"Why did you give me this?"

"I hoped it would counteract the visionary nonsense you were so busy absorbing. It's easy to get swept away on tides of history and ideals, but those people lived here, in Leeland, in world as real as ours. The 'very' world, as old frosty-nosed William said. I thought it might be an antidote for too much high-flown theory."

Poole followed her into the library while she switched on lights and opened doors. They reached her office behind the big walnut check-out desk.

"Your poor face," she said. "I must thank you—you saved my life. All our lives. I understand poor Astin will be all right."

"It warn't nothin," Poole said. "Mainly, it was pure luck, with Lainey's lousy shooting. I might have shoved you all *into* the line of fire. Yes, Astin's evidently only sore and debarred from any left-handed curling tournament or whatever winter Olympics you folks planned."

Poole shuffled pages and handed the notebook to Ann. "I need your keen insight and encyclopedic knowledge of Leeland. Can you help untangle this?"

Poole sat next to Ann, reading and interpreting his notes.

"You have most of it right," she said. "I assume Donald has a perfectly legitimate claim to the Cosgrove estate and that he is in Charles' will. I'm no lawyer, but I don't see how he could be cut out by anyone on grounds of his status as Charles' son. *And* Margo's. He was adopted by Charles and Amelia, Charles is his biological father and Margo his biological mother. He's more, um, *blood-kin* than Chance."

"A little more than kin and less than kind…"

"That applies more to Elaine and Chance. I think it will come out well. For Don, I mean. And that's good for your…corporation, isn't it?"

"Given the options, it's super." Poole was hyperconscious of Ann's closeness and warmth, the stillness of the mausoleum-like building, *The grave's a fine and private place, But none, I think, do there embrace.* Or words to that effect. He felt interested in her womanly aura and choked with shyness.

"So," she said, "you finished your work here?"

"Yeh. Unfortunately. I mean, I wish I had more time…here."

"Mmm. So do I. It's lonely here in midwinter."

"Shame on your husband for letting you be lonely," he said thickly.

"My…?" Oh, for *goodness sake!* I've been widowed five years. It *is* silly and old-fashioned to hang onto the Wilcox, but I owe something to Thomas' memory. I thought you knew…"

Poole sat up to see the stooped janitor materialize like a malevolent gnome in the office doorway. He coughed and said, "Hit's past openin time, Miz Wilcox. Thought I'd better fetch you."

Ann gave Poole a compassionate glance and rose, gathering her warder's keys. "Duty calls," she said." Poole glumly collected his notebook, coat and scarf.

He found her unlocking the great bronze front doors, and she said, "Take time to see me before you leave. Please?"

Poole stepped again into the saw-teeth of a prairie gale, warmer, sadder and wiser.

* * *

Len Howells muttered from the corner of his mouth to Poole and concentrated on following the FBI man's unmarked car. It was a dun-colored Nakajima mini-van, and Poole wondered if it were crammed full of sophisticated electronic surveillance gear, exotic weaponry or miniaturized FBI agents. Weiss drove at a steady 35 mph. on the glare ice. Howells rehearsed the facts of the impending confrontation between law and disorder, while Poole's weary mind freewheeled. Thinking about the FBI van led to speculation on the federal drug-enforcer he had met at Howell's office, a suave, compact Chinese-American named Jonathan Wong, who dressed and spoke like a young instructor at an exclusive prep school and who drove an unmarked charcoal-gray Focke-Wulf 190 roadster. Poole decided the long-term effects of the Marshall Plan had been to establish rampant yuppification, to endow the U.S. with a cadre of imported centurions from The People Who Brought You World War II and to leave everyone else baffled about winning and losing.

"...so just keep your ass out of the way now, huh?" Howells said.

"No problem. I'm here for the thrills, not the action."

In minutes, Poole sat alone in the car in Cockatoo Lot of LeeLand Mall, trying to see through misted windows. Howells had walked with two young plain-clothes officers to mingle at the back entrance. FBI and DEA cars were interspersed with those of shoppers. Poole was unsure what he was observing, but as the cold seeped into his bones, he spotted a huge truck, an eighteen-wheeler a block long, nosing toward the loading-shipping bays at the end of the mall. The tractor was red, white and green in gaudy slashes, the trailer muraled with a painting of St. Nick ensleighed, eight reindeer rampant. Vast lettering bawled *SANTA CLAUS EXPRESS* and in slightly smaller letters *DAISYCHAIN INC.* On the back doors a smaller notice:

ST. VITUS, LA.

PLAQUEMINES PARISH

TRANSPORT AND SUPPLY.

The huge truck seesawed to the loading dock. A large black man in a worn mackinaw coat climbed down from the cab and walked around the truck. Two men in nondescript work clothes— Poole recognized Weiss and Wong—drifted from the building and met the driver. He presented a clipboard. Howells and a plain-clothes minion walked across the lot from behind the truck, moving purposefully but without menace. The Federal men talked animatedly with the driver, gesturing from truck to clipboard.

Howells' associate scaled the cab. He held a small revolver discreetly against his pants leg. He shook his head down at Howells. Two more plain-clothes lawmen moved from an old black sedan and strolled around the semi. Howells waved his right arm in a saddle-up or allee-allee-in-free gesture. More men converged. Poole clambered stiffly from the car and trotted after them.

When he rounded the truck, Poole saw Wong pointing a snub-nosed revolver at the driver, while Weiss snaffled his thick wrists with a nylon-and-wire restraint, the latest police technology—disposable handcuffs. Wong held the driver's clipboard in his left hand, while he recited in pedantic tones the conditions of the driver's arrest. Poole heard Wong saying, "Are you, um, Roscoe Domino, aka. 'Fats'?" The black man was enormous, with the stacked silhouette of an NFL nose tackle. His red stocking cap was pushed to the side of a bristly semi-Afro, and he snorted a plume of vapor. In an incongruously light, treble voice he chanted, "My name is LaMothe, LaMothe is really my name. My folks was all Frenchmens..."

The Federal men gently hustled the shivering giant away, and Howells' men opened the trailer doors. The cargo bay was crammed with cardboard cartons brightly stenciled *KRAZEE KILLER KIDS*. The men methodically shifted and opened cartons. One officer toted a tape recorder and mini-cam, documenting the operation. Poole stood with Howells in the maw of the loading bay as the lawmen ransacked this mountain of cargo.

* * *

In late afternoon, Leeland police and assorted Federal agents, inspectors, field supervisors and assessors assembled in the Leeland police squad room. Evidence was heaped on tables and stacked in corners. A young man arranged big black-and-white photos on an easel. Weiss and Wong, shirt-sleeved, industriously assembled photocopied reports. Poole drifted until he located Howells, who sat in a tubular chair staring at a box open on his lap. In the box was an especially hideous doll, gnarled tiny boy-man with carrot-red hair, pustulent features and bucktoothed grin. The figure was clad in ragged clothes festooned with patches.

Howells showed the little totem to Poole. "Jeez—it looks like something out of a voodoo orgy!" he said. "I suppose if these things hit the market, my Angie will want one. You imagine coming home from a hard day looking at stiffs in the morgue and eyeballing that?"

Wong and Weiss convened the meeting, presenting a carefully choreographed exposition of evidence and charges. As the Leeland operation transpired, Federal agents in Louisiana had arrested importers and managers at DaisyChain Inc. and rounded up everyone in the offices and plant at St. Vitus and on the New Orleans waterfront. Wong said, "Kudos all around for a flawless operation, ladies and gents! The D.C. office guys are highly pleased. We have enough forensic evidence and testimony to shut down all sources of the coke and to keep the, um, dolls impounded."

Weiss wielded an overhead projector with grease-penciled charts to show how the FBI and DEA had tracked and suppressed hundreds of pounds of brown Mexican cocaine from its Louisiana point of entry. He reeled off statistics about the size and purport of the operation.

"We're ready to throw this to the media," he ended. "I want to thank you for keeping everything tight. We have all the links to make a case against Gregory Samsa and Elaine Cosgrove, and we broke the connections Nugent set up in St. Louis. We can safely say this operation is one-hundred percent in the bag. Santa's bag, in this instance!"

Poole felt mildly disappointed that Wong pronounced Ls and Rs with broadcast-standard impeccability and Weiss showed no trace of a Dr. Strangelove accent.

As the meeting ended, Poole realized it was like any office Christmas party. Backslapping and joviality all around, cookies and coffee. With the dolls, festive boxes, advertising posters and other impounded sales paraphernalia, the squad room looked like a corporate boardroom ending its pre-Christmas campaign, ready to send salesmen on the holiday trail. Poole heard a faint Muzaked carol leaking from the Celotex ceiling: "Lo, How a Rose E'er Blooming."

* * *

The crappy room at SleepyEye House felt nostalgic to Poole as he stuffed his bags. *Be it ne'er so humble,* he thought. Elbert Bastin stood by the door.

"So you nabbed the bad guys?" he asked, digging a forefinger into the mysteries of one nostril.

"Indeed we did. I told you, er, Cap—the forces of right win out."

"Yeh," Elbert said glumly. "That's what Captain Cosmo always said. And he turned out to be a crook."

"Sometimes you don't know what makes a bad guy bad. Or a good guy good. It's not that you wear a fancy uniform and make speeches. It's *who* you are and *why* that count. You have to believe it's important to do the right thing, no matter what."

"So Uncle Heck was a good guy?"

Poole sighed. "He was as good as he could be. He *thought* he was doing the right thing."

"How can you tell?" Elbert said plaintively. "I burned all that old Captain Cosmo junk I used to keep."

"I'm not sure you needed to do that."

"Ah, it was kid stuff. Besides, they got this new show on, every afternoon. Kolonel Kombat. It's about this guy who goes back to Veet-nam, see, an rescues all the Americans in slave camps, an he has this fantastic laser-aimed machine gun, an..."

Shuddering, Poole latched his suitcase. He drifted to the parking lot and the slush-stained Ferret, while Elbert walked at his elbow, in full bardic rhapsody, recounting the revisionist TV delirium in gristly detail, with daily body-count. Poole stowed his bags in the trunk, flinching as he opened the hatch, with a little *frisson;* perhaps the shade of Captain Cosmo was condemned to ride the earth in the ass-end of an undersized rental car. Talk about eternal *damnation!* He clicked the lid shut and suppressed a shiver.

He let the Ferret warm and leaned out the window toward Elbert. "Look," Poole said, "why don't you take an afternoon and go down to the library? Ask for Ann Wilcox. Tell her I sent you for a load of wholesome literature, bud. Something innocent, like *Treasure Island* or *The Moonstone* or *Murders in the Rue Morgue*, for God's sake. Take care of yourself, Cap—"

Poole drove away, not looking into the rear-view mirror. He did not want to know which hand or digit Elbert might wave in his adieux.

* * *

Margo Cosgrove sat elegantly arranged, a self-conscious study in gray and black, on a settee in her living room, while Don stood by the fireplace, staring into the empty hearth. She had just pronounced, "There will be only a small memorial service. Charles was explicit about his final wishes."

Don stared at a brass fire tool, turning it in his hands. "I'm not so concerned with the...obsequies as with putting our name right," he said. "There's a question of...image."

"You see, Mr. Poole," Margo said, "Donald is fully recovered. He thinks like a veteran manager."

Donald turned toward her. "And you're *sure* the will is sound?"

"The lawyers were reassuring. It will have to go through probate, and the instructions must be interpreted by fine legal minds. But your father was exact in assigning rights, and you retain direction of the businesses. Your position at the mall is in the hands of Mr. Poole's masters." She looked gravely at Poole, as if cuing him in an *adagio* performance of a French neoclassical tragedy.

"Er," said Poole glibly. "My immediate boss, Harvey Lewis, says AmeriMall will approve the *status quo*. At least until the next board meeting. He crawled onto a skinny limb to convince them everything was under control at LeeLand Mall."

"For which we are grateful," Don said. "Give us six months, and the operation will be tiptop. Next Christmas we'll go all-out. I've been working up a campaign. We can offset this...nonsense with a community-service program, something based on the old values— peace on earth, good will toward men. I have a designer coming in from San Francisco, one of the top media men in seasonal sales. We'll put this commercialism and corruption behind us. And, by God, we'll make money for the mall doing it!"

"The family is mended?" Poole asked Margo.

Don hesitated, and she said, "Donald has been understanding. I think he sees why his father and I practiced deceptions. We felt it was right to bring him up as Amelia's child, along with Elaine. It was... simpler than trying to explain to children such complexities. We were wrong, but it was an innocent deception. Elaine is the tragic figure. How she could ally herself with that creature Samsa, and why she believed we were out to shove her and Chance from the family circle, I don't know. All the adages about spoiled children apply, Mr. Poole."

"You don't seem concerned with the indictments against her and Chance. And Samsa."

"That's in the hands of the lawyers and the courts. Which is to say that I believe she won't suffer badly on the counts. It was Samsa and Nugent who shipped the narcotics and the, ah, illicit toys. Elaine was, as always, a pawn. And Chance is scarcely responsible for himself. I assume the juvenile authorities will see he was drawn in with bad companions. The Wilson boy and those dreadful girls."

"In other words," Poole said, "justice will take its usual course, and the poor kids will carry the weight, while Chance gets probation or a stretch in a prep school?"

"I didn't make the world, Mr. Poole, and I certainly didn't order its justice. I believe the legal system will work as well as it ever does in this case. And I think Chance will have quite enough...weight to carry. His mother may very well go to prison. At least be treated as a criminal."

"But you don't feel like the wicked stepmother?" Poole asked.

"Of course not. Elaine and Donald are both my children, as I have treated them. I only regret that Donald ever heard the, ah, tale about his conception. I never treated Elaine as anything less than my natural child, and her father was extremely responsible with her. I can't fathom why children turn out so."

Don set the brass poker among the array of fireplace utensils, brushed his hands and sighed. "I'll do everything I can for Lainey and Chance. We have a good lawyer for Heck, if that helps. At least the political squabbling will be quashed. Some good will come from it all."

"Political squabbling?" Poole echoed.

"Oh, yes. Those absurd papers of Epaphimandas' settle the city-county boundary disputes, you see. The old buzzard really *was* a century ahead of his time. He had Leeland set up as a fiefdom, no distinctions between the city and PawPaw County. And that's what people have advocated here for a dozen years. Now we have a perfect legal, historical basis for a one-government operation, which will set aside litigation about the mall site, property rights, government services, the tax base, everything. Buxtrider is on his way to drafting a city-county bill. We know who he envisions as the city-county manager. I suppose it's inevitable. But it will dissolve the disharmony and infighting. Which will benefit LeeLand Mall enormously."

"All's well that ends well," Poole said.

"Mmm," Margo said. "You may relish cheap irony, looking from outside, from your Olympus corporation or whatever. But Donald is quite right: we can put the ghosts to rest. And the shade of Epaphimandas Lee will smile on us. It's in perfect accord with his theories…"

***

Poole found Fred Toller in the LeeLand Mall management suite, conferring with Wilma and Buxtrider. Fred had appropriated Gregory Samsa's office and instantly recreated the chaos of his headquarters, down to scattered styrofoam cups hall-filled with mold culture. Equipped with a fresh cup and coffee only half-singed, Poole sat with them.

He steered Toller to the gimmicks Samsa had used in his large-scale jiggery-pokery. Toller handed Poole a stack of computer sheets.

"A preliminary report," Toller said. "When the external auditors finish, we'll fill in blanks. The old boy operated on the hairy edge. None of his schemes would of held up, so we guess he was in for a quick killing and then off to Rio de Janiero."

Poole flipped pages, scanned paragraphs and whistled aimlessly a tune that came to his lips whenever he was engrossed. He thought it was a bit from Mozart's *Eine Kleine Nachtmusik*, but a listener might have tabbed it as either "Three Blind Mice" or "Lillibulero."

Toller slouched in his swivel-throne and said, "You put me onto the dummy projects, and we tracked his paper trail till we hit Tinker's Tottery. That was the only one of the proposed franchises with a lot of computer time logged to it. He had hidden it under a blind code, but Whitman has a knack for getting around IRMA. He traced it. Samsa had the franchise running like a real operation, to front for doll shipments. It was a sweet idea—I'll give the wily bastard credit. He was not only dealing dope here and to his contacts in Cicero, but the dolls were a hot item. He was getting rich both ways—on the product and on the packages!

"He was set to retail dolls at SantaLand, with Mo and Jake shilling. That was their end of the deal. They didn't know about the dope angle until they stumbled on it. They'd let Heck into the story about Gertie and her playmates, and when they found Samsa was running coke, too, they backed out. You know the rest. They got blitzed with Ogden and decided to sabotage the scam. That's when Nugent wasted them."

"How did Lainey tie in?" Poole asked.

"She bankrolled Samsa. That's as far as anybody can track her. She's in no, er, condition to be questioned now, but Heinie—Chance—has spilled his guts. Evidently Samsa convinced her he was nudging Don out of the mall, which she thought was a great idea. She was Samsa's blind partner, see, with some notion—maybe—that she'd move into Don's slot. Or that she'd groom up Chance, God help us, as LeeLand Mall heir apparent."

Buck ruminated, "Samsa must of smooth-talked her blind. All he needed was her money, and he didn't plan to stick around for any power plays later. He'd spun his sister a yarn about a South American import-export job, and she was cheerily planning a move. All hush-hush, so she wasn't about to pry into his activities. She still thinks this is a misunderstanding and she'll be down in Rio for Carnival."

Wilma sniffed and said, "A woman is always the last to know."

Toller juggled a bronze paperweight in the shape of the trylon-and-perisphere from the 1940 World's Fair. He sucked at his teeth, yawned and said, "The Feds sewed up the dope connections, and a slew of Customs people are tracking down dolls. Another couple days and Samsa would of removed the dope and gotten Killer Kids into half the homes in Leeland. Another disaster we missed."

"Why? How is *that* a disaster?" Poole said. "They're ugly little buggers, but..."

Toller pulled a plastic bag from his desk drawer. In it was another doll, this one a warped, maniacal-looking boy in short pants, sprinkled with scabs and band-aids, sporting an eye-patch and a rubber dagger.

Toller shook the grotesque figure and said, "Shit—these things were made in sweatshops in Colombia and Honduras, and they violate every toy-safety code. They're flammable, they're covered with little bitty hard, sharp objects and the stuffing material is contaminated cotton and straw. So far, the expert from the U.S. Bureau of Toy Safety has identified a half-dozen transmittable diseases in samples. Not this one, they say." But Toller handled it gingerly through the plastic shroud.

"So even if kids weren't actively injured by the damn things," he continued, "the mall would of been open to umpteen-dozen law suits. When some worried mommy found what junior was carrying around the house and chewing on, we'd of been beyond our keesters in court cases."

"But you think the mall is clear now?" Poole asked.

"Too early to tell, but we didn't actually *sell* the damn voodoo dolls." Toller sucked his toothpick and said, "Oh, yeah—there's something weird on with security. Two little yellow whiz-kids showed up yesterday. Named something like Uncle and Whistlestop. Say TransAtlas sent them in. You in on that maneuver?"

"Oh," Poole said. "They would be my Thais."

"Mai Tais?" Toller said.

"Harvey Lewis believes TransAtlas is a parsec ahead of everyone in the electronic surveillance market, Fred. Everybody is thinking *Korea*, see? So Harve locates these geniuses in *Thailand*, who are the last word in R and D for laser heat-sensitive systems. He says they'll have IRMA hooked up and turning cartwheels in a week. Your computer jockey Whitman picked them up at O'Hare, straight from Bangkok. He's enthralled. Ahn Koh and Hu Wan S'Tah are *charmers,* I should warn you."

"Any helping hand is a good hand," Toller said. To clinch the aphorism, Poole stuck out his mitt and gave Fred a hearty handshake goodbye.

* * *

Heck Ogden's cell in the new county jail was more like a set from *Captain Cosmo* than a backdrop for *The Man in the Iron Mask.* Metal and plastic, with a Teflon-like substance on all surfaces, all bathed in bright, even fluorescent light. Heck sat on a slab bed like a low cook-top. He looked incongruous, the Duke of Bilgewater signed on for a tour of duty on the Starship Enterprise.

"I didn't set out to hurt nobody," Ogden said. Poole sat on the second slab bed facing him. "But when I seen what that bastard Nugent done to Mo and Jake, I couldn't stop myself. They never had a chance, never had no breaks. I guess I was thinking of me, too. Harry Nugent walked all over people to get anything he wanted. I was drunk and sick and tired. When I pulled that trigger, I didn't feel it. I just heard echoes. It was like Korea. You'd fire off a whole clip from your carbine and never hear it. Ain't that strange? It was like a silent movie I was watchin. But I said *This time I can make it come out right!* And it don't matter about me. You know the docs say I won't make it. *Lymphoma.* God—what an ugly word!"

Ogden rubbed at his neck. He smiled vaguely, his eyes off-focus. Poole said, "What were you trying to make come out right, Heck?"

"Ah, shit. Who knows? I just didn't want Nugent to screw things up for Don and Margo and Mr. Charles any more than he had. Those people tried to be good to me. I kept fuckin up, an they stayed with me. They was all I ever had for *family,* I guess you'd say. I knew I owed them. And I owed Mo and Jake. Shit, who knows? I looked at Nugent, and it was in his eyes. He looked at me with a nasty grin. He said, 'Jesus, they still let you loose on the streets, Ogden? I thought you crawled into a bottle for keeps.' He wasn't scared or nothing, see? It was like I wasn't even pointin the gun at him. I looked at them black eyes and I could see he thought I was a worthless piece of dogshit too dumb an scared an whipped to bother him. If he'd been wearin those goddam Captain Cosmo boots, he would of wiped 'em on my face. *That's* why I pulled. See?"

Poole nodded. He scrawled a doodle, a small Thurberesque dog, in his notebook.

"I swear I didn't exactly mean to kill him. That's dumb-ass, ain't it? But it's true. It was like I was on TV, only I was the good guy, an he was some kinda scum from another planet. I started to say, 'I got the Silver Star.' Christ, it's crazy! But he laughed. He stood there with Jake an Mo hauled up like sacks of shit on his shoulder—an he laughed. So I pulled."

Poole sighed and closed the notebook. Hector Ogden would be a weird marginal gloss in column 11-Y of his final field report form. Can I get you anything, Heck?" he asked.

Ogden scratched a thick ear. "Magazines," he mumbled. "I used to read *Argosy* an *Field and Stream*. They wrote me up once in *True*. Jesus, what a laugh! All that Korea stuff—an they thought it was true! Oh…if somebody could go to Kohler's music store an get me a couple harps."

Poole had a bizarre vision of Heck Ogden draped in a bed sheet, strumming a huge harp, auditioning for the Angelic Choir. He couldn't think how to phrase his question. But Ogden handed him a scrap of paper.

"Here," he said, "I wrote it down. A couple Hohner Marine Band harmonicas. One in C an one in G. If somebody could…"

As Poole left the jail he felt pleased at the idea of Heck Ogden equipped with harmonicas. He hoped Heck played them very badly and loudly, like a dying bagpiper. He hoped their nasal din penetrated every soundproofed and thickly carpeted living room in Leeland.

* * *

The next stop was the city jail. Len Howells led Poole back to the holding cells, also recent examples of domestic penal furnishing. Gregory Samsa sat on a metal chair in a long, open cage, staring listlessly up at a flickery TV set mounted in the corridor. Merv Griffin's blancmange countenance peered from the box like a genie waiting for release. Merv and his guests were in shades of blue.

"You up for a visitor?" Howells said through the widely-spaced bars. Samsa's pale blue eyes flickered toward them and away. He sat with his arms crossed on his chest, his legs straight, like a sullen grade-schooler serving a period of exile in a cloakroom. His face was empty.

"The Garbo of PawPaw County," Howells said. "He's probably waiting for *Captain Cosmo* reruns. Right, Greg? Watch your favorite TV actor strut and fret his weary hour, and so on?"

Poole glanced with surprise at Howells. The detective hooked an eyebrow sardonically. In a phony stage-whisper he said, "It's a new technique I worked out. Wallop 'em with literary allusions and see if they break down. You, me, Inspector Javert and Herlock Sholmes, Poole. But Greg's too hard a case for me. Whooee! They're going to put me back to handling your run-of-the-mill, dime store bad guys. Now, I can *talk* to Heinie and Ziggy. Your plain vanilla warts and pimps. When we get to gentlemen—guys who live in boardrooms—well…out of my league. I can get next to guys who steal and embezzle and sell dope and push cruddy illegal toys on kids. But not with *bonafide* big shots."

Samsa turned slowly. His face was cadaverous, immobile. He blinked and sighed. "On advice of counsel, I have no statements to make," he said in a creaky voice, the tones of someone who has not spoken in days or weeks.

Poole said, "Look. TransAtlas would like to help. Or at least *understand.* You had a good record. Standing in the community. Your sister is—"

"Leave her out of it," Samsa whispered.

"How the hell can we? Every reporter from here to Chicago is camped on your doorstep. What do you think she's going through?"

Samsa looked away. He recrossed his arms and stared at the TV set. Merv Griffin was replaced by the Pillsbury Doughboy, who doubled with silent laughter as a giant hand tickled his tummy. Poole realized the sound was off. A strip of meaningless blue-tinted pictures unreeling before Samsa's dead eyes.

"TransAtlas is interested in restitution, Samsa," Poole said. "We're not in the justice business. Don't you want to know there's something left for your sister?"

Howells leaned against the thickly enameled bars and uttered a bark of laughter. "You and little Alicine had reservations for Acapulco, right? You were going to take the money and run a hell of along way from Leeland. So, Poole, you're appealing to the wrong instincts. Alicine keeps coming in to add appendixes to her statement. She thinks she can get a book or a TV special out of it. She always wanted to be Somebody, even if it was The Other Woman. She said Farah Fawcett would be a great choice to do her on the TV. I don't know who she had in mind for you, Greg."

Samsa turned away. Poole shuffled his feet and glanced at Howells, who looked supremely bored. "Leave it," Howells finally said. "He's going to stonewall himself into a half-dozen years at a minimum-security lockup. Old Greg can take a vacation at a country club, right? Rub elbows with famous gents from Washington, tax crooks, spies, high-class con men from the Stock Exchange. Jesse P. Meister has sold him his round-trip ticket."

* * *

It was dusk as the library closed. Poole met Ann Wilcox as she slipped through the tall bronze doors, like Eve sneaking out of the Garden of Eden. She brightened and waved.

Poole ruled out the hotel or Lee's Happy Landing. They found a restaurant on the riverfront, one of the few businesses operating in a wasteland of boarded warehouses and crumbling factory sheds in a spider web of rusty railroad sidings. The place was in a low brick-and-stone building, once a small foundry or forge. It wore on its roof a big neon-fringed billboard as incongruous as a mortarboard cap. This sign blinked at one-second intervals: *KATE'S KATFISH KINGDOM.*

Ordering was easy, since the place specialized in catfish and other piscine repasts. The decor was Early Industrial Gothick, and only a few other diners were on hand so early on a gray winter evening. Poole and Ann sat at a table in a front corner, next to a big hulk of pitted wood and iron that must have been a punch press or sheet-metal roller in the mid-nineteenth century. A slim blonde waitress efficiently clocked their orders and brought drinks—a Manhattan for Ann, a double Vodka martini for Poole.

"You *must* leave now?" Ann asked. Poole found his drink amazingly good—right temperature, proportion, strength. He wondered if it were shaken, not stirred. Or was it the other way? He didn't have a license to kill, either.

"Mmm," he said around the martini. "Yeh, my boss is breathing fire over the phone, and there's nothing more to do here. We have an accounting team in, a couple of Oriental computer wizards, a sales consultant. The AmeriMall board voted yesterday to put in a maximum-effort salvage operation and give LeeLand Mall another year to prove itself."

"Pity," she said. Poole didn't misunderstand, but he played with the lead.

"You don't want to see it go down the tubes."

"I couldn't care less, Richard. With Aunt Mary all but gone, I don't have interests here. My work is, frankly, becoming a bore. Aunt Mary was right—it amounts to stacking and unstacking mountains of musty volumes."

"Maybe you should get out of Leeland. For awhile."

"I've thought of going back to school—post-grad library work. I'm supposed to be the local liaison for the computer network gizmos and systems, and I don't really know one end of a byte from the other. I could trek off to Urbana or Evanston. But I don't want to try on a Betty Coed outfit in my advanced state of decay."

"Hey, no decay is evident!"

"Ah, thanks, Sir Percival. You know what I mean. We'd be better off hiring a lithe and ambitious lad or lassie for our computer slave master and letting me decompose quietly in a corner of the reading room."

"My, oh my," Poole said, "you *do* have an advanced case of holiday blues!"

To illustrate the diagnosis, Ann sighed and drained her Manhattan. Their dinner arrived, hot and well-ordered, and they were distracted by the array of food.

Poole discovered he was famished and assaulted his large catfish in its curled jacket of breading, excavated the heaping mound of home-fries, harvested the salad. Ann was equally industrious in eating.

He decided her ennui was subordinate to the sensual pleasures. Also Poole decided his catfish was the closest thing in the world to manna. The settlers must have decided this was Utopia, if you could yank the huge, ugly channel cats out of the big river and make such a simple feast. Paradisal stuff, he decided, as he reached the backbone.

"I suppose I'm indulging myself in dramatics," Ann said, as if there had been no recess for ingestion. "Aunt Mary said I lived in a one-act play by Sarah Gaskell or someone equally morbid."

"Susan," Poole said, wondering if it were couth to order more fish.

"What? Susan?"

"Susan Gaskell," Poole said.

"How on earth do you know that?"

"I almost married a woman who was a certifiable little-theater nut. She was forever busy reviving lost masterworks. Mainly so she'd have a chance to wear weird costumes and prance in front of goggle-eyed Rotarians. She tried her level best to include a nude scene in every play they staged, hoping to get arrested and make a big freedom-of-speech case of it. Make all the newspapers, see?"

As if on cue, Norman Bates materialized from the shadows of the cloakroom next to them, aiming for their table. Poole moaned in fear.

"Hi, guys!" Bates bellowed. "I hoped I'd catch you. We're still putting together a comprehensive follow-up story on the mall business before Samsa goes to the grand jury."

"Norman," Ann said in her schoolmarm voice, "we're having a private supper. Mr. Poole is on his way out of town."

"Hey, glad to catch you," Bates said, dragging a chair around the hunk of defunct machinery. "A few little points to clarify. I want to be sure the *Eagle* gets it all straight."

Poole glanced imploringly at Ann, who leaned toward Bates and hissed, "If you get out your damn pad and pencil, Norman, I'll shove them right up...your ear."

"Hey, no personal violence," Bates spread his hands. "I have a job to do, an edition to get out. The good folks of Leeland have a right to know."

Poole extracted a small wad of papers from his jacket and slid them to Bates. "Here's a copy of the notes I made for the TransAtlas PR office. It'll do for a statement. Count yourself blessed—it's more than the PR boys will release, when they get around to it. And no attribution, no mention of my name. Right?"

Bates scanned the sheets and nodded. "This leaves questions," he said. "I mean, this barely mentions Samsa, and—"

Poole held up his hand like a traffic cop. "That's the long and short of it, buddy-boy. No amplifications, no explanations. Take it or leave it."

Bates grumbled, folding the papers away. He exited on a cloud of muttered execrations.

Then Poole stared regretfully at his trusty K-Mart watch. He had an hour's drive to the St. Louis airport and a date with the red-eye to Pittsburgh. Ann sighed and nodded. "I suppose no inducement would keep you another night?"

"Oh, *I* can think of some dandy inducements. But I must evade temptation. Harvey Lewis is sitting in his office right now, waiting for me. You were mentioning a change of scenery. I could recommend Pittsburgh, but I'd rather think about a quiet and private place. I know it's weird this time of year, but there's a cozy lodge in northern Minnesota for which I have a key. Wind and snow—but it's a million miles from anyone else. And there's firewood…"

Ann tugged at the shawl collar on her sweater. "Wrong season for that enticement," she said. "You don't have a condo in the Caribbean?"

Ann walked Poole down the street under worn Christmas decorations scattered sparsely and winking in the breeze. Errant snowflakes skittered in puddles of orange sodium-vapor light beneath the aluminum standards. The music system creaked to life with "I Saw Mommy Kissing Santa Claus."

They stood by the Ferret, where it was nosed into a frozen drift, and Ann followed the song's lead. *A good kiss, a last good kiss,* Poole thought. Good enough to last him on the highway to St. Louis. He had only a few halting words to give her in return. He hated any goodbyes, and this was the next-to-worst kind. As he started the car and let the little engine shudder awake, he watched her walk down the dim street, her figure diminishing by inexorable laws of aerial perspective as she moved from streetlight to streetlight away from him. "Not in Utopia—subterranean fields..." He tried to recall the lines, but the rest was garbled in his tired brain. He felt an impulse to pull the Ferret away and race down the dark and dreaming street after her. To hell with Harvey and TransAtlas and...He sighed, put the car in gear, released the handbrake and edged over heaps of refrozen slush and blackened snow. He aimed the Ferret's blunt snout out of Leeland, out past the fairy lights around LeeLand Mall, out onto the black interstate highway with its rows of green signboards glowing toward a mundane destination.

* * *

Poole sat wearily before the Ozark Airlines counter, watching green words scroll by on a computer terminal. All flights were delayed, and the serene smiles of the young lady at the counter were his only nostrum against despair. He had returned the Ferret, superstitiously checking the trunk one last time. For an instant, he had a horrific suspicion he would find Elbert Bastin curled elf-like in the little box, frozen but smiling beatifically at following his leader into untimely oblivion. Nothing there but a fake spare tire and old stains.

His meager luggage was checked, and his hands were empty. He found his broken briar pipe in his coat pocket, took it out and inspected it. A smell like an old boot. He resolved to give up smoking and drinking again. He thought about searching the nearly empty lounge for a bookstall. He thought about making long-distance calls, pre-Christmas greetings to scattered acquaintances. Then he remembered it was past midnight.

Poole sighed. Bits of an old show-tune tinkled in his head, transmuting themselves to fit his self-pity: "...but not for you. Christmas is coming—but not for you. Winter is ending—but not for you..."

The woman behind the counter answered a phone, smiling seraphically in Poole's direction. For a second he felt singled out. Then he realized it was a conditioned-response rictus: "Always smile when you handle customer requests." Rule No. 17B in the Ozark training manual. She hung up the phone and scribbled on a paper, eyes downcast. Poole tried to sort ways to start a useful conversation with her, but thoughts of Wilma and Ann kept drifting in and out of his head.

Giving up, he sauntered across the lobby area to the Sky Bar, hoping that a little liquid refreshment would actually refresh. The bar was nearly deserted, with only two men sitting at a table by the wall and one attractive woman alone at the bar.

As Poole approached the bar, the woman glanced at him and smiled. Poole noticed the variety of tap handles, and it occurred to him that a Fulton's Lonely Blond might be fitting, given the woman down the bar.

"Can I buy you a drink?", he asked the woman.

She smiled and said, "That'd be nice, but my flight leaves in twenty minutes, so I'd better get going." Another disappointment.

As the bartender approached, Poole waved goodbye to the woman and ordered a vodka martini instead of a beer. The Muzak revealed Bing Crosby singing "I'll Be Home For Christmas". *Well, at least there's that*, he thought.

Sipping his martini, Poole murmured, to no one in particular, "Merry Christmas to you. God bless us, every one."

About the Authors

Bill Schafer was, up to his death in 2009, professor of English at Berea College in Kentucky, where he held the Chester D. Tripp Chair in Humanities. He taught English and humanities courses there beginning in 1964. He has written extensively on African–American music, Appalachian and Southern literature, and modern American fiction for periodicals and reference works. Bill's wife and co-author, Martha, still lives in Berea, Kentucky. *Deck The Malls With Murder* is their second novel.